"I didn't come all this way to visit for a day or two."

All the glow from her interaction with the baby had left her face. "How long will you be here?"

Sean's eyes went to the baby. "As long as it takes to convince you to marry me," he answered tersely. The minute he said it, he knew it had been a mistake. He'd started out on the right path with the flowers, the gifts for the baby, trying to get her sister, Jennie, on his side. But meeting his daughter had rattled him. Suddenly it had become more important than he'd realized that he be able to stake his claim on her…and on Kate.

Kate made no reply for a long moment. Finally she leaned over, gathered the baby into her arms and stood. "Be prepared for a long stay then, Sean, because I'll never agree to marry you…!"

Dear Reader,

Entertainment. Escape. Fantasy. These three words describe the heart of Harlequin Historicals. If you want compelling, emotional stories by some of the best writers in the field, look no further.

Ana Seymour made her writing debut in our 1992 March Madness Promotion. Since then she has written eleven historical romances, from Westerns to medieval stories. Critics have described her work as "brilliant," "enchanting" and "impossible to put down." Her latest Western, *A Father for Keeps,* is no exception. It is the stirring reunion romance of a San Francisco heir who returns to Nevada to win back his lost love, who is also the mother of his child. Don't miss it!

Be sure to look for *Robber Bride* by the talented Deborah Simmons. The third de Burgh brother, Simon, finds his match in a free-spirited lady who is hiding from her despicable fiancé. In Carolyn Davidson's Americana tale, *The Tender Stranger,* a pregnant widow who runs away from her conniving in-laws falls in love with the bounty hunter hired to bring her home.

Award-winning author Ruth Langan returns this month with *Rory,* the first book in her new medieval series, THE O'NEIL SAGA. In it, an English noblewoman succumbs to the charm of the legendary Irish rebel she is nursing back to health.

Whatever your tastes in reading, you'll be sure to find a romantic journey back to the past between the covers of a Harlequin Historical.®

Sincerely,

Tracy Farrell
Senior Editor

Please address questions and book requests to:
Harlequin Reader Service
U.S.: 3010 Walden Ave., P.O. Box 1325, Buffalo, NY 14269
Canadian: P.O. Box 609, Fort Erie, Ont. L2A 5X3

FATHER FOR KEEPS

ANA SEYMOUR

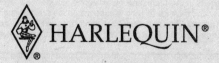

HARLEQUIN®

TORONTO • NEW YORK • LONDON
AMSTERDAM • PARIS • SYDNEY • HAMBURG
STOCKHOLM • ATHENS • TOKYO • MILAN • MADRID
PRAGUE • WARSAW • BUDAPEST • AUCKLAND

ISBN 0-373-29058-6

FATHER FOR KEEPS

This edition published by arrangement with Harlequin Books S.A.

® and TM are trademarks of the publisher. Trademarks indicated with
® are registered in the United States Patent and Trademark Office, the
Canadian Trade Marks Office and in other countries.

Printed in U.S.A.

Books by Ana Seymour

Harlequin Historicals

The Bandit's Bride #116
Angel of the Lake #173
Brides for Sale #238
Moonrise #290
Frontier Bride #318
Gabriel's Lady #337
Lucky Bride #350
Outlaw Wife #377
Jeb Hunter's Bride #412
A Family for Carter Jones #433
Father for Keeps #458

ANA SEYMOUR

The strong Scandinavian heritage of Ana Seymour's native state of Minnesota has contributed to her love of writing stories about family strength and support. She says the idea for books about two sisters came from watching the interaction between her own two daughters, now young adults, who are best friends, as well as sisters. Readers may write to Ana at: P.O. Box 47888, Minneapolis, MN 55447.

For the remarkable Liz and Bill Whitbeck—
with affection and gratitude for a lifetime
of friendship and support

Chapter One

Vermillion, Nevada
September 1882

The blood drained from Kate Sheridan's cheeks. Somewhere behind her in the house she could vaguely hear Caroline beginning to fuss, but the cries were not yet strident. She put a hand against the front door frame to steady herself.

"Hello, Kate," he said simply.

She hadn't heard the voice for over a year and a half, but the sound of it in her head was as familiar as her own breathing. She knew every contour of his face, every crinkle around those blue eyes. Without looking, she could have traced exactly the strong line of his jaw.

Out on Elm Street a buggy clopped by, the Bancrofts from two doors down. Kate's eyes were too glazed to see if it was Mr. Bancroft driving or their manservant.

Sean kept his head turned toward her, his expression

stiff. After a few more seconds of awkward silence, he said, "I should have written first. Or wired. I'm sorry if I startled you."

She gripped the wood of the door frame more tightly and drove a splinter into her finger. "Lordy!" she said, pulling her hand away and waving it in irritation.

Sean's lips turned up in a slight smile.

Kate frowned and finally addressed her visitor. "What are you smiling about?"

Immediately his expression sobered. "Nothing. I mean…it's just that you always used to say that when you were riled. 'Lordy!' It took me back."

Her wounded finger forgotten, Kate drew herself up and looked him square in the face. The words tumbled out. "Well, you can just let it take you back, Sean Flaherty. You can let it take you all the way back to wherever you disappeared to for the past eighteen months. Because you're not welcome here. Not here, nor anywhere else in Vermillion, I'd venture to say."

Sean's only reply was a wince. He was looking over her shoulder into the house. Caroline was crying in earnest now. Kate could hear Jennie singing to try to calm her, but her sister's efforts seemed to be having little effect.

"I have nothing to say to you, Sean," Kate said hurriedly. "I'm sorry." She took a step back and began to close the door in his face, but he was too quick for her. His arm shot out and stopped the heavy door cold.

"I don't expect you to welcome me, Kate," he said. "But you *will* see me. And we do have some things to talk about." He took a step toward her, crossing the threshold into the Sheridans' front hall. Kate moved backward. "To start with, you can tell me why there's a baby crying in the household of two single sisters."

Kate could feel the blood pounding in her ears. "Jennie's married," she blurted. Sean's startled look helped Kate relax. This was a safe enough topic. She continued more calmly. "She married a lawyer. His name's Carter Jones."

Sean frowned. "I don't remember anyone by that name."

"Carter's new in town since you were here." Kate's voice turned colder. "Of course, you weren't really in town long enough to remember a lot of people. You were only here long enough to…" She bit her lip.

Sean cocked his head. Now, *she* remembered that— the way he used to cock his head and flash his roguish smile. "Long enough to…what, Katie Marie?" He spoke more softly. "To make you fall in love with me?"

She shook her head and once again found herself blinking back tears. "I'm asking you to leave, Sean. Please don't make this any more difficult."

He reached out a hand and brushed a finger along her cheek. "You're pale, sweetheart. You haven't been spending enough time out in that beloved garden of yours."

Jennie, Carter and their three silver-miner boarders had harvested the garden this year while Caroline's month-long croup had kept Kate fretting indoors. But there was no way she would be explaining to Sean about Caroline's croup.

"If I'm pale, it's probably from the shock of seeing

you again, Sean. The *disagreeable* shock,'' she clarified.

He gave his half smile again. ''Well, once you're over the *shock,*'' he said, his voice gently mocking, ''I'll get to work on convincing you that having me back's not disagreeable at all.''

''Don't waste your effort. I'm not interested in having you back. And if you don't leave, I'll just have to call my brother-in-law and ask him to escort you out.'' She spoke firmly and, to her relief, her voice didn't waver.

Sean's eyebrows rose in surprise. ''You've changed, Kate. Where's the gentle little sweetheart who used to weave me chains of wildflowers out on Pritchard's Hill?''

Kate closed her eyes briefly, then faced him once again. ''She grew up, Sean. Being jilted by the only man she ever loved and losing both parents in the same month serves as a rather abrupt boost into adulthood. I don't go to Pritchard's Hill anymore.''

He edged closer and held her upper arm to keep her near. ''I'm so sorry about your parents, Kate.'' His voice was low and husky, the way she remembered it in her dreams. ''If I'd known about the flu epidemic…'' He looked away as the words trailed off, but after a moment, he met her eyes once again and continued. ''At least you're admitting that you love me.''

''*Loved.* Past tense.''

His eyes narrowed. ''That's what I've come back to find out.''

Those vivid blue eyes. Even when she'd been most

angry and bitter after he'd left her, she'd lie in bed at night remembering those eyes, and the wanting would come. She'd remember how they'd watched her, first with tenderness, then desire, as he taught her body to soar. Then she'd move restlessly between her sheets and ache for him.

"You can consider your mission accomplished. I want nothing more to do with you, Sean Flaherty. It's over."

His hair was longer, the curls more tangled than ever. He ran his hands back through them now, perplexed. "I've come a long way, Katie. I'm not about to give up this easily."

Caroline, who had been temporarily calmed by Jennie's singing, chose that moment to howl her displeasure at the continued delay of her regular feeding. Kate felt the familiar tingling in her breasts, and looked down with horror as the front of her dress grew damp.

Sean followed her gaze, his eyes widening. "That's not Jennie's baby, Kate," he said tightly. "It's yours. It's *our* child, isn't it?"

There was no way to deny the two dark spots in her light blue worsted dress. "She's my baby," she admitted, her throat constricting with sudden panic. "But that doesn't mean she's yours. You've been gone a long time. I could have been with any number of men by now."

Sean shook his head slowly. "I don't think so." He stepped around her into the center of the hall. "I want to see her."

The curtain to the parlor parted and Carter Jones'

tall form filled the archway. "Are you all right, Kate?" he asked, his eyes on Sean.

Obviously their conversation had been heard not only by Carter, but by the three miners as well, since the four men had been just beyond the curtain, engaged in their nightly card game.

Kate clasped her hands tightly at her waist. "Mr. Flaherty was just leaving," she told her brother-in-law. The look she sent Sean was half-pleading.

Sean looked from Kate to Carter. He took a step forward and held out his hand. "Sean Flaherty," he said.

After a slight hesitation, Carter shook his hand, then said, "It's a mite late for callers, Mr. Flaherty. We're early risers here at Sheridan House. Perhaps you could return with your business at a more reasonable hour."

Sean met his level gaze for a long moment, then turned to Kate. "I'll come back in the morning. Maybe you'll be over the shock by then, and we can sit down and talk things out."

Kate wanted nothing more than to be rid of him and to flee upstairs to clasp Caroline in her arms. "I've told you we have nothing to talk about, Sean. But if you need to have me tell you again, come in the morning."

Sean looked up the stairs where the baby was still crying inconsolably. "I'll be here at ten," he said. Then he walked out the door and clattered down the front steps.

Carter stood in the parlor door watching Kate with a sympathetic expression. "You're going to have to tell him, you know," he said gently.

Kate shook her head. "I don't have to tell him anything. Sean Flaherty may have been present when Caroline was created, but he wasn't around when I almost died carrying her. He wasn't around to help me or Jennie when our parents died or when we were about to lose our home. And he wasn't around to prevent the entire town from branding me a fallen woman."

"But he's come back."

Kate looked out the still-open door where Sean had disappeared into the night. "Yes." Her voice was weary. "He's come back."

"You're not telling me what it *felt* like to see him again." Jennie Sheridan looked nothing like her sister. Shorter, darker, her eyes were brown instead of Kate's crystal blue.

"Ouch! You don't have to go clear through to the nail." Kate watched with an intent frown as Jennie dug at the splinter in her finger.

"I declare, sis, you're a bigger baby than Caroline. He was as handsome as ever, I suppose. Aha, got it!"

Kate let out a relieved breath and put her finger up to her mouth to suck the place where Jennie had poked. They were sitting on the bed in Kate's room. Caroline was sleeping peacefully in her crib in the corner after taking her fill of her mother's milk. "You were the one who always said he was a scoundrel and a scalawag and I don't know what else."

Jennie bounced back against the headboard and made herself comfortable among her sister's pillows. It didn't appear that she would leave until Kate answered her questions to her satisfaction. "He is a scoundrel,'' she said. "But I never said he wasn't handsome. He's a black-haired, blue-eyed devil full of Irish blarney, but a mighty pretty one. Of course—'' Jennie's eyes sparkled "—I'm partial to blondes, myself.''

"Gray-eyed blondes. One in particular,'' Kate added. She climbed over her sister's legs to sit comfortably next to her at the head of the bed. "Yes, Sean's as handsome as ever. But that has nothing to do with me anymore.''

"There's no feeling left at all?''

Kate glanced sideways at her sister. Only sixteen months apart in age, the two had always been as close as twins. She'd never even bothered to try to lie to Jennie—it wouldn't have done any good. "My heart was pounding like the steam pump at the mine. But it could have just been the surprise of it.''

"So when are you going to tell him?''

"Jennie, I'm *not*. My life is no longer any of his business.''

"But Caroline *is* his daughter.''

"Caroline's *my* daughter.''

Jennie grabbed a pillow and hugged it to her middle. She was quiet for a moment, then said softly, "Don't you think Caroline has a right to a father?''

Kate's face was grim. "She has you and me. And she already has five men in her life—Carter, Barnaby and the silverheels.''

From the day their three silver-mining boarders had come to rent rooms, tracking silver dust into the parlor, Jennie and Kate had dubbed the men their "silverheels.'' Jennie reached for her sister's hand and squeezed it. "The silverheels love your little girl, Kate, but one of these days when the silver plays out, they'll be moving on. Barnaby's just a boy, and Carter's her uncle, not her father."

"So you think I should let Caroline learn to love Sean so that one day he can take off and leave her without warning the way he did me? I don't think so."

"He may regret leaving. After all, he came back, didn't he?"

Kate knocked the back of her head against the head-board in frustration. "I can't believe you're arguing for him, Jen. After he left, you spent months trying to convince me that I was better off forgetting about any man who would be such a cad as to leave a woman pregnant and alone."

"But he didn't know you were pregnant."

"He certainly knew we'd made love, didn't he?" Kate's voice rose in anger. "I can't understand why you're suddenly acting as if I should forget how he left without a goodbye, leaving me to face the conse-quences."

Jennie sighed. "I'm not trying to take his part, Kate. Or suggest that you forgive him. It's just that in all this time, you haven't seemed to be interested in any other man. It's as if Sean took over your heart so com-pletely there's no room for anyone else."

"Well, that's silly to say. Lyle's here almost every day."

"Oh, pooh. Lyle Wentworth is an arrogant, spoiled boy who's never done an honest day's work in his life. He's not even worth considering."

"He's a year older than you, sis, and he is working now."

"A token job in his pa's bank. No one else would have him."

Kate sighed and slid down until she was lying flat on the bed. "I'm bushed, Jennie. If I have to face Sean again in the morning, I'm going to have to get some sleep."

Jennie's face twisted with sympathy. She ran a hand over her sister's forehead. "You're working too hard for a nursing mother."

Kate reached up to squeeze her sister's hand. "You're one to talk about working hard. How about when I was in the hospital and you were running the boardinghouse all by yourself, *and* cooking for the men up at the Wesley mine?"

Jennie grinned. "You'll pay me back. When I get in a family way, I intend to let you wait on me hand and foot."

Kate smiled. "It's a deal. And the way you and Carter disappear upstairs regularly, I suspect that time will come any day." She ducked as Jennie swatted her with the pillow, then gave her sister a gentle push off the bed. "Now get out of here and let me get some sleep."

It was getting late in the season for flowers, but a two-dollar gold piece had spurred ambition in the usually indifferent hotel clerk. Within an hour after breakfast, the lad had rounded up a bouquet large enough to stir the heads of even the snobbiest Nob Hill debutantes back in San Francisco. Here in Vermillion, the offering should take Kate Sheridan's breath away. For good measure, Sean stopped at the dry goods store, balancing the flowers precariously in one arm. What did one buy for a baby? Not just a baby—his own daughter. The concept still made him weak in the knees.

The front table was stacked with bolts of heavy muslin, winter weight for the approaching cold. Did babies need winter clothes? he wondered.

"May I help you, sir?"

Sean gave an inward groan and wondered if it would be too impossibly rude to turn tail and run out of the store. Weaving her way through the colorful displays of cloth was Henrietta Billingsley, wife of the store owner and self-appointed guardian of Vermillion morality.

"It's Mr. Flaherty, isn't it?" Mrs. Billingsley continued. She had a proprietor's smile on her face, but her eyes could kill a duelist at thirty paces.

"How do you do, Mrs. Billingsley?" Sean said, fumbling to remove his hat without dropping the armload of flowers. Lord, what had possessed him to come into this particular store?

"We all thought you'd left Vermillion for good. Over a year ago, wasn't it?"

Sean had the feeling that Mrs. Billingsley knew to the day how long he'd been absent from town and also knew every detail of his transgression. Well, to hell with it. He didn't expect to be in town long enough to care what she or anyone else thought of him. He'd come to collect Kate and his daughter, and as far as he was concerned, that would be the last he'd see of Vermillion.

"Unfortunately, the family businesses required my attention," Sean answered in his most imperious tone. He'd discovered that self-righteous people were often best handled with a superior air.

"The family businesses…?"

"Shipping, banking…*Flaherty Enterprises*," he ended as if to say that anyone important would recognize the name.

"Um, of course." Henrietta's voice was a little less certain. "What can I help you with today, Mr. Flaherty?" She cast a curious glance at the flowers.

"I need something for a baby. Something warm," he ended uncertainly.

There was a gleam in Mrs. Billingsley's eyes. "And how old is the child?"

Once again, Sean was certain that she knew precisely how old his daughter was. She probably knew more exactly than he. He frowned. Hell, a man ought to know how old his own daughter was. "Around a year. No, less."

"Around the age of little Caroline Sheridan? Nine months?"

Sean felt the heat rising around his stiff collar. The annoying woman had the ability to make you feel as if she were a schoolmarm about to switch you for putting wet rags in the potbellied furnace. "Perhaps I'll come back later," he said. "After I find out what the baby needs." He backed toward the door.

Henrietta began to straighten the perfectly arranged bolts of cloth next to where Sean had been standing, as if his presence had somehow disturbed their harmony. "We'll be happy to take care of you when you're ready, Mr. Flaherty. Just let us know. If it's the Sheridan baby you're interested in, I imagine the child could use a number of items. Those girls have been plumb broke since their parents died leaving nothing but debts. I wouldn't be surprised if they've been dressing the little tyke in rags."

Sean didn't know if his sudden rage came from effrontery of the gossipy woman or from the thought of his daughter in tatters. He clapped his hat back on his head. "How much material does it take to make a dress for a baby?"

"For just a tiny one? Oh, two yards should do."

He gestured to the table of cloth. "I want two yards of each one of these sent to the Sheridan house."

Mrs. Billingsley's jaw dropped. "Each one?" she asked. "There must be two dozen different—"

"Each one. I'll be in to settle the account later this afternoon." Then he nodded and left the store, letting the flimsy door bang shut behind him.

Uncharacteristically, Sean felt his heart speeding up as he opened the gate and headed up the walk toward the Sheridan house. He hadn't realized that he would be so affected by seeing Kate again. These months back in his own world in San Francisco society, he'd managed to convince himself that his lightning love affair with a simple girl from the mountains had been nothing more than a springtime idyll. But yesterday, looking into those clear blue eyes, he'd felt a stirring somewhere deep inside, somewhere that hadn't often been touched in his comfortable life.

It was Jennie, not Kate, who opened the door. She seemed to be expecting him, but she didn't step back to allow him to enter.

"Hello, Jennie," he said. "It's good to see you again. You're looking well. Married life must agree with you."

She didn't return his smile. "She doesn't want to see you, Sean. I'm sorry. I thought..."

"Thank you for writing. It was the right thing to do."

Jennie looked quickly back over her shoulder as if to assure herself that the hall was empty. She spoke quietly. "I'm not so sure of that anymore. If she knew I'd written you about the baby, she'd be furious with me."

"Well, I won't tell her. I would rather she thought I came back for her all on my own." He shifted the huge bouquet. "May I come in?"

Jennie ignored the request and continued talking almost to herself, justifying her action. "She's fully recovered her health from the difficult birth, but she just seemed to be getting more...listless. And then there was Lyle coming around all the time trying to talk her into marrying him for the baby's sake. I didn't know what to do."

"Lyle Wentworth? The banker's son who used to lord it over you girls about growing up poor in the mountains?"

Jennie nodded and rolled her eyes. "He's been sweet on Kate since we were children."

"You'd never know it the way he treats her. I can't believe she even suffers him in your home."

Jennie bit her lip and looked at him with a pained expression. "Well, Lyle *was* a help during Kate's pregnancy when we had to take her to a special hospital. We were all by ourselves, you know, after Mama and Papa died..." Her voice trailed off.

Sean finished for her, "And with the father of her baby gone." His face grew tight. "Why didn't she contact me, Jennie? She knew my family was prominent in San Francisco. It wouldn't have been hard to find me." He stopped speaking as Kate appeared in the back of the hall at the door that led into the kitchen.

"You don't know me very well, Sean Flaherty, if you think I would go crawling to a man who left me with nothing but a terse note," she said.

Jennie turned around, startled. "He knows about the baby, Kate," she told her sister in a rush.

Kate walked toward them, grim faced. "I know. I'm afraid it was impossible for me to keep some of the more embarrassing aspects of motherhood from revealing the secret last night."

Sean stepped around Jennie and held the flowers out to Kate. "I've come to try to start over, Kate. I know you've been through a lot and there's no reason for you to forgive me, but I'm asking you to let me try and make it up to you."

Her face was as calm and hard as a statue. "Caroline's my baby, Sean. You forfeited any right—"

"I can help you, Kate. I want to help our child." He looked around the hall, his eyes resting on the faded parlor curtain. "I have money, as you know."

Jennie stepped back to allow him to move closer to Kate, who stood with her hands on her hips, bristling, making no attempt to take the flowers he was offering. "I don't want your money, Sean, or your flowers. Caroline and I don't want any part of you. I haven't changed my mind since last night. You can just pack up your bags and head back to your papa's business and your fancy big-city friends."

Sean sighed and turned to hand the flowers to Jennie. "Would you mind finding somewhere for these?" he asked with a touch of exasperation. "And give me five minutes alone with this stubborn, beautiful sister of yours."

Kate's face had colored at the compliment, in spite of herself, and Jennie's worried expression lightened slightly. She took the flowers in both arms and headed back toward the kitchen, saying over her shoulder, "You two might as well go sit in the parlor instead of standing in the hall shouting at each other like fish-wives."

Sean put his hat on the hall table and gestured toward the curtained doorway. "Shall we?" he asked.

Kate gave a reluctant nod and led the way into the parlor, where she sat on one of the high-backed chairs. Sean took the seat nearest to her on one end of the settee. He sank into the cushions, which left his head lower than hers, making him feel at an immediate disadvantage.

"Why didn't you let me know, Kate?" he asked, his voice gentle. "I would have come. You could have had the finest doctors in San Francisco."

Kate sat stiffly, her hands clasped in her lap. "It

seems to me that I'm the one who has the right to ask the questions, Sean. You're the one owing the explanations. Why did you leave? Why didn't you come and tell me you were going? What *happened* to you?'' Her voice trembled a little at the end.

Sean had a sudden urge to draw her into his arms as he had so many times during the passionate three months they'd been together. Instead he cleared his throat and said, ''I'm not making excuses, Kate. It was wrong of me to leave without seeing you. But it's just that I've never been too good at goodbyes. I thought it might be easier on both of us...''

''To leave me to have our baby alone?''

''I had no idea about the baby. Surely you believe that much anyway. I thought we'd tried to be careful. I've never had anything like this happen...ah... before.'' He stammered a little as he realized the import of his words. Kate did not hesitate to call him on them.

''You mean none of your other women has ever had the effrontery to present you with a child? You've led a charmed life, Sean Flaherty. I'm sorry to have been the one to spoil your record. But, as I've been trying to tell you since last night, you don't need to worry. Caroline and I are making no claim on you whatsoever.''

Sean blew out an exasperated breath. ''Damn it, you're a stubborn woman, Katie Marie Sheridan. Yes, I left. It was wrong, and I'm sorry. But now I'm back. I've come back for *you* and for our daughter.'' His voice softened. ''The truth is, sweetheart, I've never stopped thinking about you in all these eighteen months.'' As he said the words, he realized that they were the absolute truth. Even before he'd received Jennie's letter about the baby, Kate had been in his mind night and day. He'd had other women, but they'd been pale in comparison to the spirited, lithesome blond beauty he'd left in the mountains.

Kate was silent for a long moment. He couldn't tell if she'd been moved by the obvious sincerity of his declaration or if she was thinking of yet another way to send him packing. But before she could speak, there was a rustling of the parlor curtain. Sean looked up to see Jennie standing in the archway. In her arms was a moppet with black curly hair and blue eyes that mirrored his own.

Chapter Two

Kate jumped to her feet and crossed the room to take the baby from her sister.

"I'm sorry," Jennie said with worried eyes. "She was fussing, and I have to head up to the mine." Although the financial situation had eased when Jennie had married Carter, she still went up to the mine each day to prepare the noon meal for the silver miners, the job she had obtained when they'd needed money to keep Kate in the hospital in Virginia City before the birth.

"That's fine. You run along," Kate told her, clasping Caroline tight against her.

Jennie looked doubtfully from her sister to Sean. "Will you be all right?"

Sean stood and took a step toward them. "I'm not a monster, Jennie. Your sister is perfectly safe with me."

"I didn't mean to be insulting, Sean. It's just that…" She glanced at her sister, then back to Sean. "Well, good, then. I'll leave you to get acquainted with your daughter." She leaned over to give Kate a quick peck on the cheek, then darted out the curtain into the hall.

Sean walked over to Kate and the baby, a look of wonder on his face. "She has black hair," he said, his voice choked.

Kate looked up at him, her eyes glazed. Her voice came out in a whisper. "Yes."

He reached out a hand and ran his finger over Caroline's silky hair. Safe in her mother's arms, the baby watched him, eyes wide. "Does she…ah…is she healthy?" he asked. "Does she have everything she needs?"

Kate looked down at the baby tenderly. It was the first time he'd seen her smile since he'd been back. She was smiling at Caroline, not at him, but the expression slid straight into his midsection.

"She's healthy and happy. Aren't you, precious?"

Kate's voice went up in pitch, her eyes lit with a special glow that was answered by a gleam in the baby's own eyes. Sean watched the mother-daughter communication with awe. His own mother and father had always been too busy with their high-society world to pay much attention to the parent-child bond. Sean was totally unprepared for the wave of love that swept through him at this first sight of his daughter. Tears welled at the base of his throat.

A minute fist came up toward his finger. He twisted his wrist to let the baby's hand close around his thumb. The back of her hand was no bigger than a quarter and felt as smooth as a polished stone. "She's… beautiful," he said finally.

Kate looked up, and this time the smile was for him.

"Yes, she is. We produced a beautiful child, Sean. And she's smart, too," she added eagerly. "She's already talking."

Some of Sean's fascination with the baby was diverted by Kate's sudden abandonment of her hostility toward him. It appeared that when she was talking about the baby, she was so intensely positive that there was no room left for old resentments. "Is she now?" he asked with the light brogue he sometimes adopted when he was flirting. "I didn't think babies could talk this young."

Kate was swaying back and forth in a natural, rocking motion to keep the baby content. She seemed to not even be aware of the movement. "Well, not *exactly* talking. But she makes sounds. And I think they mean something. She says a special goo goo that I think means 'mama.'"

Kate shifted her gaze upward again, her eyes laughing. Sean stared at her, entranced. "Mama, eh?" he said softly. "Well, now we'll have to get her to start working on 'papa.'"

All at once, Kate seemed to realize how intently he was watching her, how close he was standing, and that the hand that had been stroking the baby now gripped Kate's arm. She pulled away and walked past him toward the settee.

"If you want to visit her while you're in town, I won't prevent you, Sean," she said, sitting on one edge of the couch and laying the baby along the rest of it so that there was no room for Sean to resume his seat. "But I'm going to ask you to come back and do so when Jennie's here. I don't intend to spend time with you.''

Sean's eyes darkened. "I want to spend time with my daughter, Kate, but you're the one I need to see. I didn't come all this way to visit for a day or two.''

Kate looked up at him. All the glow from her interaction with the baby had left her face. She was pale again. "How long will you be here?''

Sean's eyes went to the baby. "As long as it takes to convince you to marry me,'' he answered tersely. The minute he said it, he knew it had been a mistake. He'd started out on the right path this morning with the flowers, the gifts for the baby, trying to get Jennie on his side. But meeting his daughter had rattled him. Suddenly it had become more important than he'd realized that he be able to stake his claim on her and on Kate.

Kate made no reply for a long moment. Finally she leaned over, gathered the baby into her arms and stood. "Be prepared for a long stay then, Sean, because I'll never agree to marry you. I loved you, I won't deny it. I was young, and a fool. I thought poetry and flowers and pretty speeches meant that a man had a heart. Now I've learned that the sign of a true heart is someone who's willing to work hard for his family. Someone who's *there* when they need them. You weren't here when I needed you, Sean. And now I don't need you anymore.''

The quiet dignity of her tone left Sean feeling for the second time that day like a chastised schoolboy. So far his visit had not gone as he'd anticipated when he left San Francisco. He'd expected that Kate would be somewhat resentful over his abrupt departure, but once she'd given him a chance to explain and turn his charm on her again, he'd figured that they would resume the relationship where they had left off a year and a half earlier. She'd been a sweet, sensitive girl and he'd been her first romance. She'd been desperately in love with him, which he'd found stimulating and intoxicating. But it appeared she'd changed in more ways than one. If she was still in love with him, she was hiding it well. And the rub of it was, the more time he spent with her, the more he realized that he was as intoxicated as ever.

He looked down once again at his daughter. She was no longer interested in the stranger and had begun instead to squirm and pat at Kate's full breasts. "I wasn't around when you needed me, Kate," he agreed. "But I'm here now, and I don't intend to leave either you or my daughter to face the world alone again."

Kate shook her head, juggled Caroline in her arms and looked as if the tears she'd been staving off would finally fall.

Sean brushed his hand briefly over the baby's curly hair, then said softly, "Go ahead and feed our daughter, Katie Marie. I'll see myself out."

It started that afternoon with Barnaby slamming into the kitchen out of breath to announce that Irving, the odd-job man from the dry goods, had just left a mountain of packages on the front porch.

"A *mountain!*" he'd repeated, gulping air. Barnaby was the thirteen-year-old orphan who had been living with the Sheridans since he'd been taken in by their parents about a year before their death. He helped around the house, especially now that it had been turned into a boarding establishment, but his position was more of an adopted younger brother than a servant.

"What are they? Where did they come from?" Jennie had asked. But Kate had merely rolled her eyes. She'd expected something of the sort ever since Sean had left her standing alone in the parlor that morning. He'd had that look in his eyes that she'd seen before, a determination that sooner or later he'd get what he wanted. She'd seen the same look the spring he'd come to town and wooed her with such intensity. That time, he *had* gotten what he wanted, but, she resolved to herself firmly, he was not going to get it now.

When they went out to the porch to examine the packages, Jennie seemed to be taking Sean's side once again. "They're for his daughter, Kate. He has a right to give her something."

But after they'd opened the tenth package of expensive, heavy cloth, even Jennie had to admit that Sean's largesse had been excessive. "What in the world could one child do with so many clothes?" she asked.

"I'll keep four of the lengths," Kate announced, "and then I'm going to send the rest off to the hospital in Virginia City. There were plenty of babies there who could use something warm for the winter."

Jennie had nodded her approval and the paper-wrapped pieces of cloth had been neatly stacked at one end of the porch awaiting transportation to their new home.

That evening when Sean had once again shown up

after supper and been informed of Kate's proposed disposal of his gifts, he'd frowned and said firmly that the cloth was for Caroline. In addition, he told Jennie, he'd see that money was wired the following day from Flaherty Enterprises to the Virginia City hospital. "Enough to clothe a hundred babies," he said angrily. But Kate had refused to see him that evening and the next and the next.

Over those three days flowers arrived regularly, morning and evening. A case of champagne had been delivered for Jennie and Carter with a card: "In belated celebration of your marriage." Amanda Hill, the town milliner and seamstress had arrived saying she'd been hired to sew frocks for little Miss Caroline. By the third evening, when a huge box of sweetmeats had arrived for their evening supper, even the silverheels were urging Kate to give Sean an audience.

"If for no other reason than to make him stop," Dennis Kelly told her as they sat around the big dining room table while Barnaby and Jennie cleared away the dishes. "The man'll drive you daft, lass."

"He's driving me daft already," Kate replied.

Dennis chuckled, jiggling the jowls under his muttonchop whiskers. "Aye, but it's a nice way to go. Showered with attention." Of Irish descent himself, Dennis' speech sometimes reminded Kate of Sean's slight brogue. And both knew how to use blarney to their purpose.

"If you really have no desire to take up with him again, Kate, you may have to see him one more time just so you can convince him of that," Carter added.

"And, of course, if he really wants to see his daughter, you may not be able to stop him."

Kate looked up sharply. "You mean he might be able to see her whether I want him to or not?"

Carter nodded. "He's the father. He has certain legal rights."

Jennie swung through the kitchen door. "I don't know why you're so set against seeing him, sis. He did come back for you."

"Yes. And he only waited a year and a half to do it."

"Ah, lass, don't be too hard on him. Some laddies are just slower than others," Dennis Kelly urged.

The other two miners had been silent throughout the discussion, but finally the youngest one, Brad Connors, spoke up. "I'd throw the bastard out on his ear if I was you, Miss Kate. Excuse my language."

"I agree," chimed in the third boarder, Humphrey Smith, who had never been called anything but Smitty.

Kate suspected that neither Brad nor Smitty was being objective, since both had all but admitted warm feelings for her themselves. But it felt good to have someone taking her side. She gave both men a smile.

"If you keep turning him away, he might decide he has no recourse but to go to the courts," Carter warned.

"And what would the courts do?"

Jennie went to put a hand on her husband's shoulder as he looked gravely at Kate and answered, "They can't make you agree to see him, but they could make you allow him to see Caroline. He's a rich man, Kate.

With the right lawyers, he could even win custody of her.''

Kate gave a little gasp of horror. ''They could take her away from me?''

Carter gave a grim nod. ''With the lawyers the Flahertys could muster, I reckon they could.''

Kate looked around the table at the three miners, then at her sister, standing behind Carter. All were watching her with concern. She swallowed hard. ''No one's taking my baby away from me,'' she said. ''I'll see him tomorrow morning.''

Sean was pleased but not totally surprised when young Barnaby, the orphan living with the Sheridans, showed up at his hotel room early in the morning with the message that Kate wanted to talk with him. He'd figured she needed time to calm down and enough courting to soothe her pride, but he'd never doubted that eventually she'd give in. Some women just needed more coaxing than others. He'd calculated it might take up to a week, so four days was more than satisfactory.

He whistled as he set off toward Elm Street, his mood buoyant. What did surprise him a bit was how much he was looking forward to seeing her again. With any luck she might have softened enough for him to take her in his arms, perhaps kiss her. The very idea made his blood race in a way it hadn't for months. And the second surprise was how much he was looking forward to seeing Caroline. He'd never been one to pay much attention to babies, but he found himself daydreaming about his daughter's sweet little face and curly black hair. He flexed his hand and remembered the feel of her tiny fist around his finger. He wanted to see them both.

But once again it was Jennie who answered the door, and her smile was not as welcoming as it had been the other day. His glance went to the huge arrangement of flowers on the table, overpowering in the small hallway. They'd come from him, of course, but Jennie made no reference to them.

"Kate's waiting to speak with you in the parlor, Sean. She asked me and Carter to join you."

A family gathering wasn't exactly what Sean had had in mind, but he smiled pleasantly and said, "Fine," and followed her through the curtain into the parlor.

Kate and Carter were together on the settee. Carter stood when they entered, but Kate remained seated. She looked tired. There were circles under her eyes, and her cheeks were even paler than when Sean had first arrived. He frowned with concern. "Are you feeling all right?" he asked her without preliminaries.

She met his gaze directly. "I'll be feeling better when you leave town."

"Kate!" Jennie exclaimed at her sister's rudeness.

Carter gave a half smile and extended his hand toward the visitor. "Kate's interested to know the purpose for your stay in Vermillion, Flaherty." The two men shook hands. "What exactly are your intentions here?"

Sean looked around the group. Jennie walked over to stand next to Carter, who slipped an arm around her waist. Kate glared up at him from her seat on the settee. There was less warmth in the room than in an icehouse at midwinter.

"I came back to see Kate, to see if we could resume…if we could find…" He stumbled over the words, then cleared his throat and started again. "Of course, now that I know about my daughter, it just makes it all the more urgent." He shot Jennie a glance to make sure that she realized that he was keeping her part in his return a secret. He wouldn't reveal that he'd learned of Caroline's existence from Jennie's letter.

"Caroline's *my* daughter," Kate began, her voice shaking. Carter put a steadying hand on her shoulder.

"No one will deny that you are the father of Kate's child," Carter said in a lawyerly tone. "We've asked you here today to discuss the ramifications of that admission."

This was *not* the discussion Sean had expected. He'd hoped Kate had come to her senses. He'd hoped for some kind of tender reunion, had even pictured taking her back to his room at the hotel to rekindle the passion they'd been so quick to find eighteen months ago. He felt awkward standing before her as if at some kind of tribunal.

"May I sit down?" he asked, gesturing to the high-backed chair.

"Of course." Carter sat down again on the settee, and Jennie sank to a low stool beside him, leaving her hand in his.

As Sean took his seat, Kate spoke again. "You're not taking away my baby, Sean."

He looked up in surprise. "Is that what you think of me, Katie?"

"We just want to get this straightened out," Carter explained. "As the father, you might have certain rights."

"By all means, let's get it straight," Sean replied. He was beginning to get angry. "I have no intention of taking Caroline away from anyone. A baby belongs with her mother. But she belongs with her father, too. I'm here to try to make that happen." He shifted his gaze directly to Kate and spoke intently. "I want us to be together, Kate. I'm asking you to forgive me and to give me—to give *us*—that chance."

There was a long moment of silence during which it was obvious to everyone in the room that Sean's words had somehow reached their target. Kate's expression had softened and there was a look of something like longing in her clear eyes.

Finally Carter stood, pulling Jennie up with him. "I think I hear the baby," he said.

Jennie gave him a puzzled glance. "Barnaby's with her."

Carter lifted an eyebrow and gave a slight nod toward Sean. "Maybe we'd better go check to be sure," he said.

Jennie looked from Sean to her sister, then back to Carter, who nodded again. "All right." She let him lead her across the room and out the curtain. "We'll be close by if you need anything," she told Kate. Then the couple ducked through the curtain and Sean and Kate were alone.

"Did you really come back for me?" Kate asked finally. "To try again?"

Sean wasted little time in moving in at what appeared to be a wavering of the opposing forces. He got up and swiftly crossed the room to sit next to Kate on the settee. "I haven't stopped thinking about you in all these months, Kate." This much he could say with complete sincerity.

Kate's gaze became unfocused and drifted toward the window. "I couldn't believe it when you left," she began slowly. "We were so happy. My world had become a paradise, and then suddenly you were gone. You didn't even come to say goodbye, just that cold letter..."

He took her hand. "Ah, Katie, if it sounded cold it was because I was writing it with a broken heart. I didn't know what to tell you."

"You said you had to go back to your family's business."

"I was *forced* back by my father. He said he was tired of my foolish whim to play prospector. If I hadn't gone home, he might have disowned me."

"And he forced you to leave so quickly you couldn't even come to tell me in person?"

Her voice was growing cold again. Sean looked down at the floor. "No," he said in a low voice. "That was sheer cowardice. I think I knew if I had to look into those beautiful eyes of yours to say goodbye, I'd never be able to leave."

Kate pulled her hand out of his almost regretfully, without her earlier anger. "As you said the other day, I'm not the same person I was back then, Sean. We don't know if we would even feel the same about each other."

Sean met her eyes. "Maybe you don't, but I knew

it the minute I saw you again, Katie.'' He recaptured her hand and this time brought it to his mouth and planted a kiss on her palm. ''Tell me you don't feel it, too.''

She made no reply, and this time she didn't pull her hand away. He followed the one kiss with another on the inside of her wrist, right at the spot where her pulse was pounding. His voice grew husky. ''Since the minute I saw you, Katie, I've been wanting to do this again.''

He shifted closer on the settee and enfolded her in his arms, then bent to find her mouth with his. He was gentle, tentative almost, not at all the passionate, demanding lover she remembered. It was devastating.

She felt a swirling inside her head and then her mouth opened to accept his deepening kiss. For a moment the past year and a half receded and she was back on a hillside in the early spring, in love for the first time in her life.

He pulled her against him, her breasts hardening as they pressed into his chest. Her insides turned liquid and hot and her head fell back against his arm as his kiss became two, then three, then she lost count.

''I never forgot this, sweetheart,'' he murmured. ''All this time, I've remembered the taste of these lips.''

The sound of his voice helped clear the haze that had descended on her so abruptly. She pulled away, her cheeks burning.

''You haven't forgotten, either,'' he said. When she refused to meet his eyes, he took her chin in his fingers and gently turned her face up to look at him. "Have you?"

After a moment, she answered, grateful that her voice was steady. "They say a girl never forgets her first love."

"And I was your first, Katie. That was your precious gift to me. I was a cad for accepting it and then leaving you, but I'm here to convince you to forgive me for that. Is there any hope?"

Kate sank back against the soft cushions of the settee and sighed. "How could I ever trust you, Sean? You broke my heart once. Wouldn't I be foolish to entrust it to you again?"

He smiled. "Five minutes ago I might have answered yes, but not after those kisses. Now I'd have to say you'd be foolish *not* to give me another chance. Because you're still in love with me, Katie Marie Sheridan. A woman doesn't kiss like that unless she's in love."

She didn't bother to deny his assertion. Part of her had never stopped loving Sean Flaherty. But if she'd learned one lesson in the past eighteen months it was that sometimes loving is not enough.

"Perhaps we can spend some time together and see how we feel," she said after a long pause.

Sean gave a whoop and leaned over to buss her on the cheek. "That's my girl. That's my sweet Kate."

She slid away from him across the silk seat. "I've told you, Sean, I'm not the same sweet little Kate I was when we met, but we'll get to know each other again and see what happens."

"We'll do this any way you want," he assured her.

She nodded firmly. "For one thing, we'll have none of that kissing business for a while. It muddles my thinking."

Sean grinned. "Nothing wrong with a bit of muddled thinking now and then."

Kate gave a reluctant smile. "Well, I prefer to stay clearheaded, thank you very much."

He stood and reached for her hands. "Fine. I won't kiss you again until you ask me to. I promise."

She let him take her hands and pull her up to stand intimately close to him. The heat was instantaneous. She felt her cheeks flush again.

Sean laughed, obviously aware of her reaction. "Come on, my clearheaded darling, let's go find my daughter so I can get better acquainted with her."

Chapter Three

"Do you think I did the right thing?" Jennie asked, snuggling against Carter in their soft bed.

"To go against your sister's express wishes and write to Flaherty, putting her at risk of losing her child to his powerful family?"

Jennie winced and buried her face in his shoulder. "You don't really think he'd try to take Caroline, do you?"

"I don't even know the guy, honey. I think you were playing with fire, but I've learned my lesson about trying to make you change your mind when you get one of your notions."

His voice held laughter and a lazy, post-lovemaking indulgence. "I find *that* hard to believe, counselor," Jennie said dryly. "But, seriously, maybe this time I've made a terrible mistake. Kate and I have always tried to take care of each other."

"And you're still trying to take care of her, Jennie. That's your problem. Your baby sister's all grown-up now. It's up to her to decide what she wants to do about Flaherty. You'll just have to trust her to make the right decision.''

''I don't want her hurt again, Carter. She deserves to be happy.''

Carter sighed. ''Perhaps you should have thought about that before you wrote the letter, honey. But it's too late now. He's here, and, personally, I think Kate is perfectly capable of dealing with him.''

''Do you think she's still in love with him?''

''She hasn't said a single kind word, and her eyes flash daggers when she looks at him, so I would say...yes.''

Jennie pulled her head up to look at him. ''That doesn't make sense.''

He pulled her on top of him and gave her soft bottom a loving pat. ''It makes perfect sense. How many verbal daggers did you throw at me before I could get you to admit that you were crazy about me?''

She smiled at him in the darkness. ''I threw plenty. But that was *before* I fell in love with you.''

Carter shook his head. ''Nope. It was *because* you fell in love with me. The opposite of love is indifference, not hostility.''

''So your theory is that if Kate is hostile, it means she still cares about him?''

Carter pulled her a couple inches along the top of him, enough for her to feel evidence of his renewed arousal. ''We can have a heck of a tiff, baby,'' he said in a low voice, ''and you still do this to me. The one thing I can't be when I'm around you is indifferent. If Kate were calm and nonchalant, I'd say Flaherty should start packing, but as it is...I don't know. She just might weaken.''

Jennie shifted her legs to fit her body more closely around him, eliciting a low growl from her partner. ''If he hurts her again, I'll personally take Papa's shotgun and run him out of town. I swear.''

Carter reached his hand up to pull her head down toward him. ''I don't want to talk about Flaherty anymore,'' he said tersely. Then he proceeded to close her mouth with his own.

By the end of the week it was obvious that Carter had been right. Kate was anything but indifferent to her former lover. She tried to pretend that her interest was casual, but Jennie could recognize the signs in her sister—the extra primping before he was due to call, the starry gazes out the window when she thought no one was around, the flushed cheeks at the sound of his knock on the front door.

She hadn't agreed to go off alone with him yet, so Jennie assumed she was keeping some degree of control on the relationship, but she suspected that would change. Sean could be very charming...and very persuasive. Even though she'd been responsible for bringing Sean back to Vermillion, Jennie's misgivings grew. As the older sister, she felt as if she should at least warn Kate about giving in too far, too fast. But since the couple in question already had produced a child, the advice seemed a bit silly.

So when Kate asked shyly if Jennie would mind Caroline while she had supper at the hotel with Sean, Jennie merely agreed and held her tongue.

Kate sensed her sister's apprehension and was grateful for her forbearance. She had enough doubts herself without adding Jennie's. Sean had wanted to be alone with her all week, and she had continued to resist, though every day she felt more comfortable in his company, more tender watching his obvious delight in his daughter, and more reluctant to see him leave in the evening. He'd kept his word and had not tried to kiss her, but the tension between them as they parted each night made it obvious that at the barest nod from her, she would once again be in his arms.

The first chill of fall was in the air as they crossed the street toward the Continental Hotel. She was glad she'd worn the old silk shawl that had been her mother's. She and Jennie had divided their mother's clothes between them after her death. They were too short of money not to use them, though for weeks it had been a pang to see them on each other.

"I should have hired a rig," Sean said, looking at the glowing western sky. "I remember how you liked sunsets."

"I don't get much time for a drive in the country these days," Kate answered a bit wistfully. "I almost envy Jennie her job up at the mine. It gets her out into the mountains every day. Of course, I'd probably be intimidated cooking for all those men."

Sean took her arm to help her up the stairs to the wooden sidewalk in front of the hotel. "You cook for the three miners boarding with you."

"That's different. Dennis, Brad and Smitty are almost like family nowadays. And they're easy to please. They say anything I make tastes like heaven."

"Sweetheart, we had some of the finest cooks in San Francisco at home when I was growing up, and not a one of them could produce a brisket like the one we had last night."

"Ah, Sean Flaherty, you and your Irish blarney again," she protested. But she was pleased in spite of herself. Sean's descriptions of his wealthy childhood had always intimidated her. The luxuries of Nob Hill sounded much farther than a mountain range away from her simple Vermillion life. Meeting Sean had opened a whole new world to her, a world beyond the mountains, where men and ladies wore fine clothes, dined on exotic foods and delighted each other with their witty sallies. There had been a time when she'd dreamed of marrying Sean and being swept off to that enchanted world. But those days were over. She was happy at Sheridan House with her daughter and the rest of her family around her. Nevertheless, remembering Sean's tales of lavish San Francisco banquets, she'd worked all yesterday afternoon to be sure the supper was perfect.

"I can tell you one thing," Sean was saying with his crooked grin. "We won't be dining as finely tonight. The Continental must have recruited the hotel chef from one of the neighboring mines. His steaks are hard as ore and twice as gritty."

Kate chuckled. One of the things that had made her fall so fatally for Sean had been his humor. Though there'd always been plenty of lively talk around their table, Kate had to admit that her own family had been a serious bunch.

He did his best to keep her fascinated throughout

the meal. The laughter felt good. She hadn't laughed so hard or felt so carefree since a year ago spring, before Sean had left her, before the death of her parents in the flu epidemic, before she'd learned that she would have to face the town unwed with a baby growing inside her.

"Ah, Katie Marie, you need to laugh more often," he said as the waiter cleared away their plates including the rum cake which Kate had scarcely touched. "It makes your face glow like a freshly opened rose."

She nodded and swirled the coffee in her cup. "Yes. There was too much sadness in our household after Mama and Papa died...and then I was so sick with the baby. And Jennie had a terrible battle with Carter when the town was trying to close down the boarding-house." She straightened up in the chair and smiled. "But that's all past now. Carter and Jennie are happy as two June bugs on a screen, Caroline is healthy..."

"And her father's come back," Sean added softly.

Kate lowered her eyes. "Yes. He's come back. And I've discovered that he still can make me laugh like no one else I've ever met."

Sean reached across the table and grasped the hand that held the cup, stopping the swirling. "He can still make you feel, too, Katie. He can make you laugh and then cry from the intensity of it. Remember?"

He spoke softly, but the words drummed into her ears. She did remember. The intensity. The tears of release after Sean had brought her to incredible heights of passion. But she remembered other tears later, the ones she'd shed after he had left her. Oceans of them. She pulled her hand away and put down the cup.

"I think I'd better get back, Sean. Caroline will be wanting her mama before going down for the night."

"I thought Jennie was going to feed her a bottle."

"Well, it's always better if I feed her myself." She spoke the words in a rush and stood up abruptly, trying to tamp down the sudden panicky feeling.

Sean stood, as well, reached into his pocket and carelessly tossed three silver dollars onto the table. "Katie, it's after ten. Caroline's undoubtedly been asleep for over an hour."

"Have you become such an expert on her schedule, suddenly, with less than a week's practice?" Her voice was sharper than she had intended, but Sean didn't seem to be offended. He walked around the table and took her arm.

"We've had such a lovely evening. I'm not ready to give you back yet." He put an arm behind her waist and steered her toward the Continental's narrow staircase. "We'll have some Queen Charlotte in my room."

"What's Queen Charlotte?"

"It's a raspberry claret—very much the rage in San Francisco. I brought some with me just for you."

San Francisco. That mysterious, glamorous world he'd painted for her in tantalizing glimpses in between their magical moments of lovemaking. Yes, she wanted to go upstairs with him to drink Queen Charlotte and get heady on the elixir of faraway places and close-up passion. Her body was strumming with the wanting of it. But her mind told her that once she climbed those stairs with him, she'd be lost. She'd have unlocked her mended heart and left it vulnerable, out in the open, just waiting for him to rend it apart again.

She stopped his forward movement by holding on to the end of the banister. "I can't, Sean."

She was up on the first step so their eyes were level, just inches apart, hers anguished, his pleading. "Let me help you remember how good we were, Katie," he said, low and husky.

Kate looked around for some sign of life to help break the spell of those intent blue eyes, but the hotel lobby was empty. Even the desk clerk had abandoned his post. She turned back to him and took a deep breath. "That spring I let you make love to me, Sean, because I was young and foolish and desperately in love. But it was a mistake." He tried to protest, but she held up a hand and continued, "Mama always said the wisest people were the ones who make plenty of mistakes, because they learn so much from them."

The image of her sensible, down-to-earth mother, the woman who had wanted to raise her daughters in the simplicity and beauty of the mountains, helped Kate grow calmer.

Sean seemed to sense that he had lost the battle. He dropped his arm from behind her. "I promised that you'd do the asking next time, Katie," he said with a sad smile.

She nodded. "Thank you."

He put his hands at her waist and boosted her off the step, then left them there for a long moment. "Having a baby didn't thicken that waspish waist of yours any, sweetheart," he said, his voice a little shaky.

She slipped out of his grasp. "There are plenty of pleasingly plump girls in town if you're on the lookout, Sean," she snapped.

"Katie! That wasn't a complaint. You're...*perfect*. Just the way you are." He stepped back and took a quick glance at her graceful, slender form. "You're perfect," he said again softly, almost to himself.

Kate suddenly felt tired. She'd been up feeding Caroline before dawn. "Will you take me home now, Sean?" she asked.

He stood looking at her one more long moment, then seemed to come to some kind of resolution. His face became animated once again. "Yes, I'll take you home. But tomorrow night we're going for that sunset drive." When she started to demur, he added, "We'll take Caroline along with us. That way we won't have to trouble Jennie again. C'mon, sweetheart. I want to have a picnic with my daughter."

Once again, Kate knew the more she let this go on, the more at risk she was, but a sunset picnic with Sean and their daughter sounded wonderful. She smiled her agreement. "I'll pack us a supper."

Barnaby was the only member of the household to put it to her directly. They spoke in the kitchen as he helped her make the meat pies Kate had planned for supper. She would pack several to be eaten cold on the picnic. In his matter-of-fact voice that was just beginning to show signs of slipping into manhood, he said, "I thought Mr. Flaherty was a bad man, Kate, 'cause he left you, and you had to have Caroline all by yourself and almost died. So I don't understand why you're going on a picnic with him.''

Kate smiled slightly at the unanswerable logic. ''Sometimes adults do things that don't make much sense, don't we?''

Barnaby nodded. He needed a haircut and his body had sprouted out of his clothes, as it seemed to do regularly these days. He resembled a miniature scarecrow. ''So how come you're going?'' he persisted.

Kate gave a little shriek as her finger slipped off the towel and touched one of the hot pie tins. She set the pie on the counter and dipped the tip of the burned finger into the pan of dishwater. ''Well, for one thing, Sean is Caroline's father. I think it's only fair for me to let him get to know her and give her the chance to have a father, if things could work out that way.''

''You mean, like you marrying him after all?''

Even Kate hadn't wanted to confront the question after roundly rejecting Sean's initial proposal, but now that the issue was raised, she realized that marrying Sean was exactly what had been on her mind these past three days. It was hard to believe after all she'd been through, but suddenly it seemed the only course that would make her life perfect. She had her health back, she had Caroline. Now all she needed was Sean.

She pulled her finger out of the water and frowned at it. ''Well, I told him no once, and he may not ask me again.'' Barnaby was methodically pulling off the pieces of crust that had overlapped the edges of one of the tins and popping the bits of dough in his mouth. ''Don't burn yourself,'' she cautioned.

''Oh, he'll ask you again all right.''

Kate blushed. "How do you know that?"

"The way he looks at you...you know, all dopey eyed. And I heard Carter and Jennie talking about it. I guess it's all right. It would be good for Caroline to have a pa."

A slight shadow crossed his face. Like Caroline, Barnaby had been born illegitimately. Shortly after the baby's birth he'd been so concerned about protecting her from the stigma he'd carried throughout his own short life that he'd tried to run away with her into the mountains. It had taken Carter, who also had been born to an unwed mother, to convince the boy that the love of a close-knit family like the Sheridans could make up for the lack of a name.

Kate sensed the direction of the boy's thoughts and leaned over to ruffle a hand through his reddish hair. "Caroline would do just fine without a pa, Barnaby. But I guess it would be nice for her to have one just the same."

"Yeah. Caroline'd like that, I think. But you'd still be living here, wouldn't you?"

Kate's thinking hadn't taken her that far. "I don't know," she said slowly.

Barnaby looked worried. "You can't take Caroline away. We all love her."

"I know, Barnaby. She loves you, too. But anyway, no one's even talked about my getting married yet, so we won't worry about it, all right? Now how about you take some of these pies into the dining room? Be sure to set them on a plate so they don't scorch the table."

He nodded and began to do as she asked, but his face was glum.

Barnaby's dismal expression stayed with Kate as she and Sean drove up the gently sloping road that led west out of town to Pritchard's Hill. She was less enthusiastic than she'd been earlier in the day anticipating the excursion. There was no doubt that the feeling she had had for Sean was returning. She recognized the symptoms—sweaty palms, a giddy sensation in her head, fullness in her chest. But things were more complicated than they had been eighteen months ago when she'd been a carefree girl discovering the beauty of young love.

"You're quiet tonight, Katie," Sean said, turning his head from the horses to study her.

"I'm sorry. Caroline awoke three times last night. I'm probably tired."

Sean reached into her lap and seized one of her hands. "That wasn't a reproach, sweetheart. No need to apologize." He looked into the back of the buggy where Caroline was lying awake and wide-eyed, but peaceful. "I thought you told me she usually sleeps all through the night now. She's not sick, is she?"

Kate shook her head. "No, but I think those new teeth coming in are bothering her a little. I rubbed some of Carter's whiskey on them before we left tonight."

"Whiskey!" Sean looked horrified.

Kate laughed. "Not to *drink*. Just rubbed on the gums. It won't hurt her any."

Sean was viewing his daughter with a critical eye

as if trying to identify signs of drunkenness. "I don't know anything about babies, Kate," he said finally with a sigh.

"Most people don't until they get one. Then you learn fast."

They'd reached the grove of old cedars where they had been accustomed to stopping during their visits here that first spring. "Shall we make it here, for old times' sake?" Sean asked.

Kate's heart sped up a little, but she nodded. "It'll be too dark if we try to go farther."

Sean sprang out of the carriage and was around to Kate's side before she could climb out on her own. His arms came up around her waist and swung her down. When her feet touched the ground, she tried to take a step away, but he held her firmly against him, looking down at her. His eyes were slightly hooded, the nostrils flared. When he spoke, his voice was husky. "I won't break my promise about waiting until you ask, but a kiss for old times' sake would be nice, too."

Their faces were only inches apart, and Kate could feel an actual tingling in her suddenly dry lips. She licked them. "I think we'd better eat," she said. "Caroline will be fussing for her own supper before long."

He released her instantly, his face impassive. "I'll hand her down to you," he said, boosting himself up on the side rails to reach for Caroline's basket.

Kate felt the tension drain out of her as she busied herself preparing for the meal. They set out two blankets and let Caroline sit up in the middle of one, entertaining herself with the wooden blocks Dennis Kelly had whittled for her. On the other, they set out the food Kate had packed. Sean had brought along a bottle of wine and two glasses. "This is for you, now, not the baby," he joked as he handed her a glass.

Kate smiled. "In a manner of speaking, Caroline drinks whatever I do."

Sean looked a little embarrassed by the reference. His eyes went to Kate's full breasts, then slid away. "I don't know much about that, either," he mumbled, and began digging into one of the meat pies.

Dinner went quickly and with much laughter over Caroline's antics as she crawled around trying to explore each item on the menu. Finally when they'd finished the last of the maple cakes for dessert, Kate took Caroline in her arms and said a little shyly. "I'm afraid I'll have to feed her before we head back. She'll be hollering up a fit before long if she doesn't get her supper."

Sean jumped to his feet and picked up the extra blanket. Folding it over three times he fashioned a little seat and propped it against the nearest cedar tree. "Will you be comfortable here or would you rather be in the buggy?"

Kate stood, still carrying the baby, who was beginning to squirm. "That will be fine." She hesitated a moment, avoiding his eyes.

Sean walked over to her and took Caroline. "You make yourself comfortable there and do whatever you need to get yourself ready, and then I'll hand her to you."

Kate sank down onto the padded seat and arranged

her skirts around her. "I should have her blanket from the basket," she said.

Sean nodded but still held the baby, waiting. When she made no move to unbutton her dress, he said, "I'll go take a walk or something if you want me to, Kate, but I'd prefer to stay and watch my daughter with her mother."

Losing a little of her self-consciousness, Kate undid the top of her dress, then reached up for Caroline. Sean retrieved the blanket and tucked it tenderly around the baby, who was already finding her dinner.

It seemed, after all, natural and sweet to sit in the darkening evening with Sean while their baby tugged at her breast. Sean's eyes were mostly on her face, but every now and then he'd reach out a hand to stroke the back of the baby's head ever so gently.

When she was finished, she sat Caroline on her knee and patted her back. "Let me do that," Sean said, reaching for the baby.

"Careful, she might spit up," Kate warned, and helped him arrange the blanket over his trousers in case of any sudden eruptions. She fastened up her dress, then sat back against the tree to watch Sean minister to their baby. The sight made her throat fill.

After several minutes, she said, "She'll sleep now if you want to put her down in the basket."

He smiled and gave Caroline a final hug, which she returned by putting her chubby arms around his neck. She made no protest as he put her down and carefully arranged the blanket around her.

"She's half-asleep already," he said, his voice tender and a bit awed.

The evening was beginning to grow cool. Kate untangled part of the blanket she was sitting on to wrap it around her shoulders. "We should be heading back, I guess," she said sleepily. "But it's nice here."

Sean took a final look into Caroline's basket, then went back to drop beside Kate, dragging the other blanket beneath him. "We can stay awhile longer, if you like. Jennie said you weren't to worry about cleaning up at Sheridan House tonight."

"She and Barnaby will handle everything just fine," Kate agreed. "I don't know what I would have done without them this past year."

Sean stretched out on the blanket, propping himself on one elbow and looking up at her. "This past year when you should have had a husband with you to help in the burdens of bearing and raising your child."

Kate looked down at him, her face serious. "Perhaps I was wrong not to contact you, Sean."

"No 'perhaps' about it, Kate. But there's no way to relive the past. The question is, what are we going to do now?"

The meat pie she'd eaten seemed to be stuck at the base of her throat. She remembered the conversation earlier with Barnaby, so certain that Sean would want to marry her. And as much as the young orphan hated the thought of losing Caroline, he'd thought she'd be better off with a father. "Why did you suddenly decide to come back, Sean? You've never really explained what brought you back here." She held in a breath. Somehow the answer was vitally important to her.

Sean looked at her a long moment, his eyes unreadable in the increasing dusk. "I've told you, Kate. I never stopped thinking about you in all these months."

"Surely there have been others..."

He shook his head. "I'm not a saint, I guess you know that better than anyone. But none of them seemed to mean anything after you. Every time I was accosted by one of the society belles on Nob Hill hunting a socially acceptable husband, all I could think about was my sweetheart up in the mountains. And when I'd try to forget you by carousing in one of the gambling halls down by the waterfront, the painted ladies would turn my stomach and make me long for the fresh white skin and clear blue eyes of the beauty I'd left behind."

She wanted to believe his sincerity. But she'd believed him once before when he'd talked of love everlasting. It hadn't even lasted through the spring.

"I have more than my own heart to guard now, Sean. I have my daughter's, as well."

He was quiet for such a long time that Kate wondered if he was beginning to fall asleep. But suddenly he sat up, moved to her side and put his arms around her.

"I'm going to break my promise and kiss you," he said. "I swear it's the last promise to you I'll ever break."

Chapter Four

When he'd planned a drive away from town, Sean had anticipated that the privacy and distance would ignite the feelings that he and Kate had both been resisting for several days. But he'd planned to let her be the one to initiate things. He'd had every intention of continuing to play the role of gentleman until she gave him the word. But seeing her with his daughter had evoked emotions that he'd never before experienced. And when he'd heard the crack in her voice as she talked about entrusting him with her heart, he'd simply had to hold her. His mind, his body and something deeper than either of these were all combining to convince him that he could not live another second without feeling her in his arms.

Once she was there, nothing else seemed to matter. She'd not protested. In fact, she was willing and pliant. Within short moments, she was eager and yearning.

He kissed her, deeply, and she responded much more thoroughly than she had at her home the other day. So thoroughly that his entire body began to throb.

"Ah, Katie," he murmured. "How I've missed this. You feel so very right to me."

She lay back in his arms and smiled up at him, her eyes shining in the light of the rising moon. "You feel right to me, too, Sean. Remember, how I told you that first time...?"

He kissed her forehead, then each of her eyes. "I was the one you had waited for, you said. I remember every single detail of that night."

"On this very hill."

"Yes, up there beyond the boulder."

They smiled at the shared memory. Then Sean renewed his caresses, kissing the tip of her chin, then underneath it and along the length of her neck. He tasted her earlobe, then whispered, "I thought I never could want anything as much as I wanted you that night, Katie, but I was wrong...because tonight I want you even more than I did then."

She gave a little groan as she rocked against him, then asked, "Caroline?"

In an instant he released her, jumped to his feet and walked over to the carriage where he'd placed the baby's basket on the seat. Before the night breeze could cool the warmth where his arms had been, he was back, rearranging the blanket as he joined her once again on the ground. "We'll hear her if she stirs. Right now she's in dreamland." He kissed her again, softly. "And I'm about to take her mother into a dreamland of a different sort."

Kate had one last fleeting thought that she shouldn't let herself be carried away. She had responsibilities now. She should be discussing Sean's intentions, his plans. But all she could think about was the feel of his lips on her face, his hands moving firmly along her rib cage and coming to rest gently alongside each of her breasts. "Is it all right?" he asked, sounding suddenly unsure. "You're not too sensitive?"

She felt incredibly sensitive at the moment, but not in the way he meant. It seemed as if every inch of her was quivering, waiting to feel his touch. In response to his question she began unfastening her dress and pulled his head down toward her full breasts. "Make love to me, Sean," she murmured. And as she said the words she felt an immense need begin to build in the lower portion of her body. She moved her legs restlessly against him.

He sensed her urgency and pressed a hand against her private parts through her dress as he began an onslaught of deep, rhythmic, slow kisses. She opened her mouth to his, grasped his back and moved against his hand, the sensation building so quickly that before she knew what had happened she'd tumbled over the edge into quick convulsions of release.

Sean gave a little chuckle and held her tightly. "It's been so long," she said, hiding her face against his shoulder.

"I'm glad," he said in a fierce, low voice. "I'm glad no one else found you in all these months that I was foolish enough to leave you here by yourself. Now you're mine again, Katie Marie. And this time I'm not letting you go."

His declaration seemed to spur him to action. In short order he had discarded both her clothing and his own. Neither noticed the cool night air on their burning skin. It was enough that they were together again, flesh against flesh, their mouths seeking each other with needy, almost desperate kisses, their hands touching everywhere, relearning the once familiar paths to passion.

"I love you," Kate breathed without conscious thought as their bodies joined, and as they moved together and the feeling spiraled, the words spiraled, too, in her head. "Love you, love you, love you..." Until finally once again the wave of feeling broke over her, and this time Sean shared the moment, clutching her more tightly as he climaxed inside her.

Afterward they lay totally still for several long moments, each lost in private thoughts. Sean was the first to speak. "I'm sorry, Katie, I didn't mean for this to happen."

Kate froze, then felt her heart plunge. But even as she struggled to hold back the sob that rose in her throat, Sean continued, "I'd meant to get you to agree to marry me before we did this again."

There was a rushing behind her ears. All the doubts that had surfaced earlier when she was talking to Barnaby and on the drive up here dissipated like dust in a rainstorm. She sank back against his arm and smiled with joy and relief. "Did you now?" she asked.

He tucked her snugly against him and kissed her cheek. "Caroline needs a father."

Her smile dimmed a bit. She'd hoped for a more romantic declaration, but perhaps she shouldn't be so particular. Sean *must* love her if he wanted to marry her. After all, he'd come back to Vermillion to find her before he knew anything about the baby.

He didn't seem to notice her hesitation. Smiling at her, he gave her a playful kiss. "And who knows, we may already have started on a little brother for her. I'd say it's more than high time we were married, young lady."

She chuckled. "I'm not a young lady anymore, Sean. I'm a mother now."

He stroked her soft skin from her shoulder to her hip. "No one would believe it, Katie. You're more beautiful than ever."   •

She moved beneath his hand with a murmur of contentment. "You truly want to marry me? I'm not dreaming this?"

He stopped his caress and rolled away from her. "We keep getting things backward, sweetheart. I wanted to do this proper, but I can't think straight when I have you naked in my arms."

He gathered up her clothes and handed them to her, then stood to don his own. He was dressed before she. The first stars had just begun to appear alongside the quarter moon in the dark sky. By their light, he helped her fasten up her dress and straightened her shawl around her. When she was properly attired, he dropped to one knee in front of her and took her hand. "Miss Kate Sheridan," he said, his voice low and vibrant, "I would consider myself the luckiest man on earth if you would do me the honor of granting me your hand in marriage."

Kate felt the tears smart her eyes and her nostrils. She nodded, then, unsure if he could see in the darkness, she said, "Yes. I do. I mean...*I'll marry you.*"

She laughed. "I don't know what one's supposed to say."

He stood and took her in his arms to give her a chaste kiss. "The 'yes' was all I needed to hear."

She leaned her head against his chest, her heart bursting with happiness. "I love you, Sean," she said again. Perhaps this time he'd say the words himself.

"I almost forgot!" he said instead. He released her and began to fish in his watch pocket, finally drawing out a tiny ring box. "This is for you."

She took the velvet case and opened it. Even in the darkness, the stones glittered in regal splendor. A spectacular diamond, completely encircled by smaller rubies. Kate looked up at him in amazement. "You didn't get this in Vermillion."

He laughed. "Lord, no. It's from San Francisco. I brought it with me when I came. Are you thinking it was vain of me to be so sure I could persuade you to forgive me?"

She shook her head. What she was thinking was that this showed he really *had* come back for her, come back expressly to marry her. Which meant that his words about how he had never stopped thinking about her in all those months were true. "It's so beautiful, Sean," she said simply.

He took the ring from the box and slipped it on her finger, then held her hand out to the moonlight so that they could admire it together. "It suits you, I think."

Kate smiled and shook her head. "It's far more elegant than anything I've ever owned or expected to own."

"You can flaunt it in front of Mrs. Billingsley and

all those other self-righteous biddies who gave you a hard time about the baby."

Kate dropped her hand to her side. "I'll love the ring because you gave it to me, Sean, not for any other reason. I have no bitterness against those ladies. They were merely upholding the standards of propriety that they had been raised to believe in."

"Well, they didn't have to try to ruin your and Jennie's lives because of it."

"That's all past. Everyone in town accepts me now. And our true friends have supported us all along."

Sean shrugged, but said with a grin, "I'll still look forward to seeing old lady Billingsley's face when she sees it on you."

Kate laughed. "I might get a tiny bit of enjoyment out of that sight myself."

"He bought the ring in San Francisco, Jennie. You see what that means—he came back *intending* to marry me."

Kate's face was radiant with happiness. The two sisters were out in the little washhouse behind the main house, working on the seemingly endless task of washing linen. Dennis, Brad and Smitty came in filthy every night from the mine and went through several towels each. Carter's prosecutor job was not as dirtying, but he was a fastidious man who also liked a daily bath. And Barnaby, though he would easily forgo the bathing process if the sisters would let him, managed to track in more dirt than the four adult men combined. With so many towels, along with the sheets and other laundry, Kate and Jennie found themselves out at the washing shed almost every day.

"It's too bad he couldn't have done that a few months back," Jennie said dryly. She seemed reluctant to endorse Kate's sudden change of position on Sean. Of course, Jennie had been cynical about men in general before she'd fallen for Carter.

Kate picked up the ring, which she'd carefully set on a shelf while they scrubbed the clothes. "I never thought to have anything this pretty," she said dreamily.

"A pretty ring doesn't make a marriage, Kate. Are you sure about this? Are you sure you won't be too lonely way off in San Francisco?"

Kate's expression dimmed. "Sean said we'd come for regular visits. And you can come to see us."

"It'll be hard for all of us to let little Caroline go. The first thing the silverheels do each night when they get home is go in to check on her. Carter, too. And you know Barnaby considers himself her personal protector."

"I'll always be grateful for that, Jennie. Caroline hasn't felt the absence of a father because she's had a whole household of them. But if she can have her *real* father, don't you think that's better?"

"I just hope Sean's family will love you both as much as we do."

"I'm sure they'll be wonderful. Sean said he told them before he ever left that he was hoping to bring home a bride."

"He *was* sure of himself, wasn't he?"

Kate chuckled but then became serious. "You can't

imagine how important this has been to me, sis. When he left me that spring, I thought I'd been foolish to believe that he loved me. But now I see that he really did love me all along. It just took him a bit longer to figure it out.''

Jennie's smile was weak, but she walked around the wooden washtub to give her sister a hug. ''He'd just better have it figured out now, because it's a big responsibility to take on a wife and baby. If he's not up to it, he'll have to answer to the whole passel of us.''

''I can't believe you would be such an idiot, Kate.'' Lyle Wentworth was striding angrily up and down the front porch of the Sheridan house while Kate sat on the swing at one end trying to stay calm.

''And I can't believe you would use that tone of voice to me, Lyle Wentworth. If you came here to shout, you can leave right now.''

He spun around and walked back toward her, his long face contrite. ''I'm sorry, Kate, but, honestly, you've got to realize what a mistake you're making. This man abandoned you when you were expecting his child.''

''We've been through that, Lyle. I've listened to Sean's explanations and I've decided to forgive him. I'm sorry that this is disappointing you. I know you…''

''You know I've loved you my whole life. I've waited for you. When you had to be by yourself at the hospital in Virginia City, who was the one who stayed by your side? It sure as hell wasn't your fast-talking rich boyfriend.''

Kate stood and faced him. "I've asked you to watch your language, Lyle."

His eyes reflected his misery. "Don't scold me, Kate. Can't you see how I'm suffering?"

"I'm sorry, Lyle." And she was truly sorry. Lyle had been a help and comfort to her when she'd been so sick before Caroline's birth, and he'd been a devoted visitor ever since. If she'd let him, he would have called on her daily. Frequently he arrived with trinkets for the baby, flowers for her or sweetmeats for their table. But she'd never been able to get over the feeling that Lyle viewed her as something he wanted to possess. As the only child of the town banker, he'd had everything he wanted his whole life—everything except Kate.

"Just take some more time to think about it, Kate. The guy's been back less than a month. And you were together only a couple months in the first place. You don't really know him that well."

She could have told Lyle that she knew enough to realize that Sean's kisses made her heart soar, whereas the few times Lyle had kissed her, she'd felt nothing. But such an admission would be too cruel to an old friend. "The heart is a funny thing, Lyle. Sean and I haven't spent that much time together, but I love him. It's as simple as that, really."

They were still standing in front of the swing. Lyle grabbed the chain and moved it back and forth in frustration. "I think you're wrong, Kate. Sometimes it's not that simple at all. When you go into his world in San Francisco, you may find that love isn't enough.

And by then it'll be too late. All the people who love you will be too far away to help.''

Jennie had offered similar sentiments, but Kate was ignoring them all. Of course, Sean needed to be back in his world. He was expected to take his place in his father's business and, as his wife, it was her duty to live where he needed to be. She stopped the motion of the swing with her knee and laid her hand on Lyle's. ''It's where I belong,'' she said, her eyes sad. ''I'll never forget what you've done for me, Lyle. But you've got to let me go and give me a chance to build a life with my child's father.''

Lyle pulled his hand out from hers. ''I won't wish you luck, Kate,'' he said tightly. Then he turned around, crossed the porch and ran down the path to the street.

Kate insisted on keeping the wedding preparations to a minimum. Though everyone in the household offered best wishes, she knew that Lyle's skepticism and Jennie's concern were shared by the others. No one else in town had been invited. Some of their friends had been staunch supporters during Kate's unwed pregnancy, but she thought it was unseemly to advertise the nature of Caroline's birth with a regular wedding.

So it was just the family and the three silverheels who lined up in the parlor to listen to Kate and Sean exchange vows in front of Reverend O'Connor. An Irishman himself, the blustery minister seemed willing to overlook Sean's tardy arrival on the scene months after his daughter's birth.

"May the Lord bless you both on this holy occasion," he said in closing, and shook the groom's hand warmly before accepting just a "wee" glass of the celebratory champagne Sean had insisted on having brought from Virginia City.

Kate was kissed by each of the silverheels in turn, then Carter, and finally by a teary-eyed Jennie. "Be happy, Kate," she whispered. "That's all I want."

All in all it was a subdued evening, and by the time she and Sean left to go back and spend their wedding night at his hotel, Kate's stomach was jumping with nerves.

"Would you like me to have some food sent up, sweetheart?" Sean asked as he took off his blue suit coat and hung it on the clothes tree. "I noticed that you didn't eat anything back at your house."

"I wasn't hungry," she said, and walked toward the bed, feeling odd and lonely, as if she had already said goodbye to her family and home.

Sean came up behind her and put his arms around her. "You're tired. You've worn yourself out packing the last two days. I'm sorry I couldn't have waited longer, but I know my father is anxious for me to get back to San Francisco."

The warmth of his arms dispelled some of her gloom. "It's going to be hard to leave tomorrow," she agreed. "But as you say, we'll see them often. And I'll have the two most important people in my life with me."

Sean turned her to face him and looked down at her with a serious expression. "I heard what your sister said, Kate, and I saw the misgivings in the faces of the others. But I *do* want to make you happy. You and our daughter.''

She smiled up at him. ''Caroline's quite taken with her papa already. And, of course, her mother's been hopeless about him since the day we met.''

''On the steps in front of the Wentworth Bank.''

She nodded.

''You were wearing a blue dress, just the shade of your eyes, and I thought you were the prettiest sight I'd ever laid eyes on.''

Kate moved more fully into his arms. ''You said, 'Miss, I hope you're planning to lock some of that beauty up in the bank here, because it's not safe to have it out in the open.'''

''Did I now?'' Sean grinned.

''Yes, and I thought it was the most outrageous nonsense I'd ever heard.''

''But look where it led us.''

''Yes.''

She turned her face up for his kiss, and all the misgivings of the brief wedding ceremony faded as once again her body responded to his caresses with increasingly strident yearnings.

''Ah, Kate, you turn me to fire every time I hold you,'' Sean murmured in her ear, and the hardening of his body against her was ample proof of his words.

They were too impatient to pull back the coverlet on the bed, tumbling right on top of it and shedding clothes as they fell. ''Jennie gave me a lovely nightdress to wear...'' Kate began, but trailed off the words as Sean met her mouth with searching, skillful kisses that made her head spin. Her eyes closed and she lay back and let him stroke her into passion, her thighs, her stomach, her breasts.

"We'll put it on you later," he whispered. "For now I want just you...naked and soft and warm." The words accented his deliberate caresses. Eventually his hand slipped between her legs where she was moist and ready to receive him. He pulled himself over her and asked softly, "Now?"

She opened her eyes to look up into his, glittering blue fire above her. "Please...now," she whispered, and guided his entry.

Their union was slow perfection. The speed they had felt at the beginning was through, replaced by a delicious sense of timelessness. All their feelings were centered on their joined flesh. Kate reached the edge first, and she whimpered at the back of her throat and hugged him more closely to her, prompting him to hasten his movements into a quickened shared rhythm that sent them both crashing into completion.

His body rested on top of hers, their damp skin sticking together wherever they touched. Kate's fingers played idly through his tangled hair.

"You were magnificent, Mrs. Flaherty," he said finally.

Kate gave a slow smile. Mrs. Flaherty. It had a lovely sound. "You were pretty magnificent yourself, Mr. Flaherty," she said happily.

He rolled off her and pulled himself up to lie next to her on top of the coverlet. "To all appearances, Katie Marie, one of us was in a bit of a hurry. We didn't even undo the bed."

She loved the teasing note to his voice. "I believe we *both* were impatient, my love."

Sean smiled. "*My love...*I like the sound of that."

Actually, the endearment had slipped out unintended. Sean had still never told her in so many words that he loved her, and she had thought that she should not push the matter. But he *was* her love, and after what they'd just shared, it only seemed right to tell him so.

"Then I shall call you that every morning when I wake you up in our new home in San Francisco," she said, tapping a finger lightly on his nose.

His smile dimmed, and for a moment his thoughts seemed to wander away from her. "I may change my bedroom," he said after a moment.

She frowned in confusion. He'd already explained that for the time being they would be living at his family's mansion, which was plenty big enough to house them and Caroline. "Change it?" she asked.

"We're right down the hall from Mother, and I have a feeling if we don't do something about it, the first sound either of us hears each morning will be her knock."

"Surely your mother wouldn't intrude on a newly married couple."

For just a moment Sean looked younger than his twenty-five years. "We'll see," he said, but his voice lacked its usual confidence.

"Perhaps we should try to find a place of our own to live. Your parents might not like being saddled with a new daughter-in-law *and* a new granddaughter all at once."

Sean rolled off the bed. "We should pull back these covers," he said. His voice had lost all the warm intimacy of the previous few moments.

Kate got to her feet, feeling suddenly self-conscious at her nakedness. Without comment she opened her carpetbag and put on the light pink lawn nightdress Jennie had given her. "Do you think they'll like me?" she asked, disturbed at Sean's reaction to the topic of his home and parents.

"Of course," he said. "Everyone likes you, Katie." The offhand answer did little to comfort her. She slipped into bed under the blankets and waited while Sean put out the light and climbed into the other side of the bed. The sheets were cold and Kate shivered under the coverlet. She wanted to feel Sean's arms around her again, making her feel warm and loved. But he didn't reach for her. "We'd better go to sleep so we can get started early tomorrow," he said. He turned toward the opposite side of the bed and settled down, apparently ready to sleep.

Kate lay awake, staring into the darkness, a tightness closing around her heart. Tomorrow she would leave the only home she had ever known to travel to a new city and a new family. And all at once the man who was taking her there seemed like a stranger.

Chapter Five

The four-day trip by stagecoach to San Francisco had seemed interminable. Caroline had been understandably fussy to be torn away for the first time ever from her comfortable surroundings at Sheridan House. Kate had been long-faced after her tearful parting from Jennie and Barnaby. Sean himself had found the exuberance of the courtship and the wedding being replaced by worry over what it would be like to return home with his new bride.

Of course, it had been his father's insistence that had sent him back to Vermillion in the first place. When Sean had shown him Jennie's letter with the news of the birth of his daughter, Patrick Flaherty had given his son a stern lecture on responsibility, had written him out a bank draft for five hundred dollars, and then had basically thrown him out of the house and told him not to come back until he had the matter straightened out.

Sean was fairly certain that his father would be pleased that he had decided to shoulder responsibility by marrying Kate. But his mother…Lord. She'd be reaching for her smelling salts at the news. She'd always maintained the hope that Sean would pick out one of the pink and pretty debutante daughters of her insufferable nouveau riche friends in Nob Hill society. Sean had dutifully courted several of them. And unbeknownst to any of their parents, had even gone beyond courting with two or three of the more willing ones. But he'd never found one who had fascinated him the way Kate had from the moment he'd set eyes on her.

Well, his mother would just have to give up her matchmaking schemes now that he was presenting her with his ready-made family, a grandchild already nearly a year old. Sean leaned against the mended leather back of the old stagecoach seat and closed his eyes. Harriet Flaherty a grandmother? He suppressed a groan at the thought.

Grandmothers were people like Nonny, Patrick Flaherty's tiny Irish mother, Bridget, who lived with them. She, at least, would welcome Kate and the baby. He'd always been able to count on Nonny. With that comforting thought, he let the jolting of the coach rock him into a restless sleep.

Kate felt as if she hadn't slept a wink for four days. Sean seemed to be able to sleep even as the carriage tilted precariously over the edge of a mountain road, threatening each instant to slide into a thousand-foot gorge. But she stayed wide-awake, clutching Caroline's basket with white knuckles.

The nights had not been much better. Jammed into tiny rooms at overcrowded rest stops, Sean had made no attempt to resume their lovemaking. He seemed tired and distant, and Kate didn't know what she should do about it. At times she concluded that his mood must mean that he was already regretting his decision to link his life with someone so different from the ladies he was used to back home. Perhaps he was dreading having to present her to his parents and fine friends. Since he'd become so pensive when the subject had arisen on their wedding night, she'd been afraid to bring it up.

Caroline was the one bright spot. It gave Kate a warm glow to watch Sean play with her and delight in her antics. When she and Sean would laugh together at the baby's unintelligible attempts to formulate words or her wide-eyed exploration of each new item she encountered on the journey, it made Kate feel as if they truly were husband and wife.

Sean had become surprisingly comfortable with the baby. When she'd begin fussing, more often than not by the time Kate reached for her, Sean had already snatched her up into his arms. He never complained about her restless nights, and had even taken to changing her wet clothes now and then, though he'd let Kate deal with the washing.

But when the baby was asleep and Sean got that somber look on his face as he sat gazing out at the sage-covered hills, Kate would feel the beginnings of an unsettled dread in her stomach. She didn't know what kind of life awaited her up on that intimidating-sounding place called Nob Hill, but she was starting to get the feeling that her year of single motherhood would be a picnic in comparison.

* * *

San Francisco was already full of rich speculators, merchants, railroad tycoons and gold barons before discovery of the Comstock lode. But the unimaginably rich silver strike had ushered in a whole class of instant millionaires, wealthy "nobs" who began building their ostentatious mansions up on a hill overlooking the city and the bay, which soon became known as Nob Hill.

They fueled the growth of the city, investing in coal companies, factories, woolen mills, silk weaving, all variety of enterprise. Patrick Flaherty was among the earlier arrivals to the Paris of the West. Arriving with a modest sum obtained from a gold strike that had played out before it could yield real wealth, he had chosen to invest in exporting and shipping. The move had multiplied his wealth beyond his wildest dreams. A city full of new rich, hungry for marble from Italy for their carved mantlepieces, wicker furniture from China for their long verandas or Parisian glass for their atrium skylights increased his shipping operations tenfold, and then tenfold again.

The Flahertys were also among the early builders on Nob Hill. Their mansion was relatively simple compared to some of the ornate structures that were now being called Victorian. But to Kate, the Flaherty mansion was nothing short of a palace.

Her mouth fell open as she followed a step behind Sean into the huge entrance foyer. It was dominated by an imposing staircase with a large wrought iron candelabra sprouting up from the newel post like an iron tree. Gilt-edged mirrors went floor to ceiling along both side walls, reflecting endless images of herself looking small and lost as she stood in the simple blue serge coat that had been her mother's, holding a sleeping Caroline.

The door had been opened by a uniformed young man who had disappeared before Kate could even thank him.

Sean put Caroline's basket and bag on one of the elegant hall chairs and turned around to face her. "Welcome home, sweetheart," he said, smiling.

Kate felt as if she hadn't slept in weeks, but she managed a wan smile. It was the first time he'd called her sweetheart on the entire journey. Perhaps things would be better now that they were truly home. The strangeness that had settled over them on their wedding night would disappear. "Thank you," she said, then looked around the empty hall. They'd been there for several minutes and no one had come to welcome them. "Did your parents know we were arriving this evening?"

Sean looked ill at ease. "Yes, I wired them. But I believe they had a supper to attend tonight. Some sort of opera gala. There will be time enough for you to meet them in the morning."

It was certainly not the kind of welcome a family visitor would receive back at Sheridan House, but, Kate reminded herself, she was in a different world now. She'd have to get used to the way Sean's people did things, and she'd have to learn not to be quick to judge the new ways until she'd given them a try. She smiled more broadly. "I daresay they'll find me a more pleasant sight after a good night's sleep anyway.''

Sean nodded. "Do you want to wake Caroline to feed her?''

Kate looked down at the sleeping child. "She's so exhausted, I think she'll sleep right through the night if you want to take her basket up to our room.''

Sean looked surprised. "She'll have her own nursery, Kate. She doesn't have to sleep in your room anymore.''

Kate hesitated. "But I don't mind having her there.''

"Nonsense. This house is huge. There's no reason for everyone to sleep all cramped together like…ah…well, there's no reason to be all crowded.''

Most of the time the crowding together at Sheridan House had felt cozy rather than burdensome, but Kate didn't want to start an argument. She had slept in the same room with Caroline since her birth, and she would have enjoyed the comfort of being near her on their first night in this vast strange new home, but she supposed that it was reasonable that Sean would want some privacy with his wife. "If you take her basket to the nursery then, I'll put her down.''

Caroline stirred in her arms as if suddenly aware in her sleep that her life was about to change. Kate rocked her back into oblivion.

"We don't need the basket anymore,'' Sean said. "There's a crib all ready for her up there.''

"Oh. Well, that's very nice,'' Kate said, casting a glance at the discarded straw basket and following Sean upstairs.

Wall sconces lit the entire length of the endless staircase. They seemed to glow all by themselves. Noticing her glances at them, Sean said, "Gasworks. It goes through the house to all the light fixtures. Uses a fortune in coal."

Kate nodded as if she understood what he was saying, but in reality the bright lights seemed to be a product of magic. And then, as they rounded the curve of the stairs, a small figure appeared who could very well be the wizard who'd produced the effect. Or some kind of benevolent gnome.

"Nonny," Sean cried, and took the remaining stairs two at a time to enfold the creature in a giant hug.

By now Kate could see that it was not a gnome but rather a small woman wrapped in a quilted plaid night robe and wearing a matching pointed nightcap. By the light of the sconces her eyes danced merrily as she looked down the stairs at Kate and said, "Ah, Sean, you've brought us an angel...two of them from what I can see, one grown and one wee."

Sean turned toward Kate, his arm still around the old woman's shoulders. "This is my grandmother, Kate. Bridget Flaherty."

"How do you do, Mrs. Flaherty?" Kate murmured, mounting the last couple steps to stand directly in front of her.

"My child, you're to call me Nonny, like my grandson does. I'm your granny, too, now, from what Sean writes."

Her voice was so warm and cheerful it gave the same effect as stepping into a comforting hot bath.

Kate relaxed her shoulders and gave a genuine smile. "Thank you, Nonny."

Nonny bent toward the baby. "What a precious little love. With the Flaherty black curls, no mistaking that. She's the picture of yourself as a wee one, Sean."

Kate could literally feel her heart lightening with the woman's instant acceptance. Perhaps her new surroundings would not be so alien after all, in spite of the intimidating luxury of them. She smiled again at the little woman. "I've thought that myself ever since she was born."

"Ah, but we're keeping you here talking, my dear, when you're swaying from exhaustion. Let me help you get this little angel to bed and you right behind her."

"Caroline will sleep in the nursery," Sean clarified.

Nonny looked sharply at Kate, whose smile had faded, then gently addressed Sean. "She'll sleep where her mother says she sleeps."

Caroline was heavy, and Kate felt if she didn't put her down and get to a bed herself soon, she might sink down on the Flahertys' lush Persian carpet and spend the night there. "The nursery will be fine, if that's the way Sean wants it," she said.

Nonny looked at her for another long moment, her bright gray eyes keen. "I'll tell you what, for the wee one's first night here in a strange house, I'll just sleep by her in the nanny's bed. If she wakes up, I'll come to get you right away."

Kate nodded, her gratitude plain on her face.

"In fact, if you trust me with her, I'll put her down myself. You can go right on to bed." Gently and smoothly she reached for Caroline, who went into her arms without stirring. "She'll be just fine," Nonny whispered. "Now Sean, take this poor lass off to bed."

With a last look at Caroline, Kate let Sean take her elbow and lead her down the long hall. Her arms felt empty without the baby who had been like another appendage during the long trip. But Sean's body brushed against hers as they walked and suddenly she realized that she was alone with her husband. The husband who had not kissed her since their wedding night. Her mouth felt dry.

They reached a door at the end of the hall and he opened it. "Here's your room," he said.

She looked at him in surprise. "*My* room?"

He nodded. "Mine's next door. There's a connecting door inside. Just tap on it if you want anything. Do you need your trunk up here tonight?"

Kate shook her head, feeling a bit dazed. Once again she tried to remind herself that she wasn't in Vermillion anymore. Maybe in San Francisco fancy folk who were married didn't share a bed, but it certainly seemed as if that was one custom that the poor folk had much better figured out than the rich.

"Nonny's right, you do look tired. I'll leave you to get some rest," he said.

He leaned over and gave her a brief kiss on the cheek, and then he was gone. The door next to hers clicked shut. Kate stood in the doorway of her room looking down the long hallway at the twinkling gaslights. "Welcome home," she said to herself softly with a rueful twist to her mouth. She was too tired to sort it all out now. No doubt tomorrow things would look brighter. Then she turned to enter her bedroom alone.

Thank heaven for Nonny, Sean thought as he lay wide-awake in his bed. At least some member of the family had been there to give Kate a welcome. He'd had the feeling the entire journey that his new bride was already regretting their hasty marriage. The trip had been hard on the baby, on all of them. And when they'd arrived at his home, he'd seen how she looked at it as if it were overly extravagant and pretentious. Which it was, he supposed. He'd never really thought much about it before.

He couldn't believe it when the new houseboy had told him that neither of his parents was home to receive them. What was the lad's name? He couldn't keep track, they came and went so fast. His mother was not the easiest mistress to work for.

In spite of his exhaustion from the trip, he couldn't seem to sleep. Part of his restlessness was undoubtedly due to the knowledge that his beautiful wife was this minute sleeping not fifty feet away from him. He'd hoped to have her sleeping next to him tonight, naked in his bed. But she'd looked so tired and so distant.

Still, even after he'd left her, he'd waited up for a good hour, hoping to hear the knob turning on the door between their rooms. Hoping that she'd want to spend their first night in their new home together.

He sighed. Tomorrow would be better. She and Caroline would be rested. His parents would be there to give her an official welcome to the family. And then, perhaps, after a day of getting used to his world, to-

morrow night she'd be willing to slip through that connecting door and let him spend the rest of the night
making love to her.

Sean's knock the next morning on the door that connected his room with Kate's woke her from a sound
sleep. Without opening the door, he asked her if she
needed more water or anything else, and then told her
that he would wait until she was ready to go down to
breakfast. She dressed in the same clothes she'd worn
the previous day, then quickly put her hair up in a roll
and knocked a little timidly on Sean's door. He opened
it immediately, as if he'd been waiting just on the other
side. They stood staring at each other self-consciously.

"You slept well?" he asked.

She nodded. "And you?"

He nodded.

After a moment she said, "I should go see to Caroline."

He looked down at her breasts. "Do you need
to…ah…feed her before breakfast?"

Kate smiled. "I just need to *hug* her before breakfast. But she might be more insistent than that."

"May I come, too?"

"Of course," she answered, sounding surprised.
Sean had not only become more distant as they'd
neared San Francisco, he seemed to have become less
sure of himself.

They walked together to the nursery to find Caroline
already up, dressed and bouncing on Nonny's knee as
the old woman sat in the big padded rocker. "We were
just discussing what time you slugabeds were going to

decide to make an appearance," she said. "Caroline feels that she's overdue for some breakfast."

Kate blushed, but the twinkle in Nonny's eyes put her once again at ease. "I should feed her," she said. "Do you mind waiting for breakfast?" she asked Sean.

Nonny stood up, holding the baby in one arm and gesturing for Kate to take her seat in the rocker. "He has nothing to say about it, lass. It's the first lesson that fathers have to learn. When babies need to eat, they come first."

Sean nodded his agreement. "I think I've learned that one already."

Kate took the baby and sat down, getting ready to nurse her. "Have you met with your parents yet?" Nonny asked Sean.

He shook his head. "We'll go down when Kate's finished."

"Don't let them bowl you over, girl," Nonny warned. "Especially that hoity-toity daughter-in-law of mine. She likes to think she was raised in a castle in Paris, France, but I remember when my son found her singing for her supper in the mining camps when he made his strike back in '50."

Sean shook his head but smiled as he said, "Mother would kill you if she knew you'd told Kate that story."

"Well, it's the truth. Thirty years ago most of these highfalutin folk who pretend such concern about using the right fork with their oysters were scrabbling in the mining camps for enough to eat."

Kate opened her dress and let Caroline find her nipple. She was so fascinated by Nonny's plain speaking that she forgot to be self-conscious, even when Sean's eyes glanced over her, then looked away.

"Well, you'd never know it now, to hear them talk," Sean said.

Nonny turned toward Kate. "Just remember my words, lass, if some of them start to put on their airs. I wonder how many of them could have done what you did...birth and raise this beautiful child all by yourself." She cast a reproachful glance toward Sean as she spoke.

"Thank you, Nonny, but I wasn't by myself. I had a lot of wonderful help, especially from my sister, Jennie."

"Ah, there's love in your family. I can tell. You're lucky, child. You and your sister both. I'd like to meet her someday."

"I'd like that, too," Kate said.

"Now I'll leave you to finish up with your little one. And when you're ready for breakfast, give me a call and she and I will go for a stroll."

"I don't know how to thank you."

"Nonsense, child. I haven't had this much fun since Harriet lost her wig at the Cotillion Ball." She gave a low little laugh and left the room.

"Don't your mother and grandmother get along?" Kate asked Sean, who was looking after Nonny with amusement.

His smile died as he turned back to her. "Mother can be...difficult sometimes."

She sensed that there was more behind his words. "What will she say about us? And, um, Caroline and all?"

Sean sighed and looked up at the floral motif of the stamped tin ceiling. "I have no idea, Katie. But as soon as you finish there, we'll go downstairs and find out."

When Kate and Sean went downstairs, the senior Flahertys were still at breakfast, which was an elaborate meal set out in the imposing formal dining room. She and Sean entered through sliding mahogany doors to a table that could easily have seated all the miners Jennie fed every day up at the Wesley mine. A huge sideboard along one side of the room was crowded with silver dishes containing enough food to have fed the entire mine crew.

Kate tried not to let her awe show as she turned toward the couple sitting at the opposite end of the table. The man at the head was an older version of Sean, the black curls of his hair more than half gray. He stood immediately when they entered.

The woman seated on his right didn't look old enough to be Sean's mother at first glance. Her hair was bright red. Perhaps a little too bright, Kate decided after a moment. And her face was painted, artfully, not at all like the ladies one tried not to see when visiting the rougher areas of Virginia City, but painted nevertheless.

"Ah, there they are," Patrick Flaherty said in a hearty voice that had only vague shadowings of Sean's.

"Hello, Father, Mother." Sean nodded to each of his parents. "I'd like you to meet my wife."

"Where's the child?" Harriet asked without directly acknowledging the introduction.

"Caroline's upstairs with Nonny," Sean answered smoothly. "I thought you'd like to get to know Kate first."

"Of course we would," his father answered. "But the poor girl's probably starving after the trip. Get her some food, lad." He gestured to the sideboard.

Kate was at a loss how to enter the conversation, since she was being discussed as if she weren't even present. But she remembered Nonny's words about intimidation and took a deep breath. "I'm so pleased to meet you both," she said, her voice a little louder than normal. "And to be here. You have a beautiful home."

Harriet squinted at her. Kate noticed that a pair of spectacles lay unused near her plate. "Let me see you, girl," she said. Kate looked uncertainly at Sean and walked to the other end of the table, directly across from his mother. Harriet gestured for her to be seated, then looked over at Sean. "She's pretty enough. Bring her a plate of food, Sean."

Kate pulled out the heavy chair and sat down, aware of Sean clattering dishes behind her. "Not too much," she cautioned.

"You don't need to skimp on food here, girl," Harriet said. "I daresay we throw away more every day than you had in a week up in the mountains where you came from."

"How unfortunate," Kate murmured, but she wasn't sure if Harriet heard the remark.

"Sean told us you owned some sort of hotel," Patrick said.

"Not exactly. My sister and I opened our home to boarders after our parents died."

"You and your sister by yourselves?" Patrick asked.

Kate nodded. "We had no other way to pay the bills."

Harriet scrunched her face in distaste, crinkling the powder at the edges of her mouth. "What kind of boarders?"

"Silver miners. There was a shortage of housing for them in Vermillion after the strike at the Wesley mine."

Harriet shot a significant glance from Kate to her son, who had put a plate in front of Kate and was preparing another for himself. "You two young girls took in transient *males?*"

Kate had the same sensation she'd had when she'd been forced to explain her unexpected pregnancy to Henrietta Billingsley back in Vermillion. She felt the hair bristle at the back of her neck. "We've had the same three miners living there for over a year. They're fine men. And then we had the town district attorney move in. He's a lawyer, of course, educated at *Harvard.* He married my sister."

Even Harriet looked impressed at this and suddenly seemed to realize that her interrogation was sounding unfriendly. She gave a thin-lipped smile. "I just mean that it must have been difficult for you…two unprotected women taking in strange men."

Sean pulled out the chair next to Kate with a noisy scrape and interrupted his mother. "I think we should let Kate eat her breakfast before it gets cold,'' he said as he sat next to her.

Patrick pulled a watch from his vest pocket. "I need to be getting down to the office."

"I should leave, too," Harriet said, folding her napkin carefully and pushing back her chair. "I'm due at the dressmaker's at ten."

"I thought I could bring Caroline down to meet you," Sean said.

"We'll see the child this evening," Patrick said briskly. "I expect you'll be down at the office shortly, son?"

Sean nodded. "As soon as I see that Kate and Caroline are settled in."

Patrick stood. "Nice to meet you, miss," he said to Kate with an impersonal nod. Then he strode out of the room without bothering to take leave of his wife.

Harriet seemed not to notice. "Perhaps you could drive me to Madame Lavalier's, Sean, if you can finish up your breakfast quickly."

Sean looked over at Kate, then down at his still-full plate. "All right. Just give me five minutes."

"I'll go get my shawl," Harriet said, then turned another brittle smile on Kate. "Make yourself at home, dear. If you need anything, just let one of the servants know."

Kate forced a smile in return as her mother-in-law left the room. What a strange welcome. If Sean's parents were any indication, life on Nob Hill would be far different than the warmth of Sheridan House. She did not mind so much for herself, but she was worried about how this cold atmosphere would affect her daughter. It had taken her all of thirty seconds to determine that the one thing Caroline would not have in the midst of this Nob Hill luxury was doting grandparents.

"Do you mind if I leave you today?" Sean asked. "I've really been away from work longer than I should."

Kate shook her head. "No, it sounds as if your father needs you."

Sean gave a humorless laugh. "I doubt that. But he'll check to be sure I make an appearance. What will you do today?"

"I'll unpack my things, and then perhaps Caroline and I will explore the neighborhood a little."

"Be careful where you go. You're in the big city now, not Vermillion."

She smiled at him, pleased that he'd asked about her day and that he was concerned about her. Perhaps her strange feelings were just due to the newness of it all. Once she and Sean had time to adapt to their life here, things would be all right.

"I'll be careful," she assured him with a smile. And when he leaned over to kiss her softly on the mouth before he left the room, her smile turned into a gentle glow that lasted most of the morning.

Chapter Six

The taste of Kate's lips lingered on Sean's all through the trip down to the wharf where Flaherty Enterprises had its main warehouse and offices. He'd dropped his mother off at her dressmaker's along the way, mostly ignoring her inane conversation about which of her friends had imported what new piece of ostentatious adornment from what castle in Europe. Mansion building had become an obsession among the Nob Hill elite, and Sean found the topic thoroughly boring.

His mother had made no mention at all of Kate or the baby. Of course, she'd known his marriage was a possibility before he left to return to Vermillion, but he'd suspected at the time that she was praying that he wouldn't go though with the plan. Now that he'd come home with his wife and child, he hoped she would be willing to make the best of the situation. He knew she'd wanted to marry him to one of the pretty young debutantes who were dutifully paraded by their mothers at all the best parties. But he'd made his decision, and she would have to accept it.

As he mounted the steps of the imposing stone Flaherty Building, he felt the beginnings of the familiar dull ache in his stomach. He'd been coming to work here for four years, ever since returning from college in New York, but he still felt the tension each time he entered.

It had been an attempt to escape that sick feeling that had sent him up into the mountains almost two years ago. Against his parents' wishes, he'd gone there with another frustrated son of one of their Nob Hill neighbors. The two young men had determined to find their *own* Comstock lode and show their families that they were just as capable as their fathers. But instead of a Comstock lode, they'd barely been able to eke out enough ore to buy food. Charles Raleigh had given up first, returning to work in his father's watch factory. And when Sean had used up all his cash and began receiving increasingly harsh telegrams from his father, he'd also surrendered his dream. He'd headed home impulsively, too embarrassed at his failure to face the beautiful young girl who had been the only thing that had made his mountain adventure palatable.

He'd left Kate a note and some flowers. And a baby. Lord, it was a miracle she didn't hate him.

"Nice to see you back, Mr. Sean." Clarence Applewhite had been chief clerk at Flaherty Enterprises since Sean was a child. He couldn't remember when the skinny, white-haired man had begun calling him *Mister* Sean. It had been years now.

"Thank you, Mr. Applewhite. It's nice to be here."

But it wasn't. He started down the long corridor to his father's big office at the front of the building overlooking the wharf. Sean's own office was windowless, tucked away in the back corner.

Patrick Flaherty was with two of the company's fleet captains, men Sean had met many times but who had never seemed to consider him as anything more than a kid. They were seafaring men, with hearty laughs and rough language, not the type to worry about treating the owner's son with some kind of false respect. Neither one stood when Sean entered the office.

"My son's back," Patrick said, stating the obvious. Sean was surprised to note that he sounded pleased.

"You been digging up the Sierras again, lad?" one of the captains asked. "Strike it rich this time, did ya?"

Sean straightened the knot on his tie. More than anyone else in his father's employ, the sea captains always made him feel as if he could never make it in a real man's world. He could speak French and quote Virgil, but to them he was still a boy, working at his father's whim.

"He brought back something more valuable than silver this time, Captain Lawford," Patrick answered. "A wife. Right pretty one, too."

Both captains looked at Sean in surprise. "A wife, eh?" Captain Lawford spoke again. "Good for you, lad. Congratulations."

"Aye, congratulations," said the other man briefly. Then he turned back to Patrick. "We'll see what we can find out about that alternate route, Mr. Flaherty. I'd like to give it a try before winter sets in."

"As would I," Captain Lawford agreed and added

with a grin, "Campbell and I could make a race of it."

Both men seemed to have forgotten Sean's presence entirely. "Keep me informed," Patrick said, standing up to signify that the interview was at an end. "For now, I need some time with my boy."

The captains turned around as if surprised to find Sean still standing there. "Of course," said Lawford. The men shuffled to their feet and started out of the room. Lawford clapped Sean on the back as he passed. "Good job, boy. High time you were raising a family to uphold the Flaherty name."

Patrick sat back down when the captains had departed. He motioned Sean into the room. "Sit down, son. Now that your mother's not here busting her stays trying to figure out your wife's pedigree, you and I can talk."

Sean smiled and took the chair opposite his father. Oddly enough, it was the only place in the whole building he felt comfortable. He'd never liked his own cramped quarters, and whenever he was dealing with others in the company he always had the impression that they were too aware that he was the boss's son. But he and his father had had some of their best discussions sitting just like this, across from each other in the big, sunny office. Somehow it was easier to talk to his father away from the claustrophobic atmosphere of the Flaherty mansion.

"I'm not worried about Kate's pedigree," Sean said. "But I'm afraid Mother's not going to find it up to her standards."

"You're the one who's married to her, not your

mother,'' his father said. ''The important thing is for you and Kate to be happy together. It's not an easy thing to achieve.''

Sean knew that his father's sigh was the closest he would ever admit to being unhappy with his own marriage. ''I'm going to do my best,'' he said. ''I just hope I can make up to her all she's been through in the past year and a half. She almost died having Caroline.''

Patrick twisted his head to look out at the distant boats. ''Well, now, there's not much you can do about that, is there? If there's one thing I've learned, it's that you can't relive the past. And regrets don't help much, either.''

''I suppose.''

They were silent for a long moment. Then Patrick reached into his desk, took out a ledger and began writing. ''Here. Take this to the bank and get yourself some cash to buy her some pretty new clothes. Women like that.''

''I wouldn't know the first thing about buying clothes for her.''

Patrick finished writing the draft, waved it in the air to dry, then handed it across the desk to Sean. ''Ask your mother's woman. That Frenchie. Get some things for the baby, too. And a bauble of some sort. A necklace or something. Women like that.''

Sean slowly reached for the money. ''I should at least put in a day's work to earn this before I go spend it,'' he said with a rueful smile.

''Don't worry about it. Tomorrow'll be time enough for you to get back to your desk.''

Sean hesitated. Next week would be time enough,

for all the use he was. Next year. He folded the check and put it into his pocket. "Thank you, Father," he said, standing.

"Don't mention it," Patrick said briskly, reaching for the papers on his desk. "Buy her something pretty." Then he waved his son out of the room.

For once Sean was happy to see his mother. After cashing his father's draft, he'd returned to Madame Lavalier's, wondering how he was going to figure out something appropriate for his wife. He'd been relieved to find his mother still there, poring over plans for her winter wardrobe with the dressmaker and one of her assistants. When he explained his mission, his mother had plucked the money out of his hand and sent him off, assuring him that she would take charge of some new finery for Kate.

"And goodness knows, the girl needs it," she'd added. "She looked as if she'd slept in that dress all the way from the mountains."

"We hadn't brought up her trunk yet," Sean explained, but his mother went on without pause.

"And she's *still* feeding the baby? That will have to stop immediately. She'll be as big as a cow before you know it."

Sean looked uncomfortable. "I think that's Kate's decision, Mother."

She laughed and said to a fawning Madame Lavalier, "Men aren't expected to understand these things, are they? We'll take the poor girl in tow, won't we, my dear madame?"

And the dear madame had assured Sean that, indeed,

they would. Sean was not at all sure that Kate would want to be "taken in tow," but at least it relieved him of the responsibility for the time being. And since his father had freed him of his duties for the day, he decided that he'd head over to the Golden Garter and see if he could get into a game. At the moment, a drink and an impersonal, undemanding hand of cards sounded very close to heaven.

"You say Sean meant for me to have these things?" Kate looked with dismay at the three frilly dresses her mother-in-law had brought into her bedroom.

"Gifts for his new bride, he said. Sean always was a generous boy," Harriet answered.

Kate bit her lip and held one of the frocks up against her. "They're, ah, very nice, but I'm not sure they'll fit."

"The madame will make any alterations necessary. She'll be here in the morning for fittings."

Kate put the dress down on her bed and picked up the puffy white object that looked like a pillow in the shape of a crescent. "What's this?" she asked.

Harriet clucked her tongue in exasperation. "That's your bustle, my dear. We need to work on your shape a bit."

Kate had never thought much about her shape one way or another, but she remembered Sean's comment on how slender she was. The fuller curves of the ladies she'd seen walking along the streets as they drove into town were evidently what the men liked these days. She held it at her waist, her face doubtful.

Harriet reached over and pulled the garment out of

her hands. "It goes on the derriere, like this. And we really should get you a new corset, too, now that you'll undoubtedly want to wean the child."

Kate looked at her mother-in-law with surprise. "Wean her?"

Harriet lowered her voice in a conspiratorial whisper. "Now, my dear, it's simply *not done* to keep up this long. It's not healthy, you know. And your figure will be an utter wreck."

Kate nodded vague agreement. In the mountains women often nursed their babies until they were two or three years old. Evidently they did things differently in the big city. Or at least, on Nob Hill.

"Perhaps you could don one of the new frocks for supper this evening," Harriet continued. "I'm sure that would please Sean. Do you want me to send my maid to help you dress?"

The clothes were much more complicated than anything Kate had ever tried to wear, but the idea of requiring a servant to dress her was repugnant. "I'll manage," she said. "Thank you for bringing them to me."

"Thank your *husband,* dear."

Kate nodded, waiting until her mother-in-law left the room to seize one of the new dresses and stalk over to the cheval mirror in the corner of the room. "I can't believe Sean would have chosen such a thing for me," she said aloud to her reflection. But maybe she was wrong. She looked down at the comfortable, simple cotton gown she'd been wearing all day. Maybe now that they were back in Sean's society, he wanted her to look like the wealthy daughters of the San Francisco elite.

She peered once again into the mirror, screwing up her face in distaste. The dress had endless rows of ruffles going every which way up and down the bodice and skirt. The sleeves were poofed out to ridiculous proportions. And a *bustle*. Why would anyone want to make their rear end stick out like that?

Kate sighed and put the gaudy purple creation on the bed while she began to unbutton her gown. She'd feel ridiculous going down to supper in it, but she'd wear it nonetheless. It was Sean's gift to her, and if it would put a smile on Sean's face, she'd go to supper in a flour sack.

Sean remembered the crawling feeling he'd had in his stomach when he'd read Jennie's letter about the baby and realized what Kate had had to go through after he'd abandoned her so cavalierly. He had a similar feeling now as he mounted the steps to the Flaherty mansion. Reaching the top, he leaned unsteadily for a moment on one of the cement lions that flanked the front door. He was trying to decide what story he could offer to excuse his absence on Kate's very first night with his parents.

It was past midnight. If he was lucky, Kate would be asleep and he wouldn't have to face her until morning. He wrapped his arms around the lion's mane. Many of his mother's elaborate embellishments to their house had seemed foolish to him as a lad, but he'd always loved these lions. Through the years they'd sat stoically guarding the threshold, unmoving, undaunted by summer heat or winter rains. Unlike all the other household adornments, which came and went at his mother's whim or the latest fashion, there was a permanence to them that he found comforting.

"Shall I sleep out here with you, Leo?" he asked aloud, the words slightly slurred. He'd named the two mascots Leo and Lily years ago, before he'd been old enough to know that the only lions with manes were male.

Leo made no reply, but neither did he make any objection to having his head clutched by a shameless drunk, so all things considered he was probably a better companion at the moment than anyone on the inside of the house.

Sean rested his head on top of the lion's. What a wretch he was. He should at least have been there to introduce his parents to Caroline. How could he expect them to accept this grandchild who had appeared in their world so abruptly if he wasn't even around to champion her cause? He straightened up, still holding the statue for balance. "I'm a skunk, Leo," he told the stone head. "Do you like skunks?"

Once again the lion kept his own counsel. Sean shrugged and turned toward the door. "I'm sorry, Kate," he said, before opening it. "You've made yourself a poor bargain."

The knock on the connecting door was hesitant, but loud enough to awaken Sean, even from his whiskey-fogged sleep. For a moment he couldn't remember how he had arrived back in his own bed, but then the previous evening came flooding back, right up to his doorstep discussion with Leo the lion.

"Just a minute," he called. The words sent painful vibrations through his jaw and radiating up his temples. Lord, how much had he had to drink yesterday? Enough to have tumbled into bed fully dressed, boots and all. He dragged himself out of bed and crossed the room to open the door. Perhaps if Kate saw him in this state, she'd take pity on him, he thought ruefully.

But the expression on her face did not look sympathetic.

"What happened to you last night?" she asked. She was obviously angry, but there was still a margin of doubt in her voice, as if she would be willing to believe that his absence had had some kind of worthy explanation.

He would very much have liked to clear his head with a cup of coffee before he had this discussion, but she stood watching him, awaiting an answer. "I ran into some old friends," he said.

Her eyes widened. "All evening?"

He turned around and went back to sit on the edge of the bed, hoping he wouldn't be sick. "The time just got away from me, I guess."

She looked at him in disbelief. "You didn't remember that you were supposed to be here to introduce your daughter to your parents?"

He shook his head. The truth was, he'd remembered it every five minutes all night long, which was part of the reason one more drink kept sounding so attractive. "I'm sorry, Kate. Did you meet with them? Did they see Caroline?"

She was still standing in the doorway. Her voice shook as she answered, "Yes, Sean, I met with your parents by myself. I showed them our daughter, though with you mysteriously gone, I'm not sure if they believed she was your daughter or not."

"Katie, I'm sure there's no doubt in their minds."

"How would you know? You weren't there. Your mother had several careful questions about all the *men* I supposedly harbor under my roof, implying…I don't know what. By the end of her interrogation, even your father was looking at me a bit askance and observing that it was peculiar that you weren't there."

Sean shook his head, winced at the pain, then looked down at the carpet. "I'll talk to them this morning. We'll straighten it out, don't worry. As soon as they get to know Caroline, they'll love her…and you, too." He looked up at her and did his best to muster one of his charming smiles.

Kate's expression didn't change. "I was dreadfully worried when you didn't come home. I thought something terrible must have happened."

Sean stood again and walked over to her, putting his arms around her and drawing her resisting body close. "I have no excuse, Katie. It was a miserable thing to do. I went down to the Golden Garter to meet with some of my friends and they invited me to join a game. One thing led to another…" He coupled his cajoling tone with small circular caresses along the length of her spine. "I'm a wretch. You should hate me."

"I don't hate you, Sean," she murmured, her voice and her back softening at the same time.

"Well, you should." His hand reached her waist

and drew her more firmly against him and his lips nuzzled her neck. "I'll make it up to you, sweetheart. We'll spend the day together. And—" he straightened and his face brightened "—you got the presents I sent, didn't you?"

Kate pulled away. "Yes, your mother brought me the dresses. They're, um, very nice."

"We'll get more, too. A whole new wardrobe. And jewelry. Anything you want."

Kate looked puzzled. "Sean, it's not necessary for you to shower me with gifts just because I'm upset over your behavior. The fact that I'm angry doesn't mean I've stopped loving you. It just means that I was disappointed that you weren't here last night. And that I found it inconsiderate of you not to let me know."

Her explanation was calm and logical. It was not a type of anger that Sean was familiar with. When his father was angry, he became withdrawn, cold. When his mother was angry, she became so shrill that everyone between here and the wharf knew of her displeasure.

But Kate's composed acceptance of his transgression only made him feel more guilty. "Well, if you don't want gifts, what can I do to make it up to you?"

Kate gave him a glance up and down. "For starters, I'd say you could use a change of clothes. I believe that's the same suit you were wearing yesterday."

He nodded, embarrassed. "I should wash up and get dressed. Then we'll go get Caroline and take her down to breakfast with us. If Mother and Father are there, I'll offer them my apologies, as well."

She must have realized that his remorse was sincere,

because she gave him a slight smile. "I'll wait for you in the nursery," she said. "Caroline's quite taken to it, by the way, and to Nonny, too."

"Everyone takes to Nonny," Sean answered with a grin. Then he leaned over and kissed her cheek. "Thank you for being so nice about this, Katie."

She nodded, then left him to make himself presentable.

Kate was not feeling as charitable as her smile to Sean would indicate, but she was at a loss how to handle her husband's unexpected disappearance. In all her imaginings of what she would encounter in the Flahertys' fancy San Francisco world, she'd never once considered that she'd be facing it without Sean at her side to support her. The previous evening had been miserable from the moment she'd donned the hideous purple dress to the end, when she'd brought Caroline down for her first brief audience with her grandparents.

Patrick had been vaguely complimentary, had given the baby a distant smile, then had looked at his watch as if he had a pressing business engagement. Harriet had started in immediately. "See how pathetically thin the poor creature is, Kate? This is what I was telling you earlier. She needs to be fed in a civilized manner."

Kate had been close to tears by the time she'd fled to the comfort of the nursery. She'd sat in the big rocker and defiantly fed Caroline in the same manner she'd been feeding her since she was born, but she found herself looking down at the child's tiny arms and wondering if Harriet's words held some truth. Perhaps tomorrow she should ask Nonny where she could get some bindings to start the weaning process.

But by morning, she had other things on her mind. She'd slept fitfully but hadn't heard Sean come in. She'd awakened frantic, ready to believe that he must have been waylaid somewhere in the wicked city. Then the serving girl who brought her a basin of warm water had assured her that Master Sean was safe asleep in his room. Kate had thanked the girl, feeling embarrassed to have had to ask the question about her newlywed husband, and also abashed that she'd forgotten the girl's name, which seemed to her incredibly rude. She still wasn't able to keep straight the endless procession of servants who seemed to be required to run the Flaherty household.

Relieved of the worry that Sean might be lying somewhere with his head cracked open, she'd taken her time getting dressed, hoping that he would awaken and burst through the connecting door with desperate apologies and explanations about why he hadn't come home. But when she'd finished her toilet and there was still no sound from the adjoining room, she'd decided to knock.

Now, sitting on the thick rug of the nursery playing with Caroline, she tried to decide how she should react to the fact that his only excuse for not coming home had been that he'd been drinking and gaming. She'd heard of men who had problems with liquor. Even Vermillion had a couple of town drunks, pitiful specimens. Surely her charming, laughing, flamboyant Sean was not one of these?

In the short time she'd seen them together, she'd

already sensed the tension that existed between Sean and his parents. Perhaps he hadn't appeared last night because he was still ashamed about Caroline being born so long before their marriage. She knew something about shame herself. She'd endured it for months before the baby's birth and some time after. For Sean, it was still new.

This explanation made more sense than the drinking. He just had to work through his shame, the way she had, then he'd be normal once again. In the meantime, she'd try to be understanding, try to help him through it. It might not be easy. She sensed that Harriet was the kind of mother who could make a son feel ashamed for a very long time, if she was of a mind.

Sean appeared in the doorway looking much better than he had a few minutes earlier. He'd shaved and had on a freshly pressed blue suit and snowy-white shirt. His black hair was slicked back. Her breath caught at how handsome he looked, framed by the doorway. She smiled up at him and Caroline waved her arms in recognition.

Sean returned her smile with an expression of relief and gratitude, then came over to drop down onto the rug beside them. "How's my girl today?" he asked Caroline, planting a kiss on her cheek. His daughter crowed in acknowledgment.

"And how's her mother?" he asked more softly, his eyes seeking Kate's with a special glow.

"Her mother's fine," Kate answered, also softly. "But she missed you last night."

Sean reached out and stroked a finger along her cheek. "Today I'm not going to leave your side. We'll take Caroline for a drive through the city. How would that be?''

''We'd both like that.''

Sean moved his legs to seat Caroline on his knees and began giving her a horsey ride. ''Shall we go for a ride today, pumpkin?'' he asked her as she giggled in delight.

''Don't you have to go to work?'' Kate asked.

Sean grimaced. ''They won't miss me. It's more important for me to spend time introducing my family to San Francisco.''

Kate gave a satisfied smile. Sean's problem wasn't drinking, she told herself again. It was getting over his parents' disapproval of his forced marriage. As soon as he got over that hurdle, they could settle down to a happy life together.

Chapter Seven

They'd had a wonderful day. Kate was still brimming from it as she dressed for dinner. They'd taken Caroline down to the wharf to see the huge ships, their masts towering against the blue autumn sky. Then they'd driven to the top of Telegraph Hill for a view of the harbor and the entire city, stretched magnificently in front of them. Kate had never seen anything like it.

Caroline had behaved beautifully all day. They'd found a shelter for Kate to nurse her discreetly in the middle of the excursion, and Kate had resolved that the next day she would begin the process of weaning. If she was going to be a big-city wife and mother, she'd learn to do things the big-city way.

Even having to put on another of the gaudy new frocks Harriet had brought to her couldn't completely extinguish her good humor. The clothes were not at all her style, but evidently Sean had liked them enough to pick them out for her, so she would just get used to them.

But when Sean came to her door to collect her for

supper, the look on his face told her that somehow she did not fit the image he'd had when he picked out the gowns. Perhaps he was still thinking that she was too skinny. She smiled bravely and gave a little twirl. "I didn't thank you properly for these," she said. "It was very thoughtful of you."

Sean swallowed hard, then said, "You like them, then?"

"Well, they're a little different from what I'm accustomed to wearing. We're still old-fashioned up in Vermillion, I suppose." She looked wryly over her shoulder, trying to see her back. Then she turned so that Sean could see how her dress poofed out over the bustle. "I don't think these inventions have reached the mountains yet."

Sean laughed. "I'm afraid I'm a bit old-fashioned myself."

Kate looked up at him in confusion. "But you chose this."

He shook his head. "No, I must confess. I left the selection in the hands of my mother. And from the look on your face, I'm thinking that perhaps that wasn't the best idea."

Kate gave up trying to mask her feelings. "It's just that they're so...*frilly,*" she said with a little sigh.

Sean put his arm around her waist and said, "Sweetheart, you shouldn't worry. You look good in anything. And if you don't like these dresses, we'll give them to the servants and go get you some new ones."

It was just what she needed to hear, and after their pleasant day, she went down to supper with her heart light. But it didn't take long for her mother-in-law to dampen her high spirits.

"Isn't Kate the belle in her new finery?" she asked Sean.

He nodded. "She's beautiful in anything. But we may look for some different styles. I believe her tastes are a bit plainer than yours, Mother."

Harriet gave a little sniff. "I'm sure they're *plainer* where she comes from, but she's a Flaherty now. We can't have her going out on the streets looking like a milkmaid."

"I agree with my son," Patrick said, looking up from an earnest attack on a huge sirloin steak. "She's pretty in anything. I don't think you need to worry about her disgracing the family name, Harriet," he added with a touch of sarcasm.

Once again, Kate grew uncomfortable being discussed as if she were not around. "My mother always used to tell us that it's not the wrapping that counts, it's what is inside," she said.

"I'm sure your mother made do with the resources she had," Harriet said with one of the bland smiles that Kate was finding increasingly infuriating.

Sean looked bleak and made an effort to change the subject. "I'm sorry I wasn't here to introduce you to little Caroline last night. What did you think of your new granddaughter? Isn't she a beauty?"

Patrick had gone back to his steak. Through a big mouthful, he mumbled. "Pretty child."

"She's quite thin," Harriet observed. "We'll have to hope she gets more robust with some real food and ocean air. The mountains aren't healthy for babies, you know.''

Kate hadn't touched her supper. The steak looked bloody and unappealing. ''That's odd. All the babies I've ever known have grown up in the mountains. And most of them have been remarkably healthy.''

Sean supported his wife. ''There's nothing wrong with Caroline's health.''

Harriet seemed to find the topic disagreeable. ''Who were you with last night, Sean?''

''I ran into Wellington and later Charles Raleigh.''

Harriet beamed. ''Fine boys. Did you ask after their parents?''

''They're hardly boys anymore, Mother. Charles is starting to take over for his father at Raleigh Watch, and Harold Wellington has his own law office.''

''Of course, dear. *Such* fine families. Cynthia Raleigh is the most regal woman I've ever met. Did Charles tell you about the place they're building down on Van Nuys? Well, she's just going to be the envy of the whole city.''

''We didn't discuss it, Mother.''

Harriet looked at Kate. ''Don't take this wrong, my dear, but people always used to talk about how Sean and Charles' sister, Penelope, would make a sterling match. Of course, that was before you came along.''

Kate felt as if the starched ruffle collar of her new dress were choking her. She looked down at the slab of untouched bloody meat on her plate. Pushing back her chair, she said quietly, ''I hope you'll excuse me. I'm not very hungry tonight.'' Then she gracefully got to her feet and left the room.

No one spoke for several moments after she left. Sean took a bite of potatoes, chewed, swallowed.

"I hope I didn't hurt her feelings. She seems to be a touchy person, doesn't she, Sean?" Harriet asked.

"Nothing touchy about it, Harriet," Patrick observed brusquely. "You as much as told the girl that you'd hoped Sean would marry someone else."

"Why it's only natural to want your son to make a brilliant match. Any mother would."

Sean had taken two more bites of potatoes. He had no idea what he'd just eaten. "I'm not too hungry, either," he said abruptly, throwing his napkin on the table. "Excuse me."

He left the room and ran up the stairs to Kate's bedroom, expecting to find her lying on her bed, perhaps in tears. But the room was empty. In the nursery, Nonny was rocking Caroline and said she'd seen nothing of Kate.

He found her finally in a tiny parlor at the back of the house, which his mother called the music room, though no one in the household played any kind of instrument. She was seated on a small couch, looking out the window into the darkening twilight at a large oak tree in the backyard. She looked up at his entry and gave a wan smile. "That was probably rude of me," she said. "I'm sorry."

Sean shook his head and went to sit beside her. "There's no need for you to apologize, Katie. My mother was the rude one."

"No. She had every right to say that. I'm sure it's a disappointment to her that our marriage eliminated any possibility of you making what she would consider an eligible match with one of the important families around here.''

Sean put his arm around her shoulders and drew her close. "Sweetheart, she's been trying to marry me off to some rich man's daughter since I started wearing long pants. But I never wanted any of them. I never wanted anyone until I met you.''

Kate smiled and rested her head on his shoulder. It had grown dark outside. The tiny parlor was without the gas fixtures that illuminated much of the house. A small whale-oil lamp provided a dim, cozy glow. "Will you tell me that more regularly?''

Sean laughed gently. "Every time you remind me. Sometimes I'm not too good at remembering these things myself.''

They sat for a moment in companionable silence, then Kate moved her head in what seemed like the most natural motion and their mouths met in a gentle kiss.

Sean felt the contact all the way to his feet. He'd been trying to resist thinking about the physical side of his marriage. In a way, he was punishing himself for having taken advantage of Kate all those months ago. He'd disgraced and endangered her by giving in to his baser urges, then he'd compounded the disappointment by not being strong enough to resist his family and declare his love for her. Now he was determined that he was going to be strong. He'd be a husband to Kate and a father to Caroline, and stand with them against his parents, if necessary. And he wouldn't let his physical needs interfere.

He pulled away from her, though she seemed willing to continue the kisses. "It wasn't fair of me to bring you here without giving you some idea that my family's not like yours, Kate."

"I never expected…"

He put his fingers gently on her lips. "No, let me finish. I know that my father can be cold and distant. And my mother can be calculating and inconsiderate. They both have their good sides, too. But they're not the easiest people to live with."

"I just wish your mother didn't seem so set against me."

She was still in his arms, and he settled her more comfortably against his side. "Sometimes I think she'd be against any woman I chose, Kate. Even one of her high-society debutantes. It's just the way she is. You'll have to learn not to let it bother you. And my father is rather impressed with you, I believe."

Kate laughed. "Not so anyone would notice."

"Well, he doesn't say much, but his few words about you have been complimentary. I'll confess he was the one who suggested I buy you those dresses that turned out so disastrously."

"They're not disastrous, they're just…"

Sean grinned and kissed the tip of her nose. "Disastrous," he concluded for her. "We'll get some others that suit you."

"Sean, I don't need dresses. I don't care about them. What I need is you…*us*…talking, sitting here like this. When your arms are around me, the whole rest of the world could be at sixes and sevens for all I care."

Sean kissed her again, on the mouth this time, then

followed up the first kiss with several more. Both began breathing more deeply. "Me too," he whispered.

"So you won't go off and leave me alone like last night?" she asked a bit timidly.

He pulled away from her mouth. "I told you I was sorry."

"I know. I won't bring it up again. It's just that for a while, for these first few days, I need you, Sean. When you're here, I'm not lonely."

"Aw, Katie." He shifted against the back of the couch and lifted her into his lap, cradling her like an infant. "I don't want you to be lonely ever again." He started to kiss her once more, then stopped abruptly and said with sudden excitement, "We'll get our own place."

"We'll what?"

"You and I and Caroline. We'll find a place of our own to live. Then you'll only have to listen to my mother's nonsense when we come once a week for Sunday dinner." He sounded almost like a little boy planning a birthday party.

"Can we afford our own place?"

"I'll ask my father for a raise. Or for a share in the company. I've been there four years now, it's time I was making enough to show that I'm the owner's son. Charlie Raleigh makes three times what I do."

The idea of becoming independent and establishing his own household was suddenly exhilarating. Energy surged through him and fueled the already urgent signals of his body from the contact with Kate on his lap.

"It would be nice to have a little place just for us," she said wistfully.

But he didn't want her wistful. He wanted her as she had been on their wedding night, needy and hungry for him. He brought a hand up to sculpt a breast and even through the frills of the new dress, he found her raised nipple. "A place just for us, my darling wife, so I can make love to you in every single room."

Kate giggled and leaned back against his arm, giving full access to his freely roaming hands. She gasped as his hand found a sensitive spot through her skirts. "I've yearned for this since our wedding night," Sean murmured.

"I have, too," Kate admitted. "But you've seemed so tired and distant. And then last night you weren't in your room."

Sean nuzzled her neck, then kissed along the length of her jaw. "We should be in my room right now. Shall I carry you through the halls to my boudoir, sweetheart, and scandalize the servants?"

"How about if I just walk there?" she replied with another happy laugh.

"I don't know if I can bear to let you go long enough." He glanced at the door. "The damn thing doesn't lock."

No sooner did the words leave his mouth than, to Kate's horror, the knob turned and Harriet stood in the doorway, peering into the gloom. When she saw the two entangled on the couch, her eyes widened. "Am I interrupting?" she asked frostily.

"Yes, as a matter of fact," Sean said.

But Kate pushed herself off his lap and said with as much dignity as she could muster, "Of course not, Mrs. Flaherty."

Harriet walked into the room, not bothering to avert her eyes as Kate tried to inconspicuously smooth her rumpled skirts. "Good," she said. "I sent word to Madame Lavalier about your dissatisfaction with the dresses and she *insisted* on sending her assistant over here immediately to take measurements for new ones."

Kate's heart plunged, but Sean said, "It'll have to wait until tomorrow, Mother. This is no hour to be doing tailoring."

"My dear Sean," Harriet said, "the woman will be here any moment. It would be terribly rude to turn her away."

"I've never known you to worry about being rude to shopkeepers, Mother," Sean said bluntly.

"No, Sean," Kate chided. "Your mother's right. I wish you all would not worry about new clothes for me, but if the woman has come out in the middle of the evening, it would be discourteous not to see her."

Harriet smiled. "We'll go up in my bedroom, dear. Sean can go join his father for a glass of port." She turned to her son. "He's so happy to have you back home, Sean."

Kate followed her out of the room, looking ruefully at Sean over her shoulders as she left.

Sean punched his hand into the puffy sofa cushion. Once again his mother had exercised her uncanny ability to interfere in his life at the worst possible moment. Since he'd been a child, she'd managed to snatch away pleasures that she considered beneath the family dignity. At the same time, she'd always turned a blind eye on his drinking bouts, since his companions were of such impeccable lineage.

He closed his eyes and let his still-aroused body slump into the sofa. It had always been easier to let his mother win these contests of will. But then, he'd never before had anything he cared about enough to make it worth the fight. Behind his closed eyelids danced the memory of how Kate had looked in his arms moments ago, her lips swollen from his kisses, her eyes loving and sensual. She was definitely worth fighting for. It was time to see if he had the mettle to go to battle.

Madame Lavalier's assistant proved to be a roly-poly woman who made pleasant quips during the measuring process, apparently not bothered by the fact that neither Harriet nor Kate seemed too amused by her attempts.

Kate's thoughts were on Sean, on the kisses they'd shared in the music room, on the arousal of his body, which had been so obvious as she'd sat on his lap. Tonight, when the interminable measurements were completed, she'd open that connecting door and finally join him in his bed. The thought of it hummed through her as the round little woman worked around Kate's slender body.

When the seamstress left, Kate thanked Harriet hastily and went to the nursery to give Caroline the most abridged nighttime feeding she'd ever attempted. Then she fled to her room and took out the nightdress that she'd gotten from Jennie for her wedding night. After throwing water haphazardly on her face and washing

out her mouth, she undressed and put on the night-
gown.

There had been no sound from the adjoining room.
Suddenly a thought struck her. Sean had been out so
late last night, perhaps he had already fallen asleep.
She tiptoed over to the connecting door and hesitated,
listening. All was quiet.

For a moment, she thought she would give up and
go sleep in her own bed, but, with a frown of determination, she changed her mind. She was Sean's wife.
She didn't care what the big-city customs were. Her
place at night was beside her husband in his bed.

Slowly, she opened the door to his room. No lights
were lit, but the light from her own room slanted
across the floor all the way to Sean's bed, plenty bright
enough to see that it was still made up. The room was
empty. Her husband was nowhere in sight.

"Did he spend so much time out with his friends
before I came here?" Kate was rocking Caroline after
her morning feeding while Nonny sat nearby embroi-
dering a dress for her new great-grandchild.

"Sean's always been one to love a good time," the
older woman answered carefully.

"Which means drinking and gambling?"

"Which means whatever makes him forget that he's
never really had to accomplish much of anything."

Kate stopped the chair's rocking motion. "What do
you mean by that?"

Nonny smiled at her and put aside her sewing.
"Like many of the sons of Nob Hill, Sean was raised
in luxury. He had everything he wanted and needed,

except a challenge. And except a sense that he was worth something. Sean has never had to fight for anything in his life.''

Kate considered the older woman's words with astonishment. Since she'd met Sean, she'd considered that *he* was the lucky one. He'd had everything. Even his ill-fated prospecting adventure in Vermillion had been more like a game to him than a life's necessity, as it was for most of the men who came to try it. She'd never considered that in some ways she was luckier than Sean for having grown up with an appreciation for the struggle that life sometimes represented. The Sheridan household had been rich in love, but poor in worldly goods. They'd had the large, comfortable home that now was Sheridan House, only because her father had built it with his own two hands. She wondered if Sean's hands had ever held a hammer.

''But he's working in the family business,'' Kate said. ''His father seemed happy to have him back. Surely that gives him a sense of pride.''

Nonny shook her head. ''I don't blame my son for the way he's raised Sean. He had little example to follow. Patrick's own father died when he was only eight.''

''Oh, I'm sorry,'' Kate said quickly.

Bridget gave one of her merry smiles. ''It was long ago, dearie. And it didn't take me long to discover that there were advantages to living without a man in your life. A permanent one, that is.'' Her eyes danced. ''I've had a number of temporary adventures along the way.''

Kate was mildly shocked at the older woman's boldness but found herself smiling back. "I'm glad," she said.

"But as to Patrick and Sean...they've never quite been able to get it right. I think Patrick would give anything to have a son he can be proud of, strong enough to take over Flaherty Enterprises, but he doesn't see that it's been his own overbearing ways that have kept Sean from becoming that man."

"I've noticed that his father tends to tell Sean what he should do."

"Always has. I told him long ago that he had to start giving the boy some freedom, let him make his own mistakes and find his own successes, but Patrick just doesn't seem able to do it."

"Sean went up into the mountains by himself," Kate pointed out.

"Yes, and look how it turned out. The mining was a failure and, I'm sorry to put it this way, my dear, but in the eyes of the family, what happened with you was a failure on Sean's part, too."

Kate began rocking again, tears stinging her eyes. Coming from Nonny, the words sounded harsh. Caroline had fallen asleep. Kate looked down at her and told herself for the hundredth time that she would *not* regret the act that had brought her beautiful daughter into the world. What she and Sean had done was wrong, but they'd faced the shame and owned up to it. Now they were married and should be able to move beyond it.

Nonny spoke again, sensing her turmoil. "It wasn't anything of the kind, mind you. Falling in love with you was perhaps the most independent and sensible thing Sean ever did in his life.''

Kate lifted her head and smiled. "It wasn't right for either of us to let it happen, but I'm content with the way things have turned out.''

Nonny didn't look totally convinced. "Which is why you're sitting here with me instead of enjoying a leisurely morning in bed with your new husband.''

Kate flushed. "Things will work out with time.''

"That's exactly what I hoped when I saw Sean's proud face that night he brought you here. But I'll admit I'm disappointed he's gone back to spending time with Charles Raleigh and the like.''

"His friends at the gaming house?''

"Yes. They're all like Sean. Rich sons of self-made fathers. I think they find gambling and drinking and loose women easier than trying to prove they can match their fathers' ambitions.''

Loose women? The drinking and gambling were bad enough, but the thought that Sean might have gone from their kisses in the little parlor last night to the company of another woman was almost too painful to consider. She'd left her home and family and come all the way to San Francisco in order to make a life with Sean. She wasn't about to let it be ruined by his parents or his drinking or his gambling. And she certainly wasn't about to lose him to another woman.

She stood and went to place Caroline in her crib. "Perhaps I will go see if Sean is still in his room, after all, Nonny, if you don't mind.''

Nonny picked up her sewing once again. "Take

your time, dearie. I'll just sit here till the wee one wakes.''

''Bless you,'' Kate said over her shoulder as she hurried from the room.

''And you, child,'' Nonny said softly with a sad smile as Kate disappeared down the hall.

This time Kate didn't even knock. She marched into her room, then crossed to the connecting door and threw it open. He was still in bed, reading the newspaper, stark naked except for a blanket up to the waist. He looked up in surprise.

''Good morning,'' she said, willing herself to calm down. She walked into his room and closed the door gently behind her.

''Good morning.'' He looked uncertain.

''I was disappointed to find you gone last night.'' She came closer to the bed.

''I thought Harriet had carried you off for the evening,'' he said.

''No. The measuring only took a few minutes.''

''I'm sorry. I should have left word. I thought you were busy. And Charles Raleigh stopped by and invited me out for a game.''

Her eyes followed the quickening rise and fall of the muscles of his chest. Some of the physical frustration she'd felt last night when she'd been ready for lovemaking and found him gone returned. She hesitated for a minute, then plopped down onto the bed next to him, took a deep breath and said, ''Well, that's too bad. Because I was hoping to continue the game you and I had started earlier in the parlor.''

The words startled a pleased chuckle out of him. "Were you now?"

"I was so impatient that I snapped at the poor dressmaker trying to get her to hurry. I was terribly rude. But when I came to your room, you were gone."

Sean folded his newspaper and tossed it to the floor. He pushed himself up a ways in the bed, heedless that the blanket was now only barely covering his most private area. "You came to my room?" he asked softly.

She nodded.

"So you meant what you said about continuing…the game?"

She nodded again, her eyes growing wider.

Sean didn't speak for a moment, then said, "Well, now I *am* sorry I went out."

"I am, too."

They looked at each other. Unlike the dim music room last night, Sean's bedroom was bright, the morning sun streaming in through his triple window. He looked rumpled from sleep, but handsome as ever, the slight growth of whiskers merely enhancing the rugged line of his chin. His eyes had taken on a predatory gleam.

"I'm here now," he said, his voice low and husky.

Kate nodded. "I am, too."

Sean reached out and put his hands under her arms, boosting her toward him on the bed. "Do you think we could continue that game after all?"

She gave a slow smile and started unbuttoning her dress. "That's what I was hoping you'd say."

Chapter Eight

If his body hadn't been racing too fast for rational thought, Sean would have taken time out to curse himself for his stupidity last night. After Kate had gone off with his mother, he'd left the house in a frustrated pique. He'd been a fool. Evidently, if he'd just been patient, they could have resumed their lovemaking right at the place where his mother had interrupted. They could have finally spent the night in each other's arms like proper man and wife.

But at the moment he had no time for regrets. Kate's arms had gone around his neck and she was kissing his chin, her tender lips soft as silk against his rough beard. His arousal was immediate, total and utterly revealed by the thin blanket that covered his nakedness.

Kate was still fully clothed, but the hard nubbins of her breasts protruded under the cloth of her dress, showing that she was as excited as he. "I'm sorry I let you down again, sweetheart," he murmured.

Kate merely shook her head and sought his mouth with hers. The passions they'd begun to summon in the music room the previous evening returned in full force. "I'm going to lock the doors, darling. There'll be no interruption this time."

He rolled out of bed and Kate's eyes followed his tall, lean form as he strode across the room and locked first the outer door, then the one that connected to Kate's room. In an instant he was back beside her in bed. He smiled when he saw how she was shyly looking at him, noticing the hard length of his arousal. "I'm ahead of you, Katie. One doesn't need clothes for this kind of game."

He proceeded to help her shed her dress and undergarments, and when she reached for the blanket to cover her nakedness, he pulled it back and threw it over the end of the bed. "I want to see you. I want to see every inch of your perfect body here in the sunlight."

She lay back against the pillows with a seductive wriggle that he would not have thought her capable of. Then she gave a kind of sensuous purr and held her arms out to him. He was on fire.

He ran his hand up her long, slender leg, then followed its path with his mouth, kissing along the sensitive skin of her thigh, then along her stomach, now more softly rounded than it had been before the baby. He halted his progress at her breasts, taking time to draw first one, then the other, into his mouth, in and out, rhythmically, until she made a whimpering sound and slid down the pillows to slip beneath him.

He needed no further invitation. Holding himself carefully above her, he found the fit of their bodies and began the slow fusion. Kate was the first one to urge speed, and their movements became increasingly frenzied until finally she stiffened in his arms and he felt the tremors of her climax. His own followed instantly.

"Lordy," Kate said after several moments of silence.

Sean laughed, jiggling her chest, as well as his own. They were glued together by the sheen of their bodies. "Lordy," he agreed emphatically.

He rolled to one side and lay side by side with her, letting the sun through the window warm their rapidly cooling skin.

"So tell me," Kate said after another long silence. "Was your game with Charles Raleigh better than ours?"

Sean gave her shoulders a squeeze. "Katie, I've never even come close to having a game better than ours."

Kate smiled smugly. "Perhaps you'll remember that the next time you get the urge to run off at night, husband."

"Perhaps you'll remember it, too, wife, when you decide to sleep next door in your lonely bed instead of in here with me."

"I never wanted my own room in the first place, Sean," she answered more seriously. "But it seemed as if you wanted me there. I thought maybe this was considered the proper way for married people to behave on Nob Hill."

Sean boosted himself up on one elbow and looked down at her. "I don't give a damn what's considered proper on Nob Hill or anywhere else. We'll live the way we want to live."

"In our own house?" Kate asked happily.

Sean was a little less sure on this score than he had been when he'd boldly proposed the idea the previous evening, but he answered, "Yes, in our own house."

She pulled his head down for a kiss. "In the meantime, I'd just as soon sleep here next to you at night, if you don't mind, husband."

Sean kissed her gently, then once again less gently. Their breathing deepened. "Ah, Katie, at this rate, I'm never going to get to the office."

"Five more minutes," she pleaded, opening her mouth to his third kiss.

"Five more minutes," he agreed, taking her breast into his mouth.

Sometime later it was duly noted by Flaherty Enterprises chief clerk Clarence Applewhite that the boss's son did not arrive at work until well past the noon hour.

Nonny had warned Kate about the afternoon teas. "A bunch of ladies too rich to lace their own shoes," she'd called Harriet's friends. "They're so busy trying to be the first to tell the latest gossip that they can't hear that half the others in the room are gossiping about them."

But Harriet had made her invitation to Kate sound more like a demand than a request. And Kate did not want to disturb her newfound harmony by starting a battle with her mother-in-law. It was enough that she and Sean had been together for the past four nights— four wonderful, passion-filled nights. Sean had not gone again to the gaming hall, but he had, after that first day, arisen early and gone off to work, putting in a full day at the company offices. It appeared that he was making a real attempt to become both a valuable employee and a model husband. Both Kate and Patrick were delighted.

So with only a niggling shiver of apprehension, Kate dressed to accompany Harriet to the Raleigh mansion for tea with Cynthia Raleigh, her daughter, Penelope, and various other ladies of the Nob Hill circuit. She donned one of her simple Vermillion dresses. She hadn't worn any of the gowns Harriet had picked out for her since she'd learned that Sean had had no part in their selection. They might be more suitable for a Nob Hill ladies' tea, but Kate was not in the mood to try to be something she wasn't. She hadn't even tried to duplicate the elaborate hairstyles that seemed to be the Nob Hill vogue. Sean liked her the way she was, plain and without pretensions. That was all she cared about.

She felt her resolve crumbling when she saw the looks on the faces of the other ladies as Harriet swept Kate into the Raleighs' Italianate marble front hall. They were greeted by the Raleigh mother and daughter, Cynthia and Penelope. Harriet embraced both the women and planted kisses in the air to the left of their cheeks.

''So this is Sean's new wife,'' Cynthia Raleigh observed, her eyes taking in every detail of Kate's attire, down to her serviceable leather shoes, which Kate *had* laced herself.

She reminded Kate of Harriet, similar age, same

questionable shade of red hair and a smile that went not a tenth of an inch farther than the teeth.

Penelope Raleigh's welcome was more genuine. She gave Kate a light hug and said in a voice brimming with fun, "Be prepared to have all the mothers hate you, Kate. You've snatched one of their richest prospects."

"Don't be crude, Penelope," Cynthia commanded.

Kate smiled at the young woman who looked to be about Kate's age. She wasn't pretty, but she had sparkling brown eyes and silky, nut-brown hair that was held back in a simple bun, rather than the curlicued coiffures of most of the women. Kate liked her instantly.

Harriet had turned away to greet her other friends, leaving her daughter-in-law to make her own introductions. "We might as well get this over with," Penelope said, slipping an arm around Kate's waist and leading her into a huge room that was dominated by red—red brocade drapes, red velvet furniture, red Persian carpet, even red books lining redwood shelves all along the far wall. "The Red Room," Penelope announced with a giggle.

It was full of buzzing ladies in clusters of twos and threes and fours like bees hovering around a hive. The drone softened as Kate and Penelope entered. Kate could see heads turning to make a quick assessment of her from every corner of the room. She felt her face growing pink.

"Tiresome, isn't it?" Penelope whispered. "You're the new grist for their mill." Then in a louder voice she addressed a buxom woman who had turned in their direction. "So nice to have you here, Mrs. Wellington. Have you met Sean Flaherty's wife, Kate?"

And so it went around the room, a blur of ruffles and exaggerated coiffures and cool eyes and bland smiles until Kate felt dizzy from it all. Penelope expressed sympathy with a click of her tongue as she led her charge into the adjoining sunroom. "I'll have to circulate a little or Mother will have my hide, but you can sit in here out of the arena if you like."

"It is a bit overwhelming," Kate admitted. "Thank you, Penelope."

"I know. My debutante year, I used to go home after every party and puke," Penelope said with one of her delightful giggles. Then she added, "Please call me Penny. I'll be back as soon as I can."

She turned to head back into the "arena," leaving Kate by herself in the bright, glass-enclosed solarium. Big, leafy plants unlike any Kate had seen before gave the room an outdoors feel. Kate found it peaceful after the overpowering decor of the Red Room. She took a seat in a small wicker rocker that was recessed amongst the plants, giving her a comforting feeling of solitude.

"Well, he got her in a family way and then felt forced to go back and *marry* the chit."

Kate stiffened in her chair as one of the buzzing clusters entered the sunroom, obviously without being aware of her presence. She ducked farther back behind the cover of the plants, unable to see the women but able to hear every word.

"Now, that was his mistake. Men do need their

amusements, but true gentlemen don't go off and *marry* the unsuitable mothers of their by-blows.''

''I can't imagine what the Flahertys were thinking to let him do it.''

''It was *cotton,* don't you think? That dress? And her hair loose, as if she were a street person.''

''I heard that she'd lived in the mountains until Sean found her. Like some kind of wild thing. No family. Not a penny to her name, of course.''

''Poor Harriet. She must be devastated.''

A sympathetic murmur ran through the group, then they moved on to exit through the far door of the solarium toward the dining room where tea was being served. Kate sat frozen to her chair.

As Penny had described earlier, she felt as if she were going to be sick. She forced herself to take a couple of slow, deliberate breaths, trying to get her equilibrium. She was torn between the urge to crawl farther into the solarium greenery or get up and flee the party. The heavy tropical smell of the leaves around her was contributing to her nausea. She stood up and peered in the direction the ladies had disappeared, trying to decide what would be the safer exit. One way was the Red Room. The other was the dining room, which was now filling with guests lining up for tea.

As she stood, hesitating, Penelope appeared in the dining room door. ''Kate, come have some sandwiches. I'm sorry to have left you for so long.''

Kate managed to walk toward her new friend without revealing how shaky she was feeling. ''I'm not really hungry, Penny.''

Penelope grinned and said, ''That's good, because the sandwiches Maggie makes wouldn't fill up a hummingbird. For some reason people think ladies don't need to eat. But I do recommend the butter tortes. They're tiny, but delicious. If you take two or three, you can get a decent mouthful.''

The girl's chatter was helping to calm Kate's nerves. Her stomach still threatened to rebel if she were to insist on putting food in it, so once again she politely refused Penelope's invitation to fill a plate from the elegant array of minute delicacies arranged on the Raleighs' long table. But she was more or less able to answer Penelope's questions and nod in acknowledgment when she was introduced to yet another set of carefully polite ladies.

Were these the ones who were discussing her earlier? she wondered. Or was it the foursome over in the corner who were surreptitiously looking her way while they tried to appear occupied with their china cups and saucers?

Finally she could take no more. She blurted out, ''Penny, I'm so grateful for all your attention this afternoon, but I've developed a dreadful migraine. Do you think you could find Harriet and see if she'd be willing to leave?''

Penelope shot her a sympathetic glance and didn't bother to offer remedies for the nonexistent headache. ''Certainly, I'll take you to the foyer and bring Harriet out to you directly. If she wants to stay longer, I'll arrange to have one of our carriages take you home.''

Kate gave her friend's hand a squeeze. ''I don't know how to thank you,'' she said.

Penelope paused for a moment. The ladies nearest them had moved away and they were alone enough not to be overheard. "It will be thanks enough if you can make Sean happy." To Kate's look of surprise she smiled and shook her head. "Don't think I'm sweet on your husband, Kate. I think of him the same way I do my brother, Charlie."

"They've been friends for a long time?" Kate asked.

"We all grew up together. And Charlie and Sean are a lot alike. They both have good hearts, but they've had trouble finding direction for their lives."

Some ladies moved toward them and Penelope took Kate's arm and led her toward the foyer as she continued speaking. "I was glad to hear that Sean had fallen in love, especially with someone unconventional, you know—" she gestured with her hand back toward the throng of ladies "—not one of us."

They'd reached the foyer and Penelope looked around. "Wait here, I'll send Harriet out. I hope we see a lot more of you, Kate," she ended.

Kate nodded and thanked her, but as she watched her disappear into the red depths of the big parlor, Kate's heart was heavy. As much as she had tried to convince herself that nothing mattered in her new life except Sean, this afternoon was proof that the rest of the world *did* matter. "Not one of us," the friendly Penelope Raleigh had said. These weren't her people and never would be. She was, in Penelope's words, "unconventional."

When Harriet came out looking only mildly annoyed at having to leave the gathering early, Kate gratefully followed her to the Flaherty carriage without speaking and stayed quiet all the way home.

It was the wrong moment for Sean to decide to take off for another of his nights at the gaming tables. He'd left a tender message for her, along with a bouquet of flowers, and that should have been enough. The note said that he was joining Charles Raleigh since Kate herself would be occupied with Charles' mother and sister. It was logical. She had no reason to be resentful. But it was just that she'd *needed* Sean tonight. She needed to feel his arms around her and hear him telling her that he loved his wife, even if she was "unconventional."

But Sean was gone, and if his past evenings on the town were any example, he wouldn't be back until the wee hours of the morning. She decided to seek out her other two sources of comfort, Caroline and Nonny.

The great-grandmother and the baby had become almost constant companions since Kate's arrival on Nob Hill. It was an arrangement that seemed to work well for everyone, even though Harriet had been urging the hiring of a "real nurse" for the baby. "It's not seemly for a member of the family to be caring for her," she'd said, which Kate had taken as a prime example of the absurdity of her new life.

As it turned out, Caroline was already sleeping and Nonny had retired to her own bedroom. But the door was ajar and Nonny was sitting in a chair reading, so Kate knocked softly.

"She went down without a peep," the older woman

said immediately. "I know you ended it reluctantly, but she doesn't seem to miss the nursing."

Kate nodded. "I don't miss it either, surprisingly enough. For one thing, I'm fitting into my dresses better," she added, looking down at her chest ruefully.

Nonny laughed. "I'm sure you're much more aware of that than anyone else. You always look lovely, child."

Kate bit her lip. "I'm afraid Harriet's fancy friends wouldn't agree with you."

"Oh, dear." Nonny pulled the page marker down in her book and set it aside. "It didn't go well at the Raleighs' today?"

Kate shook her head and suddenly the tears that had been brewing ever since she heard the nasty remarks in the solarium burst forth. "Penelope said I was unconventional," she sobbed.

Nonny frowned. "Penelope did? I'm surprised. She's usually such a sweet thing."

Kate tried to explain through her tears. "No, I mean, yes. She was perfectly sweet. She wasn't the one…it was the others. They said horrible things, that I grew up wild in the mountains without a family. They made me sound like some kind of forest creature."

"Come in and sit here on the bed, Kate. Don't bother about the tears. I've shed plenty myself over parties just like the one you went to today. That's why I don't go out so much anymore. I prefer to stay home with my books and my son and grandson. And, of course, nowadays with my granddaughter and great-granddaughter."

Kate sat on the edge of the bed where Nonny had

indicated. Her sobs were gradually subsiding as Nonny continued to speak in her soothing, slightly crackling voice. "Why would you cry?" Kate asked finally, her curiosity quelling the last of her tears. "You're one of them."

"Heavens, child. I'm just a poor Irish immigrant who'd never eaten from fine china in her life until Patrick started making money hand over fist. Of course, a lot of these other women started out life just like I did, but woe be to the one who tries to remind them of it."

"I don't care if they think Sean married me only because of the baby. The only thing that's important is that I know the truth."

Nonny looked at her sharply. "The truth...?"

"That he didn't know anything about Caroline when he came back to Vermillion looking for me."

"Ah." She was thoughtful a moment, then said, "So anyway, you don't care what those ladies think, which is why you burst into tears a few minutes ago."

Kate smiled wanly. "I suppose I must care something about it. I wish I didn't."

"It's only human nature, child. We all want to be accepted by the people we live with and socialize with. But I think you're being too pessimistic. You have more brains and more beauty than any of those ladies and their insipid daughters."

"I found Penelope quite animated."

"Well, there are exceptions. But the point is, one of the main reasons they're talking about you is that they're jealous and they may even be worried. You're a beautiful woman. Once they get to know you better and see that you're really interested in Sean and none of their sons or husbands, that will fade.''

''But…'' She hesitated.

''Well, what is it? Spit it out.''

Kate didn't know how to articulate the different feelings that had run through her today as she saw herself through the eyes of the Raleighs' guests. Finally she said simply, ''They said my dress was cotton.''

Nonny laughed merrily. ''I'm sure they noticed every detail of how you looked in it, too. I think your frocks are enchanting, but if you want to play their game and wear their clothes, what's stopping you?''

Kate plucked at her skirt with both hands. ''Oh, Nonny. Didn't you see how I looked in the dresses Harriet picked out for me?''

''Oh, pooh. Harriet couldn't dress a turtle. I'll help you, if you like. We'll get you a wardrobe that will have those peahens positively green.'' She leaned back in her chair and gave Kate a critical glance. ''An updated hairstyle, some new gowns, a bit of instruction on the silly etiquette they set so much store by in these circles. In a week you'll be indistinguishable from the most aristocratic Nob Hill belle. That is, if you're sure that's what you want.''

The words from the solarium danced in Kate's head. *True gentlemen don't marry the unsuitable mothers of their by-blows.* If it took some learning and a new look to show the Nob Hill world that she was not unsuitable and that Caroline was most certainly not a by-blow, then that was what she would do.

She set her face and gave a determined nod. ''Yes,

Nonny. If you would be so kind as to help me. That is *exactly* what I want.''

The following week was a flurry of activity. Nonny accompanied her to the seamstress, the shoemaker, the glove maker, the jeweler, the milliner. They practiced dining with the confusing array of dishes and silverware currently in fashion. They even spent a merry afternoon with Nonny teaching Kate to dance, an activity she'd never tried in Vermillion.

''You'll be the belle of the ball, Kate,'' Nonny assured her.

And Kate had laughed and shaken her head, but secretly she'd hoped that Nonny's words were true, because all the activity and new discoveries of the week could not cover up the fact that Sean was once again spending his evenings out at the gaming halls. She hadn't seen him for the past four nights.

When she'd go to his room in the morning, hoping for some explanation of his renewed distance, he'd apologize and flatter her with one of his charming sallies, then say that he had to hurry or he'd be late to work.

Often the statement was coupled with a sarcastic comment such as, ''I wouldn't want to arrive tardy. Today might be the day that someone remembers I work there and gives me something to do.''

Kate knew he was unhappy at Flaherty Enterprises. Occasionally she thought of discussing the matter with Patrick Flaherty. But she found Sean's father as difficult to approach as evidently Sean himself did. And when she asked Nonny about it, the wise old woman said, "It's a battle Sean has to learn to fight himself, child. If you or anyone else tries to do it for him, it will never work."

So she'd kept silent and tried to concentrate on the new image Nonny was helping her achieve. Saturday night the entire family had been invited to a dance at the Wellingtons'. After her experience at the afternoon tea, Kate had been reluctant to accept the invitation, but as the week progressed, she began to feel more and more confident.

It was possible, she finally let herself believe, that she *could* prove to be the belle of the ball, just as Nonny had described. That would show them, she thought with a smug little smile. By Saturday she was not only ready, she was actually looking forward to the moment when Sean would enter the Wellington ball with his "unsuitable" wife on his arm.

Chapter Nine

"He knew we were due at the Wellingtons' at eight o'clock," Patrick said, looking at his pocket watch for the fourth time. "We'll just have to go on without him."

"Don't be silly," Harriet said. "Kate can't go into the ball unescorted."

"You and I will be escorting her. That's more than enough escort for any girl."

Harriet looked over at Kate and shook her head. "For a *girl* yes, but not for a *wife*. A wife goes to a dance with her husband. Any other arrangement implies some sort of scandal."

They'd been sitting in the front parlor for the better part of an hour waiting for Sean to arrive so that they could leave for the dance. Kate's face was white and unhappy.

"I just won't go," she said in a low voice. "You two please go on without me."

"Nonsense," Patrick barked. "You've got your fine new dress they worked so hard to get ready, and

Mother's been fussing over your hair all afternoon. Why, she'd have a fit if we didn't take you.''

"I was hoping she'd be going along,'' Kate said wistfully.

"Mother never goes to these things anymore,'' Patrick said. "Privilege of age, she calls it. Can't say as I blame her.''

"Nonny's never been exactly social,'' Harriet observed with a little sniff.

"Well, I'd be happy to stay right here with her. And you'll be dreadfully late if you wait any longer. Please don't worry about me.''

Harriet stood up. "She's right, Patrick. We have to go. When Sean gets back, he and Kate can come along later.''

"What if he doesn't get back? I'm not leaving her here, Harriet.''

Kate had the impression that most of the time Patrick found it easier to avoid confrontations with his wife. Generally she was the one who directed how things would operate around the house. But the few times he did take a stand, it seemed that Harriet was quick to give in. "Oh, all right,'' she said. "But it will look quite strange.''

Strange was the last thing Kate had wanted to look, but she didn't want to start an argument over whether or not she would attend. And, besides, Patrick was right. Nonny had put in a lot of time getting her ready for the event. She knew that she looked good, and that was a help. She would just go, endure the whispers of speculation behind her back as to where her husband was, and try to get through the evening without tears.

It proved to be much easier than she had anticipated. Harriet's opinion that a wife had to be paired with a husband did not seem to be shared by many in attendance. Most of the people she met did not even inquire about Sean's whereabouts. Some of the young men who were presented to her flirted outrageously, as though the fact that she had a husband was not particularly relevant. After the initial butterflies upon entry, Kate relaxed and found that she was actually beginning to enjoy herself.

Penelope came over to her side instantly, exclaiming on her new dress and hairstyle. She introduced Kate to a circle of young ladies much like Penelope herself—pretty, friendly, and much more accepting of Kate than their condescending mothers.

By ten o'clock when the waiters passed among the guests with tall glasses of champagne, Kate had almost forgotten the hurt over her husband's absence.

The Wellingtons had been the first Nob Hill home to have a formal ballroom. It had a recessed alcove for the small orchestra that was playing the newest waltzes for the elaborately dressed guests.

Sean leaned against the wall to one side of the string ensemble in the alcove shadows. He'd arrived several moments before, but when he'd spotted Kate across the room whirling around in the arms of Harold Wellington, he'd ducked into the hidden refuge. She was so graceful and beautiful that it took his breath away. Of course, she was *always* beautiful, but tonight there was a special radiance about her. Her hair was different and her gown, but it was more than that. She looked self-confident and blooming. There was something in the look that reminded him of the Kate he had first met, before she'd been weighed down with the cares of motherhood, a weight that *he* had been responsible for putting on those slender shoulders.

It twisted a worm of jealousy inside him to see Harold's hand so firm and possessive against the back of her waist. They were dancing, of course. It was nothing untoward. But the worm twisted nonetheless. He pushed away from the wall and strode across the room. The waltz was just ending, and before another could be struck up, he quickened his pace to reach her side.

Harold saw him first. "Flaherty! So you decided to put in an appearance after all."

Kate turned in surprise. She didn't speak, but her look of reproach said enough.

"How are you, Harold?" Sean asked, his eyes on Kate.

Harold's smile faded at Sean's sober expression. Harold took Kate's hand, which he was still holding from the dance, and handed it to Sean. "I guess I'll have to return her to you. You were wise to come back and stake your claim, my friend. If I were you, I'd not leave a discovery like your beautiful bride unattended."

Sean took her hand and drew it through the crook of his arm, forcing Kate to move next to him. "She's not unattended," he said stiffly.

"Not anymore, it appears," Harold said lightly. "Well, then. I'll leave you newlyweds alone. Thank you for the dance, Kate." He spun around and walked away, leaving Kate and Sean standing in the middle of the dance floor as the orchestra began another waltz.

"Are you tired?" Sean asked. "Or would you like to dance?"

Kate shrugged. For the past several days she'd pictured just this moment, when Sean would proudly take her in his arms in front of all his fine friends. But now it didn't seem to matter anymore. She'd already made her entrance, seen the admiring glances of the men and the reluctant approval of the women. She'd faced it alone. She hadn't needed Sean.

He took her silence as affirmative and swept her into his arms to the lilting rhythm of the music. "You're the most beautiful woman here tonight," he told her.

"Thank you." The compliment did nothing to soften her hurt. "I'm also the only married woman to arrive without her husband, if your mother's to be believed."

Sean sighed. "I was afraid she'd give you a hard time about it. I tried to send word to the house, but you'd already left."

Kate remained silent. She was becoming immune to his excuses.

"I'm sure Charlie caught it from his family, too. That's what kept me. I was trying to get him sober enough to be presentable." He nodded across the room to where Charles Raleigh had joined Penelope. Even from this distance Kate could see that the handsome young man looked unsteady and red eyed.

"Oh." Now this was an excuse with a bit more meat to it, as her mother would have said. But should she forgive him for choosing the needs of his friend over his wife?

"Aw, Katie, don't put that stern face with me. I'm sorry I wasn't here to walk in with you and watch every other man's face in the room turn green with envy. You *are* the prettiest, you know. I wasn't just saying that."

In spite of herself, Kate felt her coldness begin to thaw as his voice took on the low, cajoling tone. Without smiling but with a touch of humor, she asked, "Does that mean you've looked at all the others?"

He gave a relieved grin. "Only briefly. A couple of seconds each, just enough to establish that I'm the luckiest man here."

Finally she smiled, but a little sadly. "I was looking forward to coming with you. This is my first dance. I even practiced with Nonny this week."

"Practiced dancing?"

She nodded.

Sean laughed and gave her an extra whirl and dip in time to the music. Kate followed his movements perfectly. "Sweetheart, you absolutely float. You're a natural dancer."

"I just wanted everything to be perfect."

Sean frowned and pulled her closer to him. "It will be, starting now. I'm not going to leave your side the rest of the evening. The rest of the *night,*" he added more softly with a suggestive note to his voice.

"That would be nice," she said, beginning to melt in earnest as the music swelled to a crescendo close. The dance ended and there was a smattering of applause. Sean's arms were still around Kate as they stood staring into each other's eyes.

"Where in the world have you been, Sean?" Harriet's voice broke into their reverie.

Sean dropped his hold on Kate, and they moved apart. "Good evening, Mother," he said with a tinge of exasperation. "I'm sorry I was late. I was unavoidably detained."

Harriet, as usual, didn't seem interested in dwelling on her son's transgressions. "Well, never mind. I've been waiting to introduce you to the Russian ambassador. He's here with the Canfields tonight. And, Sean...he's a duke. Or a count or something." Her voice rose with excitement.

"I suppose Father has already taken care of grilling him over the shipping rights," Sean said. "Which leaves nothing for me to do other than shake the man's hand and offer to fetch him another drink."

"Don't be silly, Sean. How often do you get the chance to meet a real live duke? It's such a coup for the Wellingtons to have him here. Come on before he decides to move on to another party."

Sean gave Kate a wry smile, then offered her his arm. "Shall we go meet a real, live duke, sweetheart?"

Harriet looked at her daughter-in-law with surprise, as if she had forgotten about her presence. "I suppose Kate can come, too," she said. "But we should hurry."

The ambassador-count had not spoken a word of English, so after a round of polite nods from all sides, Kate and Sean had drifted off to join some of Sean's

younger friends. They were a lively group and seemed
to accept Kate without reservation. In fact, the young
men at times appeared to be vying for her attention, a
detail that was not lost on Sean. He stayed close by
her, as he had promised.

For the first time since her arrival in San Francisco,
Kate felt as if she might, after all, be able to adapt to
this new life. Except for the fact that a few were drinking more than she thought acceptable, she felt comfortable with Sean's friends. She may not have grown
up in a mansion and taken a tour of Europe at age
twenty-one, but she was the one Sean had chosen for
his wife. And that gave her a layer of self-confidence
that allowed her to relax and be herself.

"I'm so glad you've come to live here, Kate,"
Penny whispered as midnight approached and some of
the older members of the crowd began to leave.
"We'll be fast friends, I know. It's nice to talk to
someone who can think about something other than
mansion building and husband hunting."

"The girls I've met have been very nice," Kate protested, even though she was pleased at Penny's declaration.

Penny waved her hand. "Nice enough. But some of
them have bubbles for brains. I'm happy to see Sean
was smart enough to pick someone with beauty and a
sensible head on her shoulders, as well."

Sean overheard the last part of their conversation
and stepped between them. "I finally did something
right, didn't I, Penny? Now we need to get your
brother to follow my example."

"I wish you would," Penny said more seriously.

"He's had too much to drink again, Sean. And if I couldn't see that you're using control tonight, I might put part of the blame on you."

Sean held up his hands. "Oh no, you don't. I've plenty of sins of my own to take the blame for. I'm not about to start taking it for Charlie's behavior."

Penny sighed. "I guess you're right. Still, the two of you are trouble when you get together."

Sean looked at Kate. "Well, Charlie's going to have to begin working out his own problems, because I intend to be spending a lot more time at home." His voice lightened. "I've a wife and daughter now, Penny, in case you haven't heard."

Penny laughed and went up on tiptoe to give him a light kiss on the cheek. "I know—a beautiful wife and daughter. And I hope that means you're going to start acting like a good husband and father."

Sean put his arm around Kate. "That's my plan."

Penny gave a satisfied nod. "I should go say goodnight to my parents. Don't you two leave. Harold says that once all the old people have left, we're going to have a light supper."

Kate gave an inward groan. They'd already had an elaborate feast earlier in the evening and the rich food had been sitting heavily in her stomach as Sean whirled her around the floor. But he appeared eager to stay longer, enjoying the company of his friends.

"Perhaps we could get a bit of air out on the terrace first?" she asked him in a low voice.

Before he could answer, his mother called to him from halfway across the room. "Sean, your father wants you to say goodbye to the ambassador."

Sean looked uncertain. "Do you want to come with me or should I join you on the terrace in a couple of minutes?"

Kate looked longingly at the louvered doors that were now open to let cool air into the room of over-heated dancers. "I'll wait for you out there," she said.

He nodded. "I won't be long."

She made her way through the crowd and out the nearest door to the stone terrace that ran the length of the Wellington mansion. It was empty except for one couple at the opposite end. They were locked in each other's arms. Kate smiled at the romantic sight. Perhaps Sean would kiss her when he came out.

But it wasn't Sean who appeared in the double doors. It was his friend, Charles Raleigh. She had met him briefly in Vermillion when he and Sean had been prospecting together. He had given up and gone back to San Francisco before she could really get to know him, and this evening they'd had little chance for conversation, though she'd seen his eyes on her more than once.

"It's the fair Kate," he said with a smile that made his teeth flash in the moonlight.

"Hello, Charles," she answered, feeling unaccountably nervous remembering Penny's words about her brother. Kate wasn't used to dealing with inebriated people. "I'm waiting for Sean."

Charles sauntered over to where she was leaning against the stone balustrade. "Waiting for Sean. You waited for months and months, didn't you, poor lass? Ah, fair Kate, you deserved better than that."

It was the first reference to the circumstances of her

relationship with Sean all evening, and, coming from one of his best friends, it made Kate decidedly uncomfortable. "I'm quite content with my husband, thank you," she said quietly. She wished he would go away.

Charles gave a wobbly nod. "Well spoken. Like a proper, dutiful wife. Which is more than he deserves, I would say, the lucky bugger."

He leaned close to her, the smell of liquor overpowering on his breath. Kate slid along the balustrade trying to increase the distance between them. "I think you've had too much to drink, tonight, Mr. Raleigh. It might be time for you to go home."

He ignored her comment. "I used to tell him that when he'd go off to meet you up in the mountains. Such a lucky bastard to have found a sweet little nugget like you to while away his time." He gave a leering smile. "I tried to get him to arrange your sister for me, but he said she was too starchy, not the roll-in-the-hay type. You, however, sweet Kate, were easy prey, weren't you? Sean didn't even have to try very hard."

The heavy supper that had made her uncomfortable earlier threatened to erupt from her stomach entirely. Kate swallowed back pure bile. "You're drunk, Mr. Raleigh," she said coldly. "I have to ask you to get away from me."

"Aw, sweet Kate. Now you've hurt my feelings. C'mon and give me a little kiss to make up for it." He launched himself toward her and almost fell as she jumped out of his way.

"What the hell!" Sean came through the door and walked angrily over to them. "What are you doing, Raleigh?"

Charles blinked his eyes as if trying to clear away the haze. He put both hands on the stone railing to hold himself upright. "I'm blotto, Sean. Could you help me get to my carriage?"

Sean looked at Kate. "Is everything all right here?"

She crossed her arms and rubbed her hands up and down her shoulders, feeling cold, but she nodded.

"I'll be right back," Sean said, throwing Charles' arm around his neck. "Just let me turn this souse over to his family."

Kate leaned back against the carved stone, her expression unreadable. "Yes," she said. "Please get him out of here."

Even after they'd made tender love when they'd arrived home in the predawn hour following the dance, Kate was too embarrassed and upset to tell Sean what Charles had said to her. Of course, the man had been drunk, and was therefore perhaps unaccountable for his words, but they'd been said and she'd heard them. Nothing could alter that.

Had Sean really confided such a thing to his friend when they were in the mountains? Had he thought that she was an easy and loose woman, suitable for a quick romp while he was in town, and nothing more? The way he'd left her so abruptly would tend to validate Charles' account. But he had, after all, come back for her, though it was months later. If he'd once thought her a trivial light o' love, he must have changed his mind somewhere along the way. He'd come for her with a ring, ready to propose marriage. The memory was enough to allow her to block out his friend's cruel words and welcome him into her arms.

They'd stayed in bed most of the lazy Sunday, bringing Caroline in to join them around noon when Sean had a tray of breakfast sent up to them.

For the second time, a Nob Hill gathering had ended disastrously for her, but for the moment, Kate tried to forget about the rest of the world and concentrate on her little girl and her husband. Late in the afternoon, they got dressed while Caroline napped, then took her and Nonny for a drive down to the wharf, where they supped on freshly caught shrimp.

It was a happy day, almost enough to erase the distasteful moments with Charles Raleigh. But the next morning when Sean left early for work, Kate once again felt the uncertainty creeping over her. She'd been accepted, even admired, by the Nob Hill elite, but it would never truly be her world. There would always be someone to remind her that she was not ''one of them.''

Sean slammed shut the big ledger and pushed it to the back of his desk. Clarence Applewhite would go over all the numbers anyway, so what was the point?

He was unusually restless this morning, and he knew it was because he'd been avoiding having the conversation with his father for too long. It was odd. There'd been times that he'd been accused of having a glib tongue that could charm the claws off a grizzly, but when it came to talking with his own father, he seemed to feel as if he were still a stammering eight-year-old.

Of course, it didn't help matters that Patrick Flaherty was *always* busy when he was at work. Sean could have spoken to him at home, but then there would be the possibility of interruption by his mother, and he wasn't about to risk that.

Surprisingly, his father was alone in his office. He was reading a thick stack of papers, shipping documents it appeared, but laid them down and looked up with a smile when Sean gave a light knock, then entered.

"Ah, it's my boy. I didn't see you at breakfast this morning."

"No, ah. I slept later than normal."

"Don't look embarrassed, lad. You're a newlywed with a beautiful young wife. I'd expect no less of you." He gave a conspiratorial wink.

The topic, coming from his father, made Sean uncomfortable, but he decided to use it as his opening. "That's what I wanted to discuss with you, Father," he said, sitting in the chair opposite his father.

Patrick had picked up the papers again after his greeting. He held them ready in his hands. "What is it, son?"

As usual, Sean had the distinct feeling that he'd have a measured amount of time to say his piece and then his father would be off to the next item on the agenda. "It's the fact that I'm now a married man with a wife and daughter."

"Caroline's a sweet little colleen," Patrick interrupted.

"Yes, she is. They both are, and I'd like to be able to provide a home for them."

Patrick gave a jerk of surprise that made his spectacles slide down his nose. He reached up and took them off. "The Flaherty mansion's not good enough?"

he asked. "Lord, I thought your mother was the fussy one."

Sean shook his head. "Of course it's good enough. But it's not *our* home. I'd like to be able to have a place where Kate and I could raise Caroline by ourselves. A small place," he added hastily.

Patrick set the papers down again on the desk and looked out the window at the harbor. "You want a house…just like that?" His disapproval was obvious in his tone.

"Well…I'd need your help to acquire something. I don't think I'd have enough…"

"When I first came to California, I lived in an abandoned barn. Made my bed right in one of the horse stalls."

Sean felt his irritation rising, but he made an effort to stay calm. "Would you like me to raise Caroline in a horse stall?"

Patrick looked back at his son. "No. But it seems to me you and your family have got a pretty nice roof over your heads. I don't understand what the complaint is."

Sean let a stream of air out through his nose. "I just want to be on my own."

Patrick looked thoughtful. "Well, then, work for it, lad. I've not been too demanding when you've spent more of your time off drinking with your friends than concentrating on business. I figured, he's young—let him sow his wild oats. But if you want things in this life, you have to be willing to earn them."

"I'm not afraid of work," Sean protested. "I just never seem to have any."

Patrick looked skeptical. He took the stack of papers

he'd been reading and pushed them in Sean's direction. "Here's a start."

Sean looked at them blankly. "What am I supposed to do with them?"

Patrick snorted. "Learn!" He made a gesture that encompassed his office and out the window to the Flaherty Enterprises ships in the harbor beyond. "I got all this by learning...and by working."

Sean had heard it before. In fact, most of his conversations with his father through the years had concerned how hard his father had had to work to reach where he was today. It always made him edgy. Only the thought of Kate kept him from giving in to his overwhelming impulse to throw the papers back down on his father's desk and leave.

"If I start taking on more duties here at the office, will you help me get a house for my family?" he asked, getting back to the original topic.

Patrick hesitated. "Show me you deserve it, Sean. Then we'll see."

Sean felt as if he were going to be sick. Show me, boy. How often had he heard it over the years? Show me that you're good enough to be the son of the amazing Patrick Flaherty. The rich, successful Mr. Flaherty.

He laid the papers carefully on his father's desk. "On second thought, don't worry about it, Father," he said. "I'll figure things out my own way."

Then he stood up and left.

Chapter Ten

Kate was surprised and disappointed when Sean didn't come home for supper. After the pleasant Sunday they'd had, she'd been hoping for a nice long evening together to help further dispel the doubts that crept into her mind every time she thought about Charles Raleigh's terrible words.

As she endured another dinner alone with his parents, she tried to be understanding about his absence. She knew that dealing with them was a trial for Sean. Things would be so much better once they were established in their own home.

She put Caroline down for the night with a little sigh of relief. The baby was occupying more and more of her time each day, which Kate didn't mind in the least, but it wore her out occasionally. Caroline's afternoon naps were becoming increasingly shorter, and often in the morning she didn't want to take one at all. She'd become so proficient at crawling that she could scoot all the way across the nursery and out into the hall in the time it took Kate to fold her crib blanket. Any day now she'd take her first tottering steps.

Kate smiled and gently shut the door to the nursery. She wished Jennie could see her, she thought with a pang. By the time her sister saw Caroline again, she'd be so big she wouldn't recognize her. Of course, by now, Jennie might have a little one of her own on the way. And Kate would not hear the news until the undependable mail arrived from over the mountains. Though perhaps Carter would be kind enough to send a wire. Jennie was far too frugal for such extravagance.

The memories of home gave her a bittersweet warmth as she walked downstairs and made her way into the library. She'd determined that along with her new high-class image, she was going to spend some time each day reading to improve her mind. Of course, this was not new. There had always been reading in the Sheridan household when she was growing up. Usually the whole family read together, gathered around the little fireplace in the parlor. Kate missed those close family times. She missed the sharing. Sharing was definitely not a priority in the Flaherty home.

But Caroline was flourishing, and Sean was a tender husband in bed, if not so much out of it. As soon as they were in their own place, everything would be different. She needed to open the cookie jar and count her blessings, as her mother used to say.

"There you are," Sean said, walking into the room. She was dismayed to see that he was a little unsteady on his feet.

He crossed over to her and leaned down to kiss her on the mouth. His breath smelled of liquor, evoking unpleasant memories of the night with Charles Raleigh. But this was not Charles, this was Sean, her husband, who had spent much of yesterday making tender love to her. "I was hoping you'd be home early today," she said. "I missed you."

He grinned at her. "I missed you, too. That's why I left Charles and Harold in the middle of a game to flee to your side." He plopped down beside her on the sofa. "To your lovely side," he added, running his hand along the side of her breast.

She moved back. "You've been drinking."

His grin turned silly. "Just a little. They say it makes the beast come out in a man, have you heard that, my lovely wife?"

She shook her head, unsure how to react. This was a totally different man from the one with whom she'd spent such a happy day yesterday.

"I'm feeling the beast a little right now," he said. His hand slid to capture her breast, none too gently, and he pressed her back against the cushions and kissed her. She pushed on his chest.

"Please, Sean. I think you've had too much to drink tonight."

He let her go immediately and flopped back toward the other end of the sofa. "I think you're right," he said morosely. "I don't know why you put up with me, Kate."

"Because I love you," she said instantly.

He closed his eyes, shaking his head. "Poor Katie. She's in love with a worthless sot."

Kate was alarmed. His voice was full of self-loathing. She'd never seen him this way. "You're just tired," she said. "And I think it's difficult to balance things out with me and your parents. When we get our own home, things will be better.''

He gave a harsh laugh. ''Do you like barns, my darling Kate? Do you think Caroline would enjoy sleeping in a pile of hay?''

He wasn't making any sense. ''We need to get you up to bed,'' she said.

He pushed away her hands as she leaned forward to help him up. ''There will be no home of our own, Kate. We're not going anywhere. We're going to stay here the rest of our lives listening to my mother prattle and my father pontificate.''

''But you said—''

''I say lots of things, but the truth is, we'll have a home only when my father decides to open his purse strings. Which he's not inclined to do at the moment. Perhaps he never will be.''

Kate remained silent for a long moment, then said, ''I take it you talked this over with him?''

Sean squinted at her as if trying to focus his eyes. ''You don't talk things over with my father. He tells you what will happen and you listen.''

She frowned. ''If it's money, perhaps with Nonny watching Caroline, I could get a job. Jennie did it in Vermillion.''

''Oh, that's a wonderful idea.'' His voice dripped with sarcasm. ''Wouldn't my mother love that tale for her Nob Hill friends? Sean's *wife* has to work to keep them out of the cattle stalls.''

Kate bit her lip. ''You're in no shape to discuss this tonight. Let me take you up to bed.''

Once again he pushed her away, but this time he

lurched to his feet. Looking down at her, he said, "I shall take myself up to bed, Kate. That, at least, is one thing I can do."

Then he turned and walked carefully out of the room.

"He's your son, Patrick. You speak to him." Harriet had made one of her rare appearances in her husband's bedroom, though the purpose had nothing to do with marital relations.

"I'm sorry, Harriet, but I don't see the problem. The boy's enjoying his wife. It's a normal, healthy response."

"Day and night," she said with a huff. "Yesterday they stayed in bed *all day.* And were shameless enough to let the servants see them there."

"The Wellington party lasted all night. Everyone slept in yesterday."

Harriet ignored his argument. "He comes home from work and they go *straight* to the bedroom. It's a disgrace."

Patrick chuckled and removed his robe to slide into his bed. "There was a time when we'd head *straight* to the bedroom the minute I returned home, Harriet. It's too bad you've forgotten those days. Leave the children alone."

"They're not children. Before you know it she'll be in the family way again and then…"

"Then, what? They should have a dozen kids if they want. I always regretted that Sean was an only child. It made for a lonely life for him."

Harriet's expression was malevolently thoughtful.

"If she has another one, he'll really be stuck with her."

Patrick sat up in bed. "He's married to her, Harriet. Whether they have one or twenty children. It's time you got the notion out of your head that this is some temporary whim of his."

"It wouldn't be the first time he had a whim and later changed his mind," she argued.

"Well, a marriage is not a whim. And I don't think he's going to change his mind. Just today he came into my office asking how he could go about getting a separate house for them to live in."

"A separate house? They want to move out of here?"

"Evidently. I told him he'd have to work a little harder, but then I'd see about helping him, which made him go off in a huff, of course. But he'll get over it. I found it rather encouraging. It's about time the boy takes some responsibility for his life."

Harriet was not listening. "She wants to get him off by herself, I suspect. Cement her claim."

"She's his wife, Harriet," he said again. "That's cement enough. Now do you want to climb in here next to me or are you going to go to your room and let me get some sleep?"

She bent toward him and sent a kiss in the vicinity of his cheek. "I'll let you rest, Patrick. You've been working too hard lately. I think you're right, it's time you let Sean take on a little more responsibility."

"I just hope I can get him to take more interest in the shipping business."

Harriet's face brightened. "There! You see, if he

weren't so keyed up about getting home to his mountain woman every day, he might get more involved in the business.''

Patrick gave a heavy sigh. ''Leave them *alone,* Harriet. He's content with her. They're going to have a long and happy life together.''

She made a grimace, then turned to leave. But as she walked up the hall to her room, she muttered under her breath. ''A long and happy life? We'll just see about that.''

Sean had already left by the time Kate finished with Caroline in the morning and went down for breakfast. She hadn't slept well after their encounter the previous evening. It had been unsettling to see him in that state, not only inebriated, but so obviously unhappy. When she thought of the carefree young man she'd met over a year and a half ago, she had a sick feeling that she'd brought nothing but misery to his life.

The only thing that kept her trying to work things out was the knowledge that even when he'd tried to forget her all those months in San Francisco, he'd been unable to. He hadn't been able to live without her— he'd come back for her.

She sighed and decided to return to the library to finish the book she'd abandoned last night when Sean had appeared. Her mother had always told her that improving the mind was the best remedy for a sad heart.

To her surprise, Harriet was in the library, sitting at the little corner desk going through some papers. ''Oh,

I'm sorry. I didn't mean to disturb you,'' Kate said, beginning to back out the door.

"Kate dear, please come in. The post has arrived and there's a letter for you from home.''

Harriet looked up at her from above a pair of spectacles that made her look like the teacher Kate had despised when the Sheridans had come down from the mountains and she and Jennie had attended school for the first time. She walked across the room toward her mother-in-law and extended her hand for the letter, but Harriet continued holding it, turning it over in her hand. "I imagine you miss your family, don't you, Kate?''

Kate nodded, dropped her hand to her side and waited. She wasn't about to let Harriet see how eager she was for news from Vermillion.

Harriet gave the envelope another turn. "From your brother-in-law, it appears. Carter Jones, from Harvard, I believe you said?'' She nodded at Kate to take the chair across from her.

Sitting, Kate tried once again to tamp down her impatience. Something about her mother-in-law's expression was making her uneasy. "Do you know what the letter's about?'' she asked.

Harriet shook her head. "No, but I thought this might be a good time to give you this *other* letter. I'm sure that now that you're established here, you'll want to thank your sister.''

Kate was totally mystified. "Thank Jennie?''

"For summoning Sean.'' Setting aside the new letter from Carter, Harriet pushed a piece of paper across the desk. Kate's fingers shook as she picked it up.

It was dated the previous May. Jennie's familiar handwriting scrawled down the page. *"Your daughter is now six months old and if you have any desire at all to see her, I think you should not delay in returning…"* The paper dropped from Kate's fingers.

"My dear, you look shocked," Harriet said with a false note of concern. "So I was right? You didn't know that Jennie had told Sean about the baby?"

Kate could not open her mouth to answer. She shook her head.

"He was in turmoil over it all summer, trying to decide what to do," Harriet said. "Finally his father practically forced him to go back and see you. Of course, both Patrick and I were delighted to hear that he'd decided to own up to his responsibilities and give little Caroline a name." She leaned forward and adopted a mournful expression. "These are difficult moments for parents, Kate, when their children stray from the path. But I'm proud of how Sean did his duty."

Kate tried to take in a breath and the effort made her give a kind of gasping cough.

Harriet stood up in alarm. "Are you all right, dear? Shall I get you some water?"

It felt as if the blood had drained entirely from her face. If she didn't get some air, Kate was quite sure that for the first time in her life, she would faint. And she wasn't about to give Harriet that satisfaction. She pushed herself up out of the chair and took a deep, gulping breath. "I don't need any water, thank you," she said when she could manage.

"Goodness me, I hope I haven't upset you. I just thought…"

"If you'll excuse me, Harriet, I need to get back up to my baby."

She turned to make her way across the room, but stopped when Harriet spoke again. "Don't forget your brother-in-law's letter, dear."

Her eyes blurred with tears, she turned and snatched the unopened envelope from the desk. Then she straightened with all the dignity she could muster and walked out of the room, down the hall and up the huge staircase. By the time she reached her bedroom, the anger was surfacing. She slammed the bedroom door behind her and flopped down onto her bed. Carter's letter was still in her hand. She looked at it a moment, then threw it aside. She'd been longing for news of home, but now she didn't even want to open it.

Finally she gave in to the hot tears that had been welling in her throat. Lying on the bed with eyes closed, she let the tears stream down her cheeks, dripping sideways into her hair and ears. She'd stayed dry-eyed through all the nastiness of the San Francisco doyennes, but this was too much.

It wasn't really Jennie's letter that had left her devastated. She was furious with her big sister, but it wouldn't be the first time that Jennie had meddled in Kate's life, trying to do things she thought were best. What hurt now was Sean's deceit. And the discovery that, after all, he hadn't come back for *her*. He'd come back for *his child*.

He'd never said he loved her. And now she knew why. It was because he didn't. Looking at the way

Sean's parents were toward each other, she wondered if he would ever be able to love. He loved Caroline, of that she was sure. But loving one's own child is as natural as breathing. Even the self-centered Harriet appeared to love her only son. But the love of a man and a woman was something else. With her own loving parents as an example, it had been easy for Kate to fall in love with Sean. Though she'd wanted to believe otherwise, it appeared that he'd never truly been in love with her. He'd left her, and if it hadn't been for Jennie's letter, she would never have seen him again.

It was a devastating discovery. And now she had to decide what she intended to do about it.

It was Nonny she had to see, of course. In the short time since she'd arrived in San Francisco, the serene old woman had become more than a friend, she'd become Kate's confidante and advisor. She'd filled some of the role Jennie had played in her life.

Jennie. Kate shook her head with wonder. Even though Kate was now fully accustomed to motherhood, she still couldn't believe that her sister was about to join her in that state. Carter's letter had been brisk, in his typical lawyer's style, but between the lines she could detect his concern. Kate shared it. After all, she herself had nearly died having Caroline. And Jennie was much more petite than Kate and worked far too hard both running the boardinghouse and trudging up the mountain to prepare lunch every day for the miners.

She knocked softly on Nonny's door and opened it

when she heard the older woman's voice telling her to enter.

Her tears had all been cried out. Dry-eyed and calm, she sat down on the bed where the older woman patted in invitation. "I'm going home," she said.

Nonny's wrinkled face registered little surprise. She grasped Kate's hand. "I'm so sorry to hear that, honey. I take it the party at the Wellingtons' didn't convince you that you could fit into Nob Hill life."

Kate carefully squeezed the bony hand in hers. "No, the party was fine. In fact, I enjoyed myself most of the time."

"It's my grandson, isn't it? The drinking and gambling."

Kate shook her head. "I know that Sean's life before our marriage was very different and that he had a family thrust on him rather abruptly. I was prepared to be patient—but that was when I thought that he loved me, that he had come back to Vermillion specifically to be with me."

In short, painful sentences she explained to Nonny about Harriet's revelation in the library. From the older woman's lack of surprise, she surmised that Nonny, too, had known about Jennie's letter. It seemed that Kate herself had been the only one foolish enough to think that Sean's return had been for her and her alone.

"You need to talk to Sean, child," Nonny said after Kate had finished her recital. "He may have gone back to Vermillion because of your sister's letter, but he didn't *have* to ask you to marry him. He made that decision because of you."

"Because he thought it was what his father would expect of him."

Nonny shook her head. "You don't know that. That's why it's important to talk with him."

Kate rocked back and forth in silent misery. "The only thing that's kept me going is the knowledge that Sean came back for me. It was what made me able to stand up to Harriet and her catty friends and Sean's crude drinking buddies."

Nonny's eyes widened at the catalogue of difficulties Kate had evidently encountered, but she didn't press her for details. "But, dearie, it's nothing but the truth. He did go back for you...for you and the child both."

"After he took the entire summer thinking about it."

Nonny sighed. "As I've told you before, Sean's a lad who's taken longer than some in coming into his own, but these past few weeks I've seen a big change in him. I honestly believe he wants to be a father to Caroline and a husband to you."

"Charles Raleigh was right after all. Sean went after me to have a good time. He thought I was easy prey, and I was. I acted like a hussy. He just never expected that his little mountain adventure would come back to haunt him months later in the form of a real live daughter."

"Now, Kate. You're beginning to talk nonsense. You know perfectly well that you're the farthest thing in the world from a hussy. You were in love with Sean. You still are, if you ask me."

Kate shook her head. "Maybe so, but I've learned

my lesson. He's happier drinking and playing with his friends at the gambling house than he is here with me. I wish he'd never returned to Vermillion.''

"Do you really mean that? Deep down?''

Kate hesitated. These past few weeks with Sean had taught her a lot about life and about herself. And she couldn't deny that it was of some satisfaction to know that Caroline would go through life with a legitimate last name. But it was time for her to see reality. She and Sean came from different worlds. It was time for her to go home where she belonged, home to people who were like her. People who needed her.

"There's another reason I'm going back." She pulled Carter's rumpled letter from her pocket. "My sister's going to have a baby. She might have some of the same problems I had at the beginning of my time with Caroline.''

"And you want to be with her.''

"At least there I'm of some use." And she'd be with a family who loved her and didn't have to be ashamed at how she dressed or where she came from.

Her look of determination evidently convinced Nonny that her decision was more than a temporary low moment. Her voice took on an urgency. "Kate, you can't just leave. Sean would be devastated. Promise me you'll talk this over with him. Perhaps he would take you back to see your sister himself.''

Kate's mind was made up, but the decision made her feel shaky inside. Nonny was probably right that it would be foolish to try to leave before morning. And maybe she should at least talk to Sean before she left. "All right. I'll talk with him when he comes home for

supper. But one way or another, tomorrow morning
I'm going back to Vermillion.''

Sean threw his cards down on the table and pushed
his small pile of chips toward the dealer. "Cash me
in," he said.

The dealer nodded and slid the chips toward him.
They were at one of the tables in the back room, re-
served by the management of the Golden Garter for its
regulars, which meant the San Francisco rich or sons
of the rich. In the back room rules were suspended.
No limit. Unreserved credit. Dealers were discreet and
did not ask questions.

"You can't leave yet, Flaherty," Charles Raleigh
protested. "You've taken all my money tonight."

"It's late. I need to get home."

Charles grinned and looked around at the others at
the table. "I guess the rest of us know why he wants
to get home, eh, gentlemen?"

Sean gave a good-natured smile and got to his feet.
"She's a lot prettier than you rummies," he joked. He
was feeling guilty for spending yet another night at the
gaming tables. Last night he'd behaved appallingly
when he'd arrived home drunk. Tonight he wasn't
drunk, but he wasn't looking forward to facing Kate,
either.

He knew she was disillusioned with life in San Francisco. After the dance on Saturday, she'd been quiet
and withdrawn. He was failing to make her happy.
He'd failed in his efforts to provide a separate home
for them. He'd really done nothing but fail her almost
from the day they met. So once again he'd run away

to joke and drink and act the life of the party with his friends. It was a coward's response, an easy escape that he was only now beginning to realize didn't really solve anything.

Charles put his cards in a pile and stacked his chips on top. "Hold my place," he said. "I'll walk out with Flaherty and then I'll be back."

Sean looked at his friend in surprise, but chatted pleasantly as they sauntered through the outer room toward the frosted glass doors to the street. When they reached them, Charles put a hand on Sean's arm and said, "Let me buy you one last beer for the road. There's something I need to get off my chest."

Sean was suddenly anxious to get home, but his friend looked disturbed, so he said, "All right. A quick one." They crossed over to the Golden Garter's polished bar and sat on two stools. "What's bothering you?" Sean asked.

"I need to apologize for Saturday night."

Sean had almost forgotten Charles' inebriated state at the Wellington ball. Though Charles' continued drinking was becoming of concern to both Sean and Charles' family, his behavior Saturday had been no worse than Sean had witnessed many times in the past. He slapped his friend's shoulder and said, "You need to slow it down, my friend. You may have noticed that I'm cutting back. It's partly because of Kate, but also because I'm seeing what it's doing to you. The stuff's like poison sometimes."

Charles nodded. "I know. Penny's laid into me about it, too. But I wasn't talking just about the drinking. I was talking about Kate."

Sean lifted his eyebrows in surprise. "What about Kate?"

"What I said to her. I was drunk out of my mind, Sean. I scarcely remember the words. But I remember the expression on her face." He ran a hand back through his short brown hair. "Do you mean to say she didn't tell you about it?"

Sean shook his head, dumbfounded. Now that he thought back, he recalled that Charles had appeared to be lunging toward Kate when Sean had arrived on the terrace, but she hadn't seemed upset, and he'd figured that what he had seen had just been Charles staggering drunkenly. Suddenly the picture took on a more sinister interpretation. "What did you do to her?"

Charles shook his head. "I didn't do anything, but I…I think I insulted her, Sean. You should have seen that look…like a wounded deer."

Sean *had* seen that look, on more than one occasion, and each time he'd known that he'd been the cause of it. But he couldn't imagine what Charles could have done to put it there. "What the devil did you say to her?"

"I was just blithering nonsense. Something about how I'd envied you in the mountains because it had been so easy for you to get yourself a woman and I didn't have one…and I think I mentioned her sister. Remember how I tried to bribe you into talking her sister into seeing me?"

"I remember it vaguely." Sean was silent for a long moment, then he spoke harshly. "It was another of those occasions when you were sotted out of all good sense." His irritation rose with such intensity that he could actually feel the warmth of it prickling under his collar. He could only imagine how Charles' babbling had sounded to Kate—as if the two of them had been women-hungry predators out to take advantage of the innocent local inhabitants.

"Well, your Kate didn't like the sound of it. As I say, I think she was insulted. I would even say hurt. I can't believe she didn't tell you. All evening I've been expecting you to come at me and try to knock my head off."

"I still may," Sean said grimly.

"Look, I'm sorry, man. I'm cutting back, honest I am. I've promised Penny, too. And please tell Kate I'm sorry if I upset her."

Sean twisted around on the stool and planted his elbows on the bar. His voice tight, he said, "There's no way to take back words once they've been said, Charlie."

"I know." Charles mimicked his friend's action. The bartender walked over to them, and Charles said, "Two beers."

"I thought you were cutting back."

Charles stared morosely at the polished wood of the bar. "After tonight," he said glumly.

Sean felt the beginning of tears sting his eyes. Lord, what must she think of him? It wasn't enough that she was probably beginning to realize that he was a spoiled, rich man who had done nothing of note in his entire quarter century of life. Now she would also think that he was a womanizing bastard.

The bartender brought the beers. He pulled his over

and took a long drink. "Yeah," he said glumly to Charles. "We'll cut back after tonight."

It was almost midnight by the time he left Charles and walked unsteadily out to the hitching rail where he'd left his horse.

All the way home he went over and over his discussion with his friend. He'd made Charles repeat the conversation with Kate as exactly as his drink-fogged brain could remember, so he knew the full extent of how deeply hurt she must have been by the thoughtless words.

So why *hadn't* Kate told him about Charlie's crude remarks? Sean wondered as he made his way through the dark streets toward home. Although, it wasn't really such a mystery. He and Kate were magically suited within the confines of their bed, but so far they hadn't been too good at communicating outside of it. At times he wondered if he was destined to go through life without being able to talk to the people closest to him. He'd never been able to communicate well with either of his parents. Nonny was the only one who really seemed to listen to him. Nonny and the lions on the front stoop, he thought with a humorless chuckle.

But he would have been willing to listen to Kate, if she'd chosen to confide in him. How hurt she must have been by Charles' words, especially when the damned fool had involved Jennie. The two sisters were nothing short of fierce in their protectiveness of each other.

He spurred his horse ahead. She'd be sleeping. He'd sent word after work not to expect him home that evening. But suddenly he had a desperate urge to see her and be sure she was all right. It had taken him a long time, but he finally realized that Kate was the very best thing that had ever happened to him in his life. He needed her...and he loved her. And it was high time he told her so.

Chapter Eleven

It was the first time he'd tried to open the connecting door between their bedrooms in the middle of the night, and he was surprised to find it locked. He stood for a moment dumbfounded, his hand still on the knob. Would she be that angry with him for staying away at the gambling parlor yet another late night?

He walked over to his bed and sat down. His declaration could probably best be made in the morning anyway with a clearer head, but it was a disappointment not to be able to say his piece tonight. He'd planned on asking her to forgive him for his inattention, to tell her he loved her and then make such passionate love to her the rest of the night that Charles' thoughtless words would be forever erased from her mind.

Flopping back onto the bed made waves of sickness roll through his middle. He'd had too much to drink again. That was something else he planned to stop. He had a sweet, bright, perfect wife and a beautiful daughter, and he intended to begin working to prove that he was worthy of them.

He'd start first thing in the morning by bringing Kate breakfast in bed. An early breakfast made by his own hands, not a servant's. And then there would still be time for some of that lovemaking before he'd have to leave for work.

"What do you mean *gone?*" The poor kitchen girl cowered as the normally charming and easygoing son of her employer roared out the question.

"I don't know, sir. They left—Mrs. Kate and the baby. Perhaps you should talk to your grandmother about it, sir."

Sean felt a tremendous surge of panic deep in his gut. "They can't just be gone. Where did they go?"

The girl ducked around the end of the counter as if to put some distance between her and the shouting man. "I'm sorry, sir. I...I don't know. I heard Mrs. Flaherty, the older, your grandmother, sir, talking with Mrs. Flaherty, your...ah...wife."

"Well, what were they saying, girl?" Sean laid his hands palm down on the counter to steady them. The serving girl looked as if she were afraid he was about to put them around her neck to try to wring more information out of her.

"I heard them talking something about going home, sir, but that was all. Honest, I'd tell you if I knew anything more."

Sean took three deep gulps of air. He'd come down to the kitchen in good spirits, intending to prepare breakfast to take up to his wife. But after a couple minutes of rooting around the cupboards, he'd decided that he had absolutely no idea how to go about preparing a meal, even a rudimentary one. So he'd fetched the timid young serving girl from the dining room where she'd been laying out the dishes for the family breakfast. It was when he'd smilingly confided why he wanted her help that she'd given her shattering news.

"When did they leave?" he asked more calmly.

"Last night, sir, when you didn't come home—"

"Where's my grandmother now?" he interrupted.

"I believe she's in her room, sir," the girl answered, then sagged against the counter with a sigh of relief as Sean turned and raced out of the kitchen.

"I *did* argue her out of it, Sean," Nonny said calmly. "I made her promise to talk to you last night. The problem was, you sent word that you weren't coming home last night. When she heard that, she packed up her things and left. Your wife can be one determined little lady, in case you didn't know it, Sean."

Sean was sitting in his grandmother's rocker, his head in his hands. "I can't figure it out. Charlie said those things on Saturday night. Why did she decide to leave now?"

"I don't know what he said to her, Sean, but she didn't leave because of Charles Raleigh, she left because of you."

Sean looked up sharply. "Because of the nights out?"

Nonny leaned toward him, her face stern. "The nights out would be enough reason if I were your wife, Sean Flaherty, but Kate has a more forgiving nature than I."

He looked confused. "We'd started working things out, I thought..."

"She left because your mother showed her Jennie's letter."

Sean blanched. "The letter telling me about Caroline?"

Nonny nodded. "Kate herself had told me that the one thing that convinced her of your love, in spite of the problems you two have had, was the fact that you'd come back for her all on your own before you knew about the baby."

Sean dropped his head in his hands again. "I know. She told me the same thing. That's why I never told her the truth."

"I hate to say this, my dear grandson, but if you'd given her enough reason to believe that you love her, the letter wouldn't have been so devastating."

Sean groaned. "I'm afraid life with me was a disappointment to her." He raised his head to look at his grandmother, his eyes hollow.

Nonny narrowed her eyes. "I'm going to forgive you this bout of self-pity, Sean, because I know you're hurting now. But when you stop hurting long enough to think with some sense, you'd better think hard about what you're saying."

His voice was dull. "I'm saying the truth."

"The truth, Sean, is that you're an educated, charming, cultured, funny, warm person. Your family loves you. Your friends look to you for strength. You've managed to capture the heart of an intelligent, spirited woman, and together you've produced a beautiful daughter. So I don't want to hear any more talk about failing and disappointing."

Sean got to his feet, his expression haggard. "Kate's intelligent, all right," he said harshly. "Intelligent enough to know she's better off without me."

Nonny shook her head with frustration. "As long as you continue thinking that way, Sean, then you're right. She *is* better off without you."

Harriet was out for the evening attending the opera with friends. Patrick had declined the invitation, saying that three operas a year was his absolute limit. He'd asked his mother to join him for supper. The massive dining room table made her look as tiny as an elf.

"You're the only one he's ever listened to, Mother," Patrick was saying, sawing angrily at his pork chop.

"You're very wrong there, Paddy. Sean listens to every word you say to him. In fact, he's grown up wishing you would take the time to say a lot more to him." She stopped, watched him for a moment, then asked with gentle humor, "Would you like me to cut that meat for you?"

Patrick looked down at his plate, suddenly realizing how he was mangling the piece of meat. He set his knife and fork down. "Well, he's not listening to me now. I don't know what to do. He's been out all night every night for the past two weeks. He gets to the office after noon and bites everyone's head off when he's there."

"His wife left him, Paddy. It's not an easy pill to swallow."

"I know. That's why I resisted laying into him about it, but how much longer is this going to go on?" He picked up his utensils and started attacking the chop with more deliberation. "Tragedies happen to other people, too. They don't go all to pieces and drink themselves into oblivion every night. You lost your husband and survived."

Nonny pursed her lips. "You were too young to know just what that cost me, Paddy. But you're right. I didn't take the route Sean's taking to escape from my pain."

Patrick lifted his head to look up sharply at his mother. The sudden sadness in her voice was rare. After a moment he looked down again and said gruffly, "Well, you could tell Sean that."

"I don't think it would do any good at the moment. I know that no one would have been able to tell me that it was wrong for me to build up the walls I did and refuse to consider loving again after I lost your father."

Patrick shifted in his chair, obviously uncomfortable with this rare moment of his mother sharing her inner thoughts. "You never fell in love again after Pa," he said, frowning at his plate.

Nonny smiled at her son. "I never let myself fall in love, son. And I have no complaints, really. I've had you all these years and Sean. But..." She stared across the big table at the far wall, lost in thought. After a moment she said, "I hope Sean doesn't do that to himself."

"Then talk to him."

Nonny sighed. "I'll talk to him when he gives some

sign that he wants to talk. It would be a waste of time to try before he's ready to hear what I have to say.''

Patrick slid away his plate, the food half-eaten, and pushed back his chair. ''Well, I just hope that time comes before he drinks himself to death.''

Nonny had been unable to sleep. She'd wandered into the nursery, looking at the empty crib and wondering how Caroline and Kate were settling back into their life in the mountains. It had been three weeks. Sean had not been home a single night since that morning he'd come to her after he'd found Kate gone.

She knew that that morning he'd checked on the stage schedule, and she'd had a secret hope that he'd ride after Kate, haul her off the coach and get this whole thing worked out once and for all. But she'd given him too much credit. For too many years Sean had had his problems solved for him by his father. He wasn't yet quite up to dealing with them by himself. It had been easier to drown himself in beer every night.

She put aside her book and was reaching to put out the lamp next to her bed when she heard a series of thumps outside her door. Alarmed, she got out of bed with surprising alacrity for her age and hurried out to the hall. Peering over the railing to the hall she could see Sean sprawled in an upside-down jumble at the foot of the stairs.

''Saints preserve us!'' she said under her breath, and ran down the stairs.

''Hello, Nonny,'' Sean said with a silly grin.

Her heart slowed its frantic beat. ''Sean Flaherty,

you scared me out of ten years' growth. Are you all right?''

Still upside down, he patted his hands along his torso, then down each thigh and finally to his right knee. ''Banged my knee up, I think,'' he said with a frown.

''You could have broken your fool neck.''

''Damn. Too bad, missed my chance,'' he said.

She put her arms around his shoulders and helped him boost himself into an upright position. Then she sat on the lowest step. ''You could run up to the top and try again. You might get luckier next time.''

Sean looked over at her a bit confused. Nonny spoke again, sharply. ''Don't look surprised, Sean. You're not going to get sympathy from me. If killing yourself's the only solution you see to your troubles, then I'm not going to be the one to talk you out of it.''

He used his hands to push himself from the floor up to the first step to sit next to her. ''I thought you'd be the only one to understand, Nonny.'' He spoke slowly, concentrating on forming the words. ''Mother and Father are just as happy they're gone, I think, but you loved them, too.''

''Yes, I do love them, and I intend to continue doing so. They're not dead, you know. They just live somewhere else. I'll travel into the mountains to see them one of these days soon. And I don't see that anything's stopping you from doing the same thing.''

Sean's expression grew sullen. ''She doesn't want me, Nonny. I think that's pretty damn clear. A wife doesn't run away from her husband if she still loves him.''

He was rubbing his knee and Nonny reached out to rub it along with him. "Sometimes a wife might if she thinks that her husband doesn't love *her.*"

"She knows I love her," he said, but his voice was uncertain.

"How does she know that, Sean, when you spent your nights gambling and drinking instead of here with her? How does she know when you gave her no help in entering a totally new society and left her alone to figure out how to look and act and be a part of that world?"

Sean blinked slowly in confusion. "What's that supposed to mean? She was nothing short of a sensation at the Wellingtons' ball. I thought I was going to have to resurrect the custom of dueling to get my friends to leave her alone."

"Yes, she was a sensation. And did you ever think to ask her how she magically went from being a simple country girl to looking every inch the Nob Hill lady? Did you tell her how proud you were to have her as your wife?"

Sean just stared at her, a dazed look on his face. Nonny's voice grew softer. "Did you ever even once tell her you loved her, Sean?"

He turned toward her and uttered an oath as his knee twisted. He closed his eyes on the pain. "She left me, Nonny. She doesn't want me."

Nonny pushed herself up, looking regal in her flowing robe in spite of her short stature. "Sean, you're my grandson and I love you more dearly than life. But looking at you right now, I'd say Kate made a wise decision."

Then she gathered the front of her robe in her hands and made a graceful exit up the stairs.

By morning Sean realized that his tumble down the stairs had jarred several other joints beyond the knee. He lay in bed cataloguing the aches—his neck, his right shoulder. There was a sensitive spot all along his right hip if he rolled too far in that direction. Not to mention the ringing in his head, which was starting to become his constant morning companion after his nightly drinking bouts. Hell.

He stayed motionless for a long time, trying to decide if there was any point in getting up. Perhaps he could go back to sleep and when he awoke it would be tomorrow. That would be one less day he'd have to face.

From the strength of the sun flooding his bedroom, it was already near noon. He didn't relish the thought of going downstairs and running into Nonny. Or his mother or father, for that matter. Or anyone.

With a sigh he rolled upright and swung his legs to the floor. His right knee was swollen and there was a stabbing pain in it when he moved. Once again, he considered going back to bed. The leg would be enough excuse. But if he notified the household of his injury, his mother would be there the next instant with poultices and hot soup and her never-ending prattle.

Yesterday morning as he'd tried to sneak out of the house, she'd tackled him with her gleeful speculations on how Kate's abandonment, "as unfortunate as that was," had now freed them to look for a more suitable match for him. After a decent interval, a civilized divorce…

He'd practically slammed the front door in her face.

Lord, he'd give a tidy sum not to have to see any of them today. That is, if he had a tidy sum of his own to give, which, of course, he didn't. He still drew his money from his daddy's purse. He hobbled to the washstand and looked at his face with disgust.

What was wrong with him? He was smart enough. Handsome enough. He could be funny and witty and charming. That much was amply proved by the number of women who threw themselves at him nightly at the Golden Garter. There'd been one especially pretty brunette who'd been flirting with him all week long. Last night she'd invited him to her room. ''No charge for you, Sean,'' she'd purred.

He'd looked at her lush breasts half spilling out of her satin gown, had thought of Kate, lithe and sweet and loving, and had almost been sick right there on top of the polished mahogany bar.

He splashed water on his face. It was dirty water from yesterday or perhaps two days ago or three. He'd told the servants not to enter his room unless he specifically directed, and evidently they'd taken him at his word. There was no towel on the rack. Then he spotted it thrown on the floor half under his bed.

His knee throbbed from his upright position. He looked in the mirror again. What had Nonny said last night? That Kate had made a good decision. He gave a harsh laugh. Well, hell, hadn't he always said that Nonny was the wisest person he'd ever known?

He limped back across the room and sat on the bed.

What was Kate doing right now? he wondered. And Caroline? Her first birthday had passed, and he hadn't been there to celebrate it. Was she walking yet? Or talking? When the hell did babies start to talk anyway?

He squeezed his eyes tightly shut as tears burned behind his eyelids. God, he missed them.

With a groan he rolled back on the bed, pulled the covers over himself and went back to sleep.

Chapter Twelve

"You might as well give up and agree to marry me, Kate," Lyle said as they sat together on the front porch swing.

"Lyle, we can't even talk about such a thing. I'm already married."

"A technicality. My father's lawyers can have that taken care of in a month. Then you can forget you ever heard of that big-city scoundrel and settle down to a nice life here with me."

Kate shook her head. She put her hand on Lyle's arm. "Don't think I'm not appreciative, Lyle. You've been loyal to me for so long…"

"Years," Lyle inserted.

"Yes, years. But it's not just a matter of lawyers. Sean is Caroline's father."

Lyle gave a snort. "A lot of good it does her to have a father she never sees. Kate, you've got to face the facts. If Flaherty wanted you, wouldn't he have come racing after you when you left San Francisco?"

Kate had already admitted to herself and to Jennie as well that in the most secret part of her heart, this is exactly what she had hoped would happen. She'd been bitterly disappointed when the weeks went by without word from him. But she wasn't about to share this with Lyle.

"I'm sorry, Lyle. I'm just not ready to talk about things like this."

Undaunted, the banker's son stood and reached his hands out to her. "You will be before long. I'll give you another couple of weeks. In the meantime, come with me. I have something to show you."

Mystified, she followed him down the path to the street. Lyle had arrived in his family's big phaeton rather than on his horse as he normally did, but Kate hadn't paid much attention. When they reached the carriage he gestured to the backseat where a beautiful painted rocking horse perched on the cushions.

"Oh, Lyle!" Kate exclaimed. "It's precious."

"It's for Caroline. A Christmas present." His voice was smug. "Shall I bring it into the house now or do you want me to wait until Christmas?"

Kate reached out a hand to touch the shiny surface. It was elaborately detailed with a real leather saddle and bridle. "I've never seen anything quite like it," she said. "But Lyle…it must have cost a fortune."

"Nothing's too good for the daughter of my future wife."

Kate shook her head but smiled. "You *are* good to us, Lyle. I want you to know that I appreciate it."

"I don't want appreciation, Kate. I want a wedding date. But—" he held up a hand as she began to protest "—I said I'd let it go for a while longer. So just consider this a present for Caroline from Uncle Lyle. It should brighten up her Christmas.''

''It certainly will. It'll brighten up Christmas for all of us.'' Just yesterday she and Jennie had tabulated the bills on the house and the remaining medical bills from their parents' deaths and Kate's hospital stay to see if they'd have any money left for a proper celebration. They'd concluded that they would be wise to make it another year of homemade gifts.

''I'll bring it by on Christmas,'' he said. ''I'd like to watch her face when she sees it.''

Kate gave him an impulsive hug. He *was* good to them, and genuinely fond of Caroline. Perhaps she was foolish to discount his offer of marriage just because he didn't make her heart race the way Sean had. There were more important things in life than that, she told herself firmly. Things like loyalty, stability, responsibility.

She said goodbye to Lyle, then stood watching for a long time as the phaeton rumbled down Elm Street toward town. In San Francisco, Nonny had told her in so many words that Sean still had growing up to do. Well, maybe Kate did, too. Maybe it was time she put aside the foolish romantic notions of her youth and set herself on a course that made sense for both her own future and that of her child.

''What would you say if I told you that I'm considering marrying Lyle after all?'' Kate asked casually.

Jennie dropped the pan of butter beans. ''Damn it! Whoops, sorry, the men's language up at the mine is infecting me.'' She bent to retrieve the mess.

"It's time you let me take over for you up at the mine, sis. When I was carrying Caroline, you wouldn't let me so much as dust the banister."

Jennie ignored her sister's comment and returned to the original subject. "What would I say to you marrying Lyle? I'd say you were plumb out of your head and tell you to go take a powder and lie down until supper."

Kate laughed. "Seriously, Jennie. It's not so crazy. He's been in love with me since—"

"Since grammar school. I know. And all those years have not made him one whit more likable."

"You should see the Christmas present he's bought for Caroline."

Jennie looked up at her sister and narrowed her eyes. "Katherine Marie Sheridan, do you mean to tell me you're about to sell yourself out to some man you don't love and never have loved and never will love because he's able to buy you pretty things? As Mother used to say, there's a name for ladies like that, and it's not 'lady.'"

Kate plopped down onto the stool alongside the big wooden counter and rested her elbows on the table, her chin in her hands. "I guess you're right."

"You know darned well I'm right. Lordamercy. Anyway, how can you talk about marrying Lyle? Last I heard you were married to Sean. Am I missing something here?"

Kate waggled her head on top of her folded hands. "No. I'm still married, as far as I know. Though I wouldn't be surprised if Harriet had already put the machinery into gear to have us divorced or annulled or whatever she plans to cook up so that she can marry Sean off to some Nob Hill debutante.''

Jennie was silent for a moment. ''Kate, I'm never going to forgive myself for being responsible for you going through this. I honestly thought that things would work out differently.''

Kate's smile was brittle. ''I know you did, sis. I've forgiven you for writing to him. Maybe it's all for the best.''

''What do you mean?''

''Well, this way I know for sure that he doesn't really love me. As Lyle said a few moments ago, if he did, he'd have followed me back here.''

''Maybe his pride got in the way. You were the one who left him, after all.''

''I know. But, Jennie, if you want something desperately, you don't let pride stand in the way.'' She reached across the counter to pick up two errant beans that had sloshed there. ''No, I just have to face the fact that he's not in love with me and probably never was.''

Jennie finished washing the spilled beans in the basin and scooped them back into the pan, holding it out for Kate to drop in the two she had retrieved. ''So when are you going to stop being in love with him?''

Kate leaned back and tried to stretch the tension out of her neck. She could maintain a facade to the rest of the world, but it did no good to dissemble with Jennie. They knew each other too well. ''I don't know,'' she said.

Jennie put the beans on the counter, walked behind Kate and put an arm around her shoulders. ''Would it

help to get the marriage part over with?'' she asked
softly. ''Shall I ask Carter to see about it?''

''Jennie, I don't have any money to pay lawyers
right now. I'm not even paying for Caroline's and my
share of the household expenses. You and Carter take
care of everything.''

''Of course you and Caroline eat so much it'll put
us into the poorhouse.''

''Before long we'll have new doctor's bills to face,
especially if you end up having to go to the hospital
like I did. The lawyers can wait,'' Kate ended firmly.

''Not if it will help your peace of mind to do something now. Besides, I don't intend to have my baby in
any hospital, and as soon as we catch up with the bills,
there will be plenty of money with the rent from the
silverheels.''

Kate ducked out from under her sister's arm and slid
off the stool. ''My state of mind is fine. I don't want
you or Carter worrying about me. And no lawyers.''

Jennie looked at her doubtfully. ''Whenever you're
ready, let us know.''

''I will.'' She smiled. ''I'd better get Caroline up
from her nap. The silverheels promised to bring home
a Christmas tree tonight.''

''Lord, and I promised to make popcorn,'' Jennie
cried, looking at the watch pinned to her dress.

''I'll be back down shortly to help you with supper,'' Kate said. ''You'd better put your mind on
Christmas instead of on trying to solve my problems.''

Jennie looked thoughtfully after her sister as she left
the kitchen. Kate had been unusually vehement about
not wanting to begin divorce proceedings. Though

she'd blamed her reluctance on money, Jennie had the feeling that it had a deeper root than that. She was still in love with Sean Flaherty. She'd admitted it.

Jennie sighed and picked up the pan of beans once again to set it on the stove. She could rely on Carter to find a legal remedy for her sister's marriage, but she was darned if she knew what kind of remedy to apply to Kate's heart.

The previous Christmas had been subdued at Sheridan House. It had been the first one since their parents' deaths and Kate had still been recovering from her difficult childbirth. But this year Jennie had announced that the occasion would be celebrated with due honor. She and Kate had started making pies four days ahead of time and Carter had secured a large goose for the feast.

Kate received her Christmas present on Christmas Eve morning. One month after her first birthday, Caroline had taken her first step. When the silverheels had arrived home early from the mine, the feat was repeated, and by evening she was beginning to prefer upright to all fours, much to young Barnaby's delight.

"I'll take you for walks in the woods now, Caroline," he told her. "And before long, we can drive out of town in the cart and play on Pritchard's Hill." Kate's face had shadowed a little at this last comment, but in general the mood was too festive to stay gloomy.

The previous day the silverheels had brought home a huge blue spruce. Fortunately, John Sheridan had had a penchant for high ceilings, and the mammoth tree fit in the parlor, though it took up nearly a quarter of the room.

"I've never seen such a big Christmas tree," Jennie had laughed, half-protesting.

But Caroline was delighted with the sight of a tree sprouting inside the house, and Barnaby was thrilled at the prospect of decorating such a monster.

They supped on oyster stew, which had always been the Christmas Eve tradition in the Sheridan household. Neither Kate nor Jennie mentioned their parents, but their eyes met regularly over the table and each knew where their shared thoughts lay.

Then, leaving the dishes for later, they trooped into the parlor with bowls of cranberries and popcorn, a box of candles and a tray of the paper star ornaments that Jennie and Kate had made years ago. "We should have made some new ones," Barnaby said, pulling out one that had two of its points crumpled.

"What's wrong with these?" Kate demanded. "I'll have you know Jennie and I labored for *weeks* on these stars."

Barnaby, who was always so eager to please, looked immediately contrite. "They're very nice, Kate," he assured her.

She laughed and gave him a hug, then took the mangled star and crumpled it up. "I'm teasing, Barnaby. Some of these can be retired, I think. There's not time tonight if we're going to get the popcorn and berries strung, but tomorrow afternoon after Christmas dinner we can make some new ones."

Dennis Kelly came over to kneel next to where Barnaby was sitting on the floor, holding the tray. "Ah, lad,'' he said, plucking one of the ornaments, ''perhaps the Christmas elf will come during the night and change these poor tattered stars into real ones.''

''The Christmas elf?'' Barnaby asked.

Which was enough prompting to launch Dennis into one of his Irish tales that soon had them all holding their sides with laughter. Caroline squealed right along with the rest of the group.

Kate picked her up from the floor and gave her a long hug. It wasn't the Christmas she'd anticipated having, but it was a blessed Christmas after all. She wondered if the Flahertys were dining at one of their elegant dinner parties tonight. No doubt they would be horrified at canned oyster stew. And, she supposed, they'd have a *proper* Christmas tree, decorated by servants, of course, with stars made of real silver.

Caroline gave her equivalent of *mama* and patted her hands against her mother's cheeks. Kate closed her eyes and smiled. This was all she needed—her daughter, her family, good friends, stories, paper stars and love.

''Are you all right, Kate?'' Carter asked, leaning over her.

She opened her eyes and smiled at her brother-in-law, who had half a string of popcorn draped around his perfectly tailored suit. ''I'm just fine, Carter,'' she beamed. ''In fact, everything's just fine.''

''There's someone coming up the walk,'' Smitty said, peering out the parlor window. He straightened up and turned to Kate with a sober expression on his normally jolly face. ''I think it's that husband of yours.''

Caroline continued cooing and patting her cheeks as Kate felt the blood drain from her limbs. "Are you sure?" she asked hoarsely.

Jennie walked over to the window and looked out. "Lordamercy. What'll we do, sis? Do you want me to send him away?" She turned to her husband with a pleading expression. "Carter?"

"I'll tell him to leave if you want, Kate," Carter said. "You don't have to see him."

There was a sudden sober silence in the room and everyone stopped what they were doing. After a minute Dennis Kelly said, "Let's throw the bastard out, Carter." The other two miners nodded agreement.

Kate stood and held Caroline out to Jennie. "Take her, will you? I'll deal with this myself." She looked around the room. "I'm sorry to interrupt everyone's celebration. Please go on as before."

Jennie took the baby but said, "Don't you want me to go out with you, sis?"

Kate shook her head. "I shouldn't be long," she said, her face grim. Then she went through the curtain to the hall.

For a moment more nobody spoke, then Barnaby said, "Is Sean going to come for Christmas?"

Jennie swayed back and forth, rocking Caroline. "I don't know, Barnaby. I guess that will be up to Kate."

"She didn't look very happy," the boy observed.

"No."

"Do you want me to go out there?" Carter asked his wife.

Jennie kissed the top of Caroline's head and hugged her more tightly. "No," she said after a moment.

"Sean Flaherty is Kate's problem. I guess we're going to have to let her handle him in her own way."

It was like a bad dream that kept reoccurring, mutating, slight changes each time but with a never-changing core of unhappiness. There he was again, standing on the other side of the front door, his hat in his hands. It had only been two months this time, not eighteen, but it might as well have been two years, Kate told herself. She'd changed that much.

There was no shaking of her voice, no tremor of her hand as she opened the door and said, "This is unexpected, Sean."

"I should have wired," he said in an echo of the earlier occasion when he had reappeared in her life.

"Yes, you should have." She waited.

"Ah, Kate, think about it for a minute. How could I say what's needed to be said in a wire? There were no words. I had to come in person."

"And so promptly," she observed.

He didn't reply. "How's Caroline?" he asked.

"Fine." She hadn't intended to elaborate, but before she could help herself, she'd added, "She took her first steps today."

Sean's blue eyes gleamed. "Did she now? I can't wait to see." He looked over Kate's shoulder into the house.

Kate's expression hardened once again. "As you said, Sean, you should have let us know of your arrival. We're in the middle of decorating the Christmas tree, and I don't want to ruin everyone's celebrating by bringing our problems into the middle of it."

Sean gave her one of the smiles that she still felt all the way into her middle. "Then how about we leave our problems out here on the porch? They'll keep just fine in the cold night air. C'mon, Katie. I want to see my daughter."

It was the one reason why she would never truly be rid of Sean Flaherty. There was no way to deny that he was the father of her child. She'd never be able to change that. But she could change how she'd opened her heart only to be disappointed time and again. She'd finally, utterly, learned her lesson when it came to Sean Flaherty. And no amount of flashing smiles would change her mind again.

"Sean, you can come in and see Caroline. But don't expect a very warm welcome from the rest of my family. And don't expect that you can coax me off to an encounter on Pritchard's Hill and make everything all right again. You and I are finished. If you're not willing to accept that, I'll have to ask you not to come here again."

Sean looked tired, older even. He didn't try to smile this time, just looked at her gravely and said, "Let me see Caroline, Kate. That's all I'm asking."

She nodded and stepped back, allowing him to enter. "Everyone's in the parlor."

"Kate, it's Christmas. He's all alone, and, by the way, he happens to be your husband." Jennie was bustling around the kitchen to finish the dinner preparations and to avoid Kate's accusing stare. "Lord, Kate, I wouldn't condemn a criminal to eat the Continental Hotel's food on Christmas Day."

Kate refused to smile at her sister's quip. "It was bad enough to have him there last night. I invited him in to see Caroline, and he stayed all evening."

Jennie opened the oven and began basting the goose. "I didn't notice you asking him to leave."

"How could I? Within five minutes of his arrival he had everyone in the room laughing at his jokes and treating him like the prodigal son."

Jennie frowned at the golden brown bird. "This is done. It's going to fall apart if we cook it anymore," she said, swiping back the hair that had fallen into her eyes. "He's a charming man, Kate. You know that better than anyone. But our loyalty is to you, not Sean. I hope you have no doubt about that."

"Well, sometimes I wonder, when my own sister invites him to dinner without even asking me."

Jennie straightened up. "Fine. I'll uninvite him. I'll meet him at the door and say, 'Merry Christmas, Sean, we've changed our minds. Please go away.' Is that what you'd like me to do?"

Kate walked over to her sister and put an arm around her shoulders. "I'm sorry, Jen. I know that you've put up with a lot of my ups and downs ever since I found out I was going to have Caroline. You've been the best sister in the world. But it's just that I was hoping this Christmas would be a happy one for Caroline."

Jennie returned Kate's hug. "It will be happy, Kate. And if you're honest with yourself, don't you think it will be a happier one for *Caroline* with both her father and mother present?"

Kate was silent a moment. "Maybe."

"So I don't have to arm myself with a broomstick and shoo Sean away at the door?"

Kate finally gave a reluctant smile. "I might have enjoyed seeing that, but no. Let him come. I'll try to act civilized."

"That's my girl," Jennie said. "Now get busy and mash those potatoes before my goose melts all over the pan."

By the end of dinner, Kate had to admit that Jennie had been right about Caroline and Sean. The toddler had been wreathed in smiles since her father's arrival. As she tottered around on increasingly steady legs, she kept returning to Sean's side over and over, putting up her arms and saying something that sounded to Kate like "hay."

"She's calling me papa," Sean announced with delight, and no one bothered to argue with his interpretation.

The baby sat through the long dinner without a moment's fuss. Sean had brought wine for a Christmas toast, and the three silverheels surprised Kate and Jennie with a huge box of marzipan candies in the shape of little soldiers.

"They're too pretty to eat," Jennie had declared. But Caroline had sucked on one contentedly, ending up a sticky mess.

Finally Kate stood up from the table and said, "I'd better take her up for a bath, then I'll see if she'll go down for her afternoon nap."

"May I come?" Sean asked, getting to his feet.

After a moment's hesitation, she nodded. She hadn't

intended to be alone with him again, but she couldn't very well refuse to let him help her put their daughter to bed.

He took Caroline from her, heedless of the melted candy she was getting all over him with every pat of her hands. "I'll carry her," he said.

They mounted the stairs to Kate's room, then Sean put Caroline on the bed and undressed her while Kate prepared the basin and towels to wash her. He glanced at the crib in the corner. "So she sleeps in your room again?"

Kate nodded and answered stiffly. "There's no other room for her to sleep in, Sean. We rent out the extra bedrooms in this house, in case you've forgotten."

Sean didn't reply for a long moment, then he said, "You're going to have to let me help you, Kate. With money, I mean."

Caroline cooed contentedly as Kate began washing her with a warm cloth. "I don't need anything from you, Sean."

"If I paid the rent for one of the rooms, you could use it for Caroline. She'll want her own bedroom one of these days."

"This isn't Nob Hill. In the mountains you sometimes find families of ten living in a two-room cabin. Caroline will learn to make do with what we have."

Sean picked up the basin from where Kate had put it on the bed and sat down, holding the basin so that she could reach it to rinse the towel. "You have an extra room now that Carter sleeps with Jennie." Before their marriage, Carter had rented one of the six Sheridan House bedrooms. The silverheels rented the other three extras. Barnaby slept in a small area behind the kitchen.

"We're trying to rent that one out again. Jennie's put a sign up at the mine."

"Well, if I gave you the rent money, you could set up that room as a nursery for Caroline."

Kate rolled her eyes. "Children don't have *nurseries* in Vermillion, Sean. Maybe because they're raised here by their *parents,* not by a nurse."

Sean cocked his head in her direction. "By parents I assume you mean a mother *and* father?"

"Under ideal circumstances. But, as we know, in this life circumstances are rarely ideal." She finished washing off the candy and put a fresh diaper on the baby. "Hand me her dress, will you?" she asked.

Sean stood, depositing the basin on the washstand, then fetched a dress from a neatly folded pile on top of the bureau. "I'm not going away, Kate," he said softly as he turned back toward her.

She stopped fussing with Caroline and met his eyes—blue, intense and determined. So determined it gave her a bit of a jolt. She'd never seen an expression on his face quite like it. "I'm sure your father will be calling you back to San Francisco before long," she said with a brittle smile.

"He can't. I don't work for Flaherty Enterprises anymore."

That came as a shock. "You quit your job?"

"Yes."

"Lordy. What did your father say?"

"As usual, not much. But somehow, I think he understands why I left. In fact, I believe he was a little proud of me for having the gumption to do it.''

Kate was still trying to digest the news. ''What are you going to do?''

''For the moment, I thought I'd try to get a job up at one of the mines.''

''Here? In Vermillion?''

''Yes, here. This is where my family is.''

She finished putting on Caroline's dress and wrapped her in her blanket. Sean was *staying* in Vermillion? Her mind was racing, but she wasn't sure exactly what she wanted to say. She needed time to sort it all out in her head. For the moment, she'd stick with the safer topic of their daughter. ''I know she's tired, but she may not be able to go to sleep after all the excitement.''

''Let me put her down.'' He took her from Kate's arms and rocked her back and forth, crooning low and tunelessly. The baby's eyelids drooped. Slowly he walked over to the crib, still rocking her, and put her inside. ''She's half asleep already,'' he whispered.

Kate shook her head in amazement at his easy way with the baby. He appeared to have a devil of a time figuring out how to be a husband, but fatherhood fit him like a glove.

They tiptoed out of the room and closed the door gently behind them. Kate was starting to regain some of her composure. As they stood in the hall facing each other, she confirmed, more calmly, ''So you *are* serious? You're going to work in Vermillion as a miner?''

''I did it once before.''

''But that's when you and Charles Raleigh were

playing at prospecting. The two of you were still living on your fathers' money.''

"I know. I'm not taking any more of my father's money. That's why I need a job.''

Kate was skeptical. "The silverheels work ten hours every day—hard, sweaty work. And they make a few dollars a week.''

Sean grinned. "Doesn't sound too attractive, does it? I'll be looking around for something better. But I have to eat in the meantime.''

"If you don't have any money, what was all that talk about wanting to pay extra rent money so that Caroline could have her own bedroom?''

"I'm not entirely destitute, sweetheart. I do have some savings. I've drawn a salary from Flaherty Enterprises for years without ever having to spend any of it, since my father was always there to cover everything I needed.''

His eyes were roaming over her. She'd been planning to wear one of the two stylish dresses she'd brought with her from San Francisco for Christmas dinner, but when she'd learned that Sean would be there, she'd chosen one of her older gowns. It had a tight-fitting bodice and scooped neckline. His gaze lingered there a moment. Then he moved closer and put his hand around her upper arm. "Let's not talk about money,'' he said in a low voice.

She couldn't pretend that being near him again wasn't affecting her. Her heart was beating noticeably in her chest, but she was determined not to let her weakness show in any way.

"Let's not talk, period,'' she said. Then she slipped out of his grasp and headed down the stairs.

Chapter Thirteen

Sean stayed the entire afternoon. He shared his intentions of settling in Vermillion with the others, receiving guarded reactions. Jennie glanced worriedly at her sister and Carter frowned and rubbed his chin. The miners, who seemed to have fallen under the spell of Sean's easy charm, offered advice on job prospects.

"They lost a lot of men this fall up at Wesley," Dennis Kelly told him. "You could hire on there in a minute."

"They've all headed down to Virginia City. The Comstock pays a lot better than any mine in Vermillion," Smitty added.

Kate looked around at the three men, suddenly aware that they'd been exchanging uncomfortable glances. "It's not anything *you* men have been considering, is it?"

Dennis shook his head and tried unsuccessfully to make his smile as bright as normal. "Ah, lassie, Christmas Day is no time to be discussing work. I say it's time for the presents."

Kate looked at Jennie. If their boarders left, they'd

really have trouble clearing up the rest of their debts. Perhaps Kate could find a job cooking at one of the mines like Jennie did, but, as the silverheels were saying, more and more miners were leaving the Vermillion area and heading for Virginia City, where work was steady and paid well. The local mines might not be interested in hiring a cook any longer.

"Hurray, presents!" Barnaby yelled. He jumped to his feet and ran to kneel next to the Christmas tree where a pile of packages had been accumulating since yesterday. "Can I give them out, Jennie?"

"We can't do the presents without my daughter here," Sean protested.

Kate stood. "I'll fetch her. She's slept long enough." She addressed Barnaby. "Go ahead and begin sorting out the gifts. I'll be back down in a couple of minutes."

By the time she and a sleepy-eyed Caroline returned, Barnaby had the presents distributed to their proper recipients and was jumping from one foot to another in excitement waiting to open them. "Can we start now?" he asked as soon as Kate appeared through the curtain. His pile was the largest of anyone's.

Kate nodded, smiling, and there was a flurry of activity as everyone began opening and exclaiming all at once. Kate sat with Caroline on her lap and helped her open her gifts, a fur-trimmed jacket from Jennie and Carter, a storybook from the silverheels and a paper of candy sticks from Barnaby.

"I gave her some of mine the other day and she liked it, Kate, honest," the boy said as they opened it.

"She liked the lemon one. And since she's eating real food now…"

"I'm sure she'll love them, Barnaby. You can help her eat them. But not until tomorrow. I think the marzipan was enough sweets for today."

He nodded happily and went back to exploring his own pile of gifts.

Sean had brought Caroline a doll from San Francisco, with a china head and real hair, much more beautiful than the stuffed rag doll Kate had made for her. But Caroline seemed equally delighted with both.

Most of the gifts were opened, and Jennie was moving around the room collecting stray paper and bits of string when Sean moved to a seat next to Kate and put a velvet box in her hand.

Kate looked up at him in surprise. "I don't have anything for you," she said.

"I should think not," he answered with some amusement. "Your gift is letting me be here with you and my daughter today."

She lowered her eyes. "That was Jennie's doing. I was going to make you eat at the Continental."

Sean laughed. "Ouch. Now I see the true depths of your anger with me, sweetheart. But never mind, I intend to work very hard to make you forgive me." His voice became low and serious. "To forgive me for all the ways I've hurt you."

Kate's throat closed. "It won't be with presents," she said, nodding at the still-unopened box.

"No. That's a Christmas gift, nothing more."

He scooped Caroline off her lap and put her on his

knee, saying, "Let's watch Mama open her present, pumpkin."

Kate opened the box, expecting expensive jeweled ear bobs or something of the sort, suitable for Nob Hill balls, but too elaborate for simple Vermillion fashions. Instead, nestled against the velvet was a small enamel pendant in the form of a bluebird.

"It's a Pritchard's Hill bluebird. We saw one there…that first time," Sean reminded her, unnecessarily.

Kate nodded, her eyes blurring as she looked down at it.

"You pin it on your dress," he explained, sounding almost shy as he waited for some sign of approval.

She lifted it from the box, holding it away from Caroline, who reached toward it immediately. "It's lovely," she said. It was not only lovely, it came dangerously close to opening up that soft place in her heart that she was determined to leave closed forever. She placed the pin back in the box and snapped the lid shut. "I'd better put it away so it doesn't get lost in the mess here," she said, keeping her voice indifferent. "I'm sure you spent far too much on it for a man who's wondering how he's going to pay for his meals."

Sean shook his head. "I had it specially made, but how much I spent is not the point.…"

Before he could finish his sentence, Barnaby, who'd been carrying gifts out of the room, poked his head between the curtains and said, "Mr. Wentworth's here, Kate. You should see what he's brought for Caroline."

Lordy. She'd forgotten about Lyle and the rocking

horse. She looked at Caroline, still sitting in her father's lap. "He has a Christmas present for her," she told Sean.

She held her hands to take Caroline from him, but he shook his head and stood with the child still in his arms. "I'll take her," he said, and ducked through the curtains to the hall.

Kate closed her eyes a moment. From across the room, Jennie was witnessing her sister's consternation. Her smile was amused but sympathetic. "Shall I throw them both out for you, sis?" she asked.

Kate opened her eyes and shook her head. With a little groan she boosted herself up and followed Sean out into the hall. The two men were sizing each other up like rival bull elk while Caroline, on her feet, was leaning against the polished horse and crowing with glee.

Lyle cast Kate a reproachful glance. "I didn't know you were expecting company today," he said.

"Sean's arrival was unexpected. He wanted to give Caroline a Christmas present."

Sean looked from Kate to Lyle to the horse, which was causing a much greater sensation than his china doll had.

Lyle bent to pick up Caroline and place her in the saddle of the horse. She made no protest when he touched her, obviously familiar with his presence. He held her carefully while he made the horse rock back and forth. Caroline shrieked with laughter.

"I guess she likes it," he observed to Kate with a self-satisfied smile, ignoring Sean's dark expression.

"Of course she does," Kate agreed.

"She's not old enough for a rocking horse," Sean observed. "She'll hurt herself, break an arm or something."

Lyle continued addressing Kate. "You'll have to hold her on for a while until she gets a little stronger."

Barnaby, who was watching from the parlor doorway said eagerly, "I can do it. In fact, the two of us could fit on together. I'll hold her. Can I?"

Lyle picked Caroline off the seat and nodded for Barnaby to mount the horse, then placed her in front of him. With Barnaby's arms fast around the baby, the two children began rocking. It was hard to tell who was more delighted.

Sean's expression was unreadable, but after a moment, he said, "I think I'll head back to the hotel. I'm kind of tired after my trip."

He *did* look tired and a little melancholy. Kate had a sudden urge to comfort him, but she fought it back. Sean's moods were no longer her problem. "All right. Thank you again for the gift," she said, gesturing with the jewelry box she still held in her hand. Her voice was as formal as if he had been the minister come to tea.

Sean gave a sad smile. "You're welcome. And please thank your sister for the hospitality. Dinner was wonderful."

"I will."

He took a last look at Lyle, then leaned forward to put his hand on Caroline's head in a light caress as she still rocked contentedly with Barnaby. "I'll talk with you tomorrow, Kate," he said. Then he was gone.

* * *

He lay in the Continental's shabby room and stared at the peeling paint on the ceiling. Earlier he'd considered going downstairs for supper. Then he'd remembered the Continental's choice of cuisine and had decided that the big Christmas meal was enough to last him until tomorrow. For most of the evening he'd lain on his bed, thinking about the change in the path of his life.

Two weeks ago, when he'd awakened from weeks of pickling his brain and his soul in alcohol and self-pity, he'd allowed the words of his conscience and his grandmother to finally penetrate his brain. From there, the preparations had gone swiftly. To his mother's horror and his father's secret pride, he'd given up most of what he'd grown up with, the comforts and the security, in exchange for the mere possibility that he could recapture something better up in the mountains.

But perhaps it had been foolish of him to think that he could make Kate love him a *third* time.

The possibility seemed more remote now than it had when he'd left San Francisco. Except for the gleam of interest he'd seen in her eyes earlier when they'd stood close together in the upstairs hall, she'd not softened toward him all day.

And he'd forgotten about Lyle Wentworth, her long-faithful suitor. Wentworth was an arrogant, dull chap with little to recommend him, as far as Sean could see. But at least *he* had never abandoned her. He had never deceived her and broken her heart.

A rocking horse. What a ridiculous gift for a little tyke just barely able to toddle.

Sean rolled over and stuffed the pillow underneath

him with unnecessary force, as if the helpless pillow were Lyle Wentworth's head.

How could he expect Kate to give him yet another chance? He couldn't, unless they had time together. That was the key. No trips to Pritchard's Hill, she'd declared, in that determined way of hers. Fine, he'd already known that this time it would take more than a bluebird and some lovemaking to make her accept him again. But he needed to be able to spend time with her alone, without the rest of the family looking on, ready to pounce on him if he should dare to wound her again. And without Lyle Wentworth, handling Sean's own daughter as if he had some kind of proprietary interest.

He rolled over, once again switching his view to the ceiling. Jennie hated Lyle. And she'd helped Sean once before when she'd written to tell him about his daughter. She'd invited him to Christmas dinner. Jennie desperately wanted her sister to be happy. The more he thought about it, the more he was sure that Jennie was the answer. All he had to do was convince her that she and Sean shared a common cause.

He rolled out of bed and stood up. Perhaps he was hungry after all.

"I'm sorry, Sean," Jennie said sadly. "It's not that I don't believe what you're saying, but you must admit that your record isn't too good."

"You're in this with me, Jennie. It was the discovery of your letter that convinced her to leave San Francisco." Sean had already decided that if pleading didn't win his case, he'd not be above resorting to making Jennie feel guilty.

But Jennie was not playing. She gave him a look of reproach and said, "If she'd been happy there, Sean, finding out about the letter wouldn't have affected her."

They were in the makeshift kitchen up at the Wesley mine. Sean had walked up to the mine that morning to inquire about work, and decided that it would be an ideal time to put his case to Jennie, who was preparing the noon meal for the miners as she did five days a week. He figured that it would be easier to talk with her away from Sheridan House.

"She was happy part of the time, Jennie. But I know it wasn't easy moving into the world of my mother's friends. And it didn't help matters that I was often not around when she needed me."

"Which wouldn't be the first time you weren't there when she needed you," Jennie added pointedly. She was cutting vegetables into a big pot for stew. "Bring me some of those potatoes."

He picked up several and went over to her, holding them while she took them from him one by one. "You can't make me feel any more guilty than I already do about not being here when Kate was having Caroline, Jennie. But there's nothing I can do about that, is there?"

"Nope. But you can't blame me for trying to protect Kate from being hurt by you again. Why *did* it take you so long to come after her, anyway?"

He patiently held out another potato. "Honestly, Jennie, I was so shattered when she left that I spent the next few weeks trying to drink dry every bar in San Francisco.''

Jennie looked up from her cutting. ''Did you succeed?''

''Just about. But I'm not making excuses. Once again, I was at fault. If I tried from now till doomsday I wouldn't be able to make up for all the things I've done *wrong* since I met Kate. So all I can do is start in from this moment trying to do everything *right*.''

''And that's why you're here.''

''Yes.''

Jennie sighed and threw the last couple of potatoes in whole. ''Well, I wish you luck, Sean. I know Kate better than anyone, and I'm afraid she's not as over you as she'd like to think. But as to letting you move in with us, I can't do it. Not until I get some sign that it would really be in Kate's best interest.''

Sean nodded, hiding his disappointment. ''Well, then I'll just have to work hard to make that sign happen soon,'' he said firmly. ''I'll see you tonight.''

''At home?''

''Why, yes. She will let me see my daughter, won't she?''

Jennie gave an uncertain nod. ''I suppose so.''

''Then I'll see you tonight after supper,'' he said, ''and tomorrow right here.''

''Here?''

''I start work here tomorrow.''

''You're going to be a silverheel?'' Jennie's jaw dropped with amazement.

Sean laughed and he turned up his right foot. ''Starting tomorrow,'' he repeated.

"Well, I'll be hornswoggled," she said.

Sean grinned, tipped his hat, then turned and walked away down the path.

He'd come every night without fail for a week. Each night Kate brought Caroline down to him, said a polite "good evening" and then retired to her room until nine o'clock, at which time she would walk down the stairs, her heart pounding a little heavier than normal, and collect Caroline for bed.

Sean had not asked again to go upstairs to her room. He'd not tried to get close to her or made any suggestive remarks. He'd not called her "sweetheart."

But to Kate's immense annoyance, each day she found herself looking more often at the time in the late afternoon. On the fourth day, she'd taken out one of the two San Francisco dresses she'd brought with her when she'd left. It was the blue taffeta that matched her eyes. She'd left it on the bed all afternoon, and each time she went up to her room to change Caroline or put her down for her nap, she'd look at the dress, trying to decide if she should wear it that evening. In the end, she'd angrily hung it back in her wardrobe and worn the simple green cotton she'd had on all day.

But it was obvious to herself, if not to the rest of the household, that she was weakening. The following day was a Sunday. There was no work at the mine, and Sean had asked to be permitted to come earlier in the afternoon to have more time with his daughter. Jennie had invited him for supper.

Telling herself that it was in honor of the Sabbath Day and nothing more, Kate put on the blue taffeta.

She hadn't expected that Sean would recognize it, but he did, and his own blue eyes danced as he gave her a thorough perusal from her piled-up hair to the kid leather shoes that had also been a San Francisco acquisition.

"I'm glad you took this dress at least," he told her as she joined him in the parlor with Caroline before supper. "I couldn't understand why you left so many of your new things. I would have brought them all with me when I came, but I thought maybe you'd left them because you didn't like them any better than that first batch my mother got for you."

"Oh no," Kate exclaimed. "They were beautiful. But I didn't feel right since I was, well, you know. I *was* leaving you, after all."

"Running away," he said.

"Coming home," she corrected.

He smiled. "We'll send for the rest of the things. Your beauty needs no adornment, Kate, but I like to see you in pretty things."

The compliment brushed a blush up her cheeks. She held Caroline out to him. "I'll see you at supper, then," she said.

He took Caroline and kissed her, but said to Kate, "Couldn't you stay with us until supper? Maybe Caroline would like some time with both her parents together."

Kate hesitated. "I should see if Jennie needs help."

"Barnaby's helping her. I went back to the kitchen to say hello when I got here." When she still hesitated, he sat down on one end of the settee with Caroline on his lap and nodded at the opposite end. "C'mon, Katie.

Sit there and let me at least look at you for a few minutes. Give a starving man a crumb.''

Kate laughed. ''You don't look to be starving, Sean.''

''You wouldn't say that if you could sample the food at the hotel.''

''You're trying to make me feel sorry for you, and it won't work.''

''Hmm. Not the right tack, eh?'' He jiggled Caroline and made her giggle. ''Your mama's got a cold heart, pumpkin. Did you know that? Hard to believe in someone so beautiful.''

''Flattery won't work, either,'' Kate said, but she was smiling.

Sean leaned toward Caroline's ear and told her in a conspiratorial whisper, ''We'll have to think of something else, pumpkin. She's on to us.''

By the time Jennie arrived to announce that supper was ready, Sean and Kate were sitting on the floor with Caroline between their outspread legs. Kate's hair was mussed and her cheeks were bright. Her eyes were shining with laughter in a way Jennie hadn't seen in months.

The good humor lasted all the way through supper. Carter entertained them with a story of an unusual case he'd handled—a rancher who'd willed his ranch to his cattle, which were now roaming the surrounding territory causing all kinds of commotion. That story had set Dennis off on one of his Irish tales. The meal lasted two hours and could have continued if Caroline hadn't decided that she'd had enough of behaving for one night. She started fussing, and even Sean's cajoling wouldn't quiet her.

"I'd better take her up for her bath and put her to bed," Kate said, standing. "You all can continue talking, if you like."

But the three miners had grown suddenly serious. "Before you go, Kate, we need to make kind of an announcement," Dennis said, looking from Kate to Jennie.

Kate picked up Caroline from her high chair and stood rocking her. "What is it?"

Dennis looked down at his coffee and cleared his throat. "You know we love you two gals as if you were our own sisters."

"That's for *darn* sure," Smitty agreed, and Brad nodded vehemently.

"But we're miners," Dennis continued, "and the Wesley's beginning to play out, just like a lot of the mines in this area."

Caroline continued her fidgeting, but Kate merely brushed a kiss on the top of her head and said, "Shh."

Jennie folded her napkin carefully and put it on the table. Her expression was strained. "Are you thinking of leaving Vermillion?"

Dennis looked from Smitty to Brad, then back to Jennie. "We've taken jobs down at the Comstock."

"All of you?" Kate gasped.

"We wanted to stick together," Smitty explained. "It's bad enough having to leave you two, and Barnaby here," he added, reaching over to rough up the boy's hair.

"This will be our last week," Brad added.

Jennie bit her lip and looked around the table with a brittle smile. "We'll miss you dreadfully, you know."

Dennis' round face was mournful. "We'll come back and see you. I promise."

She nodded without speaking, her eyes brimming.

"What about the rooms? Do you know of anyone who might want to rent them?" Kate asked. She had also felt the tears rising at the thought of their kind, protective silverheels leaving them. But she had learned over the past two years that sometimes sentimentality had to give way to practicality.

Dennis shook his head. "That's part of the reason we're feeling so bad. More and more fellows are leaving. There are rooms to spare these days."

"No one has responded to the advertisement I posted up at the mine," Jennie said, glancing quickly at Sean.

Caroline let out a wail, irritated by the delay. "Well, we'll think of something. It'll work out," Kate said firmly. "I need to get her to bed, and I'll probably just go on to sleep myself, so I'll say good-night."

The others around the table bid her good-night. Sean stood and said, "Do you need help?"

She barely glanced at him. "No, thank you. I'll manage." Then she looked at Jennie. Compared to what they'd already faced together, this setback was minor. "We'll manage, sis."

The two sisters exchanged a nod of understanding before Kate turned to go upstairs.

Chapter Fourteen

"I want to be out of the house when you tell her." Carter's voice was lazily amused.

They were lying together in bed after a particularly satisfying session of lovemaking. Jennie snuggled against him. "I always knew you were a coward."

"I'm not a coward, I'm just a lawyer. We deal with people in trouble and learn how to stay out of it ourselves." He pulled the blankets around them. "For example, I don't intend to say anything to rile you for the next few months. I've heard that mamas-to-be can be very touchy."

Jennie gave a low laugh. Although her stomach was becoming gently rounded, she still wasn't totally accustomed to the idea that soon she would have a precious son or daughter of her very own. "I'll try not to make this pregnancy too hard on you," she teased.

Carter grew serious. "I just hope it's not too hard on *you*. I wish you'd agree to visit that special baby doctor who helped Kate."

"I've never felt better, darling. And as long as my

sister doesn't tear my head off for renting a room in our house to her husband, I'll be fine.''

Carter leaned over to put out the light. He liked to leave it on when they were making love, and after her initial shyness, Jennie had decided that she liked it, too. ''You're sure about letting him come to live here?''

''No, I'm not sure. But, first of all, with the others leaving, we need the money. And second, Sean's been working hard every day for two weeks. The silverheels say he works almost harder than anyone up at Wesley. Then he comes here after work every day without fail and plays with Caroline. She adores him—''

''Kate avoids him,'' Carter interrupted.

''Yes, but she's not as adamant about it as she was at the beginning. I think she's weakening.''

Carter chuckled. ''Or you want her to weaken.''

Jennie found his chin to kiss in the dark. ''I just wish she could find the happiness you and I have found.''

He kissed her in return. ''I do, too, love, but it's not something that a third party can engineer. People have to find their own happiness when it comes to love.''

''I know. I can only do so much. But Sean's a different man than he was on his previous visits here. I think Kate should give him a chance to prove that to her.''

''Well, it will be kind of hard for her to ignore him if she has to run into him every time she heads to the outhouse.''

Jennie gave him a gentle shove. ''You can think of a more romantic encounter than that, I hope. I seem to remember you and I having some trouble staying away from each other when we were both living here.''

"Even though you thought I was an arrogant, undependable male.''

"And you thought I was a stubborn, independent female.''

"Which you are.''

"Oh, yeah? Then how come you married me?''

"That's easy. I couldn't get you in bed every night any other way.''

Jennie pulled away with a gasp. "Carter Jones!''

He laughed and pulled her back. "All right, honey, I married you because I thought you were the most beautiful, desirable, intelligent, noble-hearted, stubborn minx I'd ever met. There, does that satisfy you?''

"That's better,'' Jennie said.

"But like it or not, you have to admit that lovemaking did have something to do with our rather, ah, uncontrolled attraction to each other. And when two people live in the same house, that kind of thing becomes quite clear.''

Jennie smiled to herself in the dark. "Well, now, that's exactly what I'm counting on.''

"Kate, if you're absolutely opposed, I'll find another place.''

Sean had just come down from putting Caroline to bed. Most evenings, Kate continued to busy herself in the kitchen until he left, but tonight she'd waited for him in the parlor to tell him, angrily, that she did *not* want him moving in just down the hall from her bedroom. "Well, I'm absolutely opposed,'' she said.

When he didn't answer for a moment, she asked, "Why can't you just keep staying at the hotel?"

"On a miner's salary?"

Kate threaded her fingers through the magic shawl that covered the arm of the settee. "I thought you said you had money saved."

"Well, I won't have if I keep living at the hotel at twelve dollars a week."

Kate winced. "I didn't know it was so much."

"That's all right. Don't worry about it. I'll ask up at the mine if anyone knows of a place I can go."

"Do you think you'll be able to find something?"

Sean leaned back into the cushions. "You heard what the miners said. With all the men leaving town, there are a lot of places available. And anyway, I guess a place for me to stay is not your problem, is it?" He shot her a look out of the corner of his eyes.

"Well, you are here in Vermillion because of me…and Caroline."

"Yes, I am."

"But I didn't *ask* you to come."

"No, you didn't."

Kate gave a long sigh. "Sean Flaherty, you're trying to make me feel sorry for you again, and I've already told you, it won't work."

Sean shook his head and smiled. "Katie, if I'd thought making you feel sorry for me would change things between us, I'd have started that campaign the day after I arrived. For example, I could have showed you these." He held out his hands, palms up so she could see the red welts where blisters had evidently turned into open sores that were just beginning to heal.

"Lordy. You've been working at the mine with your hands like this?"

"Working at the mine was what *made* my hands like this. But they're getting better." He held them up and twisted them around in the air. "See, no play for sympathy."

Kate stared over at the fireplace where the fire she'd laid earlier was dying out. "What if I said it was all right for you to stay here for a while. Do you think we could act civilized around each other? You know…like friends?"

Sean didn't answer for such a long time that Kate shifted her gaze from the fire and turned around to face him again. Finally he spoke with deliberation. "Katie, the easiest thing would be to say, sure. Anything to get you to agree to have me here. But perhaps you haven't noticed that I'm not trying to do things the easy way anymore. I'm trying to do them the right way."

"Which means?"

"Which means, I won't lie to you. The reason I want to move in here is not to be your friend. It's to be able to spend as much time as possible around you and perhaps little by little begin to convince you that there still is some hope for the two of us."

Kate sighed. "I don't think there's any way you can do that, Sean."

"I know you don't. And maybe you're right. But if we don't spend some time together, we'll never know, will we?"

Kate still had trouble recognizing this new, serious side of him. She kept expecting him to burst out laugh-

ing and make a joke or to tell her that he was tired of
playing working man and had decided to go back to
San Francisco and the good life. But day after day he'd
stuck it out. "Jennie says you've changed," she said
after a pause.

"I always thought Jennie was a smart woman,"
Sean said, but his grin was not the carefree, taunting
one she remembered.

"I'm not saying I'd spend time with you," she said,
hedging.

Sean must have sensed his victory. He carefully kept
his face even, but his hands tightened on the velvet
cushions of the settee. "I wouldn't force my company
on you. I think you know that, Katie."

"And it would just be a trial. If things don't work
out, you'll have to agree to find somewhere else."

Sean nodded and risked a small smile. "I knew your
big heart would win this battle, sweetheart," he said.

"And you're not to call me 'sweetheart.'"

"That will be a tough one. What would you like me
to call you, Mrs. Flaherty?" His grin was more like
the old, cocky Sean.

Kate stood up with a little huff, already regretting
her change of heart. "Just behave yourself, Sean. I
mean it. Or else you can go spend your nights in the
mine shaft for all the difference it'll make to me."

"Thank you, Katie," he said, his voice serious
again. She looked at him with a despairing expression
as if she had just lost a battle that she'd once thought
won. "You won't regret it, I promise," he added.

She bit her lip, then nodded her head and turned to
leave. "I hope not, Sean," she said wearily.

Her back was long and straight as she walked out of the room. Even that small moment of watching her move was enough to arouse him. He'd been without her too long. And he had the feeling that if they could wade through all the emotions, she'd welcome the renewal of their passion as much as he.

He'd not do anything to risk getting banished to sleep in a mine shaft. But he'd have to figure out some way for them to spend time together. Alone. Because there was no doubt about it. The place he really wanted to be spending his nights was his wife's bed.

By Wednesday, Sean had moved into the room once occupied by Carter. It was done with little fanfare. No one dared make jokes about the room's previous tenant having subsequently moved in with one of the house's owners. After agreeing to the move, Kate had been touchy all week, as if she regretted her weakness in giving in.

Jennie hoped that her sister's ill humor would fade after she got used to Sean's presence in the house. Jennie herself would see that he behaved impeccably and did nothing that could disturb her sister. She was convinced that part of the reason for Kate's mood was her fear that she would *enjoy* being around him again. Which, Jennie confided to Carter, was exactly the point. "If two people are meant for each other, the universe will move in mysterious ways to put them together," she'd said.

And her practical-minded, attorney husband had merely smiled and kissed her.

But two days into the experiment, Kate was not enjoying much of anything. Caroline had been particularly fussy, perhaps because a streak of cold weather had kept her indoors. And Jennie had seemed unusually tired. She'd been late heading up to the mine three mornings in a row, and twice had asked Barnaby if he would help Kate with the washing up so that she could go up to bed.

Kate had to admit that Sean was keeping his promise to be a gentleman. But that didn't help when her unruly, illogical body seemed so ready to jump to attention every time he was around, which was now entirely too much of the time.

The first morning he was there, she'd walked out of her room and practically run smack into him as he carried a basin of water from the backyard pump up to his room. He was wearing his boots, trousers and a rolled-up towel around his neck, leaving a good portion of his upper body naked. She'd tried to keep her eyes from his bare chest, in particular refusing to notice how it tapered down to his lean waist, how the shadow of dark hair made a vee into the top of his low-slung belt. But she'd headed down to breakfast flushed and irritated.

That night he'd insisted on helping her put Caroline to bed. When the baby had spit up on his shirt, he'd carelessly pulled it over his head without bothering to unbutton it and tossed it aside. "I'll wash it out later," he'd said. Kate had had to stand to one side and watch as he proceeded shirtless to bathe and change Caroline without the slightest self-consciousness, the muscles rippling in his arms each time he moved. When he'd reached toward her across the bed, she'd actually jumped, which made him straighten, smile slightly and say, "Will you hand me a fresh diaper?"

By Saturday, Kate was almost ready to go to Jennie and plead with her to send Sean packing. She probably would have done so if Jennie hadn't begun acting tired and listless. When Kate had first arrived back from San Francisco, it had appeared that Carter had merely been overprotective with his worry over Jennie's pregnancy. But now Kate was beginning to believe that his fears might have some basis.

In any event, it wouldn't help Jennie's condition to worry about money. Tomorrow the silverheels would be leaving for Virginia City, leaving Sean as the only boarder. Perhaps it was selfish of Kate to want him gone. At least he was a paying tenant. It was self-centered of her to put her own comfort over the welfare of the whole family. She would give the arrangement a little more time and see if she could become immune to Sean's presence.

With the decrease in production, the Wesley mine had begun working half-day Saturdays. The silverheels had been happy to have the afternoon to pack up their belongings before a final farewell celebration that evening, but Sean was hoping to put the time to better use.

"I've rented the rig for the day," he told Kate. "Caroline's been cooped up for most of the week and now that the weather's turned, a drive in the country would be good for her."

Kate eyed him suspiciously. "I told you there'd be no repetition of Pritchard's Hill, Sean."

He blinked innocently. "We can go anywhere you like, Kate. I just want to take my daughter for a drive. I'd take her with Barnaby, but Jennie tells me he's spending the day at the Colters'."

"You and Caroline could go by yourselves."

He held up his hands. "I can't drive the carriage and hold her at the same time. It wouldn't be very safe."

"I suppose not."

Sean ducked his head to look into her face. "You could use a drive in the fresh air, too, Kate. You look tired."

Since she reckoned she'd been averaging about two hours of sleep per night, she wasn't surprised. "Oh, all right. We can go. Just for a drive."

They'd set out well bundled in blankets against the late January air, but before long the brilliant sun was warming them enough to throw the covers into the backseat. Sean had been right. The sun and brisk air were reviving her spirits. She felt better than she had all week.

"We should have asked Jennie and Carter to come along," she said. "Jennie's looking tired, too." She hadn't yet told Sean about her sister's pregnancy.

"Perhaps she and Carter don't get enough sleep," Sean said with a mischievous grin.

Kate ignored the reference and concentrated on the beautiful winter day. "Isn't the sky blue?" she asked, throwing her arm out expansively.

Caroline, sitting in her lap, duplicated the gesture, making both her parents laugh.

"See if you can get her to say it," Sean suggested. "Sky," he said loudly, pointing up.

Kate turned the baby slightly to get her attention and repeated, "Sky."

"Kee," Caroline gurgled.

Sean whooped with pleasure. "She said it!"

Kate looked at her daughter with amazement. "She did, didn't she?" She repeated the experiment, and once again Caroline obliged with a "kee."

"Soon she'll be reciting the Declaration of Independence," Sean said proudly.

"It's wonderful to see the changes, isn't it?" Sharing the moment made Kate feel a warmth entirely different from the uncomfortable physical sensations she'd felt around Sean all week.

"My daughter's going to be president of the United States," Sean declared.

Kate giggled. "A woman president?"

Sean nodded firmly. "If women can vote, they can be president."

"Women can't vote. Not most places anyway."

"They will, one of these days. Maybe Caroline will grow up to be one of those suffragist ladies and help make it happen."

"I just want her to grow up happy," Kate said.

Sean stroked Caroline's bonnet, then let his hand slide down to capture Kate's hand, which was resting on the baby's knee. "That's all I want for her, too, Katie."

She let her hand stay in his. It felt right, somehow, to be holding their daughter together this way, hands clasped, sharing their hopes for her future.

But as they turned the carriage around and headed back toward town, her mood began to change. It was happening again, she thought with a momentary surge of panic. The drive had proved what she'd been trying to deny to herself all week long. The ice crystals that had formed around her heart weeks ago in San Francisco were beginning to melt.

"You must have had a nice ride," Jennie said, looking up from kneading the bread as they came in the back kitchen door. "It's almost supper time."

Kate looked guilty. "I'm sorry, Jen. Did you need help?"

"No. I'm doing fine. You can go get changed."

Kate looked down at her dress, which had not been much soiled by the drive. "I hadn't really planned on changing."

"Oh. All right. But you do remember that Lyle's coming to eat with us, don't you?"

"Lordy. I forgot." She looked over at Sean, who still held Caroline in his arms. "Can you watch her while I get dressed?"

"Of course," he agreed without smiling. After she picked up her skirts and ran from the kitchen, his expression turned to a downright frown. The drive hadn't been as intimate as he'd hoped, but he'd felt they'd been closer than they had in a long while. And he fancied that some of the soft glow in her cheeks when they'd returned home had come from more than the fresh air. So why had she raced off to primp for Lyle's visit like a girl before her first social?

"She's not serious about Wentworth, is she?" he asked Jennie.

She dusted the flour off her hands. "Serious? I don't know. He's certainly been loyal through the years. Sometimes persistence is enough to wear women down."

He had a feeling that Jennie was trying to give him a message about his own course of action, but all he could think of was the look on Kate's face when she'd remembered Lyle's visit and said, "Lordy!"

"He's a bag of wind," he observed.

Jennie smiled quietly and began covering the pans of dough with towels. "Perhaps. But he's good to Kate."

Caroline started to squirm, demanding attention. There was a knock on the front door and sounds of Barnaby admitting someone. Sean bounced Caroline in his arms and said, "C'mon pumpkin, let's go for a walk in the garden before supper." He turned to leave. "Holler for us when it's ready, Jennie, will you?"

She nodded and as the voices from the front hall grew louder, he strode quickly out the back door.

The silverheels' last supper at Sheridan House was not a happy occasion. Though everyone tried to put a bright face on things, there was no way to avoid the reality that the close knit household was breaking up. The three miners had stood with the sisters when the town had wanted to shut their boardinghouse down. They'd helped Jennie keep the place running after Kate had had to go to the special hospital in Virginia City. They'd even learned to garden and helped to harvest their own food. When Caroline had arrived, they'd been like three favorite uncles living in the same house. Now they were leaving.

Jennie's face had traces of tears when she came from the kitchen bringing a special farewell cake she'd made them. When each one of the miners had got up from his place to plant hearty kisses on first her cheek, then Kate's, Kate's eyes had misted also.

Sean understood that the goodbye was an emotional one, but he was bitterly disappointed that the close mood he and Kate had managed to achieve on the drive that afternoon had totally disappeared. And he was even more disappointed to see that Kate was leaning more on Lyle than on Sean for comfort.

Lyle seemed to be aware of the fact as well, and ready to take advantage of it. "How would it be if I send a carriage for you fellows one month from today?" he asked the miners halfway through the supper. "Then you'd all know a definite time that you'd see each other again."

Both Jennie and Kate had brightened at his offer, and Kate had sent him an affectionately grateful glance that was not lost on Sean.

By the end of the meal, Sean was feeling more hopeless and surly than he had since the day after he'd hurt his knee back home. When Dennis Kelly asked if he wanted to join the silverheels for a farewell drink in town, he agreed readily. He'd sworn off the stuff for weeks, but tonight a drink or two sounded like exactly what he needed.

Kate had taken Caroline up to bed, and Lyle was waiting for her in the parlor. She probably wouldn't even notice that he had gone, he decided as he shrugged into his coat and followed the miners out into the cold night.

He had a sudden vision of Lyle sliding closer to her on the velvety settee, putting his arm around her. It made his gorge rise.

Dennis waited for him to catch up, then clapped a hand on his shoulder. "I have to admit, Flaherty, I didn't think a pantywaist rich lad like you would ever become a real miner, but you've proved me wrong. You're all right, man. The boys and I will miss working with you."

"It won't be the same at Wesley without you three," he replied, trying to set aside the picture of Lyle and Kate.

Smitty came up alongside them. "Yeah, Flaherty, we like you so much, we'll let you buy the first round tonight."

Sean grinned. "As long as you buy the second."

Dennis put an arm around the neck of each man. "Don't fight over it, boys. There'll be rounds enough for everyone. I, for one, intend to get stinking drunk."

Sean closed his eyes briefly. Kate was probably descending the stairs this minute and joining Lyle in the parlor. Jennie, Carter and Barnaby had gone up to bed before Sean left. Kate and Lyle would be alone.

"Stinking drunk sounds good to me," he agreed.

"I've heard this from you before, Kate," Lyle said. He was standing with his back to her in front of the parlor fireplace.

"I know. I feel dreadful that I haven't been more

firm in my purpose when it comes to you, Lyle. I think I've treated you shabbily, and it makes me feel guilty.''

He turned around angrily. "I don't want you to feel guilty, damn it. You know what it is I want you to feel.''

Kate clasped and unclasped her hands as they lay in her lap. "I know. Believe me, my life would be a lot easier if I could feel for you what you say you feel for me. But I can't, Lyle.''

"It's Flaherty again, isn't it? Somehow he's managed once more to make you forget all the misery he's put you through.''

Kate drew in a deep breath. "I don't know. I don't think I've forgotten it, but there is definitely an attraction between Sean and me that won't go away. And he is, after all, the father of my daughter. If we can have a life together, I think I owe it to her to try to give that a chance.''

Lyle's face was red with frustration. "I've given you every chance to see what a fool you're being, Kate. But I'm not going to keep begging forever. There are plenty of women in this town who'd throw themselves at my feet if I looked their way.''

"Oh, Lyle. I'm sure there are. And I'm telling you that you have my blessing to go out and find them.''

When she was twelve years old, Kate would have given anything to see the pretentious Lyle Wentworth so deflated, but now it only made her heart ache. She'd tried to be as gentle as possible, but her ride today with Sean had made her realize that what she was saying was the truth. There still *was* a definite pull between her and Sean, and sharing the ever-expanding world of their daughter made that pull a hundred times stronger.

As Lyle sputtered for more argument, she stood and said once more that she was sorry, then told him that she was too tired for more talk this evening.

When he'd left, she turned toward the stairway, her heart picking up its beat. She paused, her hand on the newel post. Sean was just steps away from her, lying all alone in his bed. She'd been fighting it all week, and for what? Sean was her husband. He was Caroline's father. There was absolutely nothing to prevent her from going to his room and telling him this very minute that she would like to give their love one more final chance.

With a deep, determined breath, she started up the stairs.

Chapter Fifteen

The silverheels left at midmorning. None of them had awakened in time for breakfast, and when Jennie had offered to cook something for them before they set out, they'd all held their stomachs, rolled their eyes and explained that after their binge the previous evening, the last thing they needed on the bumpy road to Virginia City was food.

Kate had slept poorly after the all-too-familiar experience of finding Sean's bed empty the previous evening. Her ill humor mitigated some of her sadness, but she still had tears in her eyes when the men climbed into the freight wagon that had been sent by the Comstock people to fetch them and their belongings.

The sisters linked arms as they walked back up the path to the house. "The place'll seem empty as a barn," Jennie said with a sigh.

"Yes, but in some ways it will be easier. I've been waiting to talk with you, Jen. I'm worried that you're wearing yourself out."

Jennie shook her head. "You and Carter worry too much."

"No, you've been working too hard. And I've been thinking. We've paid off most of the debts. With Carter's help, maybe we won't even need to take boarders anymore. We could just be family—you two, Barnaby, Caroline and me."

Jennie glanced sharply at her sister as they mounted the stairs to the front porch. "What about Sean?"

"There are lots of empty places in town now. He could find somewhere else."

"Funny, I thought you were becoming reconciled to having him here. Maybe even liking it?"

Kate knew that it was irrational of her to feel so angry at Sean for having gone out to celebrate with the silverheels the previous evening. They'd worked together. It was a perfectly natural thing for him to do. But when she'd finally gotten her courage up to go to his room and found him gone, it had brought flooding back all the hurt from those unhappy days in San Francisco.

"No," she said quietly. "It would be easier for me not to have him around."

Jennie frowned. "Well, now we have a dilemma."

They stopped on the porch, neither one opening the front door. "What do you mean?"

Jennie reached for her sister's hands and said, "Come sit on the swing with me for a minute." Her voice was grave.

Kate felt a wave of sick fear. She was right. Things weren't just fine with Jennie as she'd been pretending. The two sisters had taken care of each other their entire lives. After their parents' deaths, when Kate had been so ill with her pregnancy, Jennie had filled the roles of sister, parent, friend and provider. Things were a little different between them now that Jennie was married to Carter, but even so, Jennie served as Kate's touchstone in facing the ups and downs of life.

She felt a chill as she sat on the cold wood of the swing. "Tell me, Jennie. What's going on? How are you feeling?"

"I've talked to Dr. Millard. He thinks it might be a good idea for me to see that female specialist who took care of you."

"Then you should," Kate said firmly.

"But we haven't paid off the bills from yours yet."

Kate reached for her sister's hand. "We'll manage. Your health's the important thing."

Jennie gave Kate's hand a squeeze. "I remember the way you held on to my hand as we sat here a year ago last spring."

Kate knew at once that she was referring to the day when Kate had had to tell Jennie that she was going to have a baby—without a husband to give it his name. The sisters had been newly orphaned, without money, and now were about to confront the greatest disgrace a woman can endure. "Those were bleak days, Jennie. But with your help, I made it through. Now it's my turn to take care of you. Along with Carter, of course. He's going to make such a proud papa," she concluded with a smile.

Jennie smiled back. "I hope he'll be as attentive as Sean is to Caroline. I've been amazed to see him changing her clothes, putting on her diapers—"

Kate interrupted. "He's attentive when he's in the mood to be around, I guess."

Jennie looked puzzled. "He's been around constantly since he came back to Vermillion this time."

"He wasn't around last night." Kate gave the swing a little push, then stopped it again almost immediately. "This isn't making you sick, is it?"

Jennie laughed. "Not right now, though this morning it might have been a problem." She returned to the topic of Kate's husband. "Kate, Sean was out with the silverheels for their last night in town. Surely you can't fault him for that. Especially when you were with Lyle, remember?"

Put that way, it made Kate's pique seem irrational, but she couldn't help the way she'd felt the previous evening when she was greeted once again by his empty bed. She tried to push the thought out of her head. Jennie's condition was the important thing at the moment. "This morning? So you have been sick?"

Jennie nodded. "A little. Not any more than most women in the family way."

"You're going to see that baby doctor, Jen."

"Carter's insisting on the same thing. The problem is, Carter and I would have to stay in Virginia City a night or two. Barnaby could stay home from school to take care of Caroline when you go up to the mine, but at night—" Jennie swallowed and looked away. "I'd feel better if you and the children had a man around." Suddenly Kate understood the dilemma Jennie had been talking about. Now that the silverheels were gone, if Carter and Jennie left, she and Sean would be alone in the house with only Barnaby and Caroline for chaperons. Lordy.

She leaned over and gave Jennie a kiss on the cheek.

"I'll be fine, sis. The important thing right now is your health. You and Carter go and stay as long as you need to have them give you a good checkup."

"It's silly, you know, I could just continue to see Dr. Millard in town."

"That's what I said, too, remember? As a result I almost lost Caroline. No, you let Carter take you down to that hospital and don't worry about things back here. I'll go up and cook the noon meal at the mine while you're gone. In fact, I'm going to start doing that anyway." At her sister's shake of the head she continued, "At least on any day when you're feeling tired. We'll switch jobs. You can stay home and watch Caroline and I'll go take care of the miners."

Jennie gave her a grateful smile. "I don't know how to thank you, sis."

Kate pulled her sister into another embrace. "Jen, I can never repay all the things you've done for me. If it wasn't for you, I wouldn't have Caroline. No, we're going to do whatever it takes to make sure that five months from now she has a beautiful little cousin to play with. Starting with...I'm going to get you out of this cold air, Mama." She pulled her sister up from the swing.

They went into the house arm in arm, laughing, but after Jennie went back to the kitchen, Kate climbed the stairs, her expression growing sober.

She would do whatever she had to in the next few months to help her sister, even if that meant spending one or more nights in the same house virtually alone with Sean. But she wasn't about to make the mistake she'd almost made last night. Sean could spend his nights at the bar or down in the red-light district, for all she would know, because she never intended to be anywhere near his bedroom ever again.

Kate looked at the meager larder and few utensils in dismay. The cookhouse at the Wesley mine was nothing more than a rough lean-to with two sides, a makeshift stove fueled by wood, a long table for food preparation and two bins with a motley assortment of cooking equipment. The food, what there was of it, was stacked on shelves running along one of the walls. Kate had visited the mine before, but until today she'd never stopped to consider how Jennie had managed to prepare the magnificent meals the silverheels had raved about under such primitive conditions.

She sighed and began to unpack the two burlap bags of meat she'd brought with her that morning. Sean had volunteered to ask permission to drive down to fetch her midmorning, but Jennie had been accustomed to walking up the mountain to the mine each day, so Kate had politely refused his offer.

She'd known she would see him, however, and wasn't too surprised when he popped his head into the shelter shortly after she arrived. "You made it here all right, I see," he said.

"Yes." She had spoken little to him all week, particularly since Jennie and Carter had left the previous day for Virginia City. She wasn't about to risk a resumption of the feelings that had begun to surface on their drive the past Saturday.

He sauntered into the kitchen and began helping her to empty the bags. "You carried all this up the mountain? Sweetheart, you should have let me come for you."

"I've asked you not to call me 'sweetheart,'" she said.

Sean grinned. "Sorry, it just slipped out."

"Well, slip it back in again," she said curtly.

The food bags were empty, so he turned and boosted himself to take a seat on top of the table and watch her while she began peeling the potatoes. "Aw, Katie," he said. "When are you going to stop being mad at me?"

She looked at him in surprise. "I'm not mad at you."

"Yes, you are. You've hardly talked to me since Saturday. It's because I went out with Dennis and the boys, isn't it?"

Kate shifted her potato pile toward the far end of the table to avoid flipping a peeling right in his lap. "It's immaterial to me what you do with your Saturday nights, Sean."

"No, it's not. Otherwise you wouldn't be mad. I take it as a good sign."

She shook her head. "Please don't."

"You were with Wentworth, you know. Did you expect me to be happy about that?"

"I didn't think about it one way or another."

"Well, I sure as hell did," he muttered, swinging his legs back and forth until the table began to wobble.

"You're going to have all my food on the ground in a minute," she said irritably. "Aren't you supposed to be working?"

"I am working. I'm seeing if the new cook needs any help."

"She doesn't."

"I got the assignment because the new cook happens to be my wife," he added with a grin.

Kate stopped her peeling for a moment to look at him. "You've told people that?"

He nodded. "Darn right I've told them."

She paused a moment, then went back to her peeling. "I would have thought you might be reluctant to say anything."

"Why's that?"

"I'm sure your mother would be mortified for the folks on Nob Hill to know that her daughter-in-law was peeling potatoes in a scruffy mining camp."

Sean laughed. "It would almost be worth a trip back to San Francisco to tell her."

"But it doesn't bother you?"

"Katie, I think it's remarkable what you and Jennie have done to survive and keep your family thriving after your mother and father left you with nothing but debts."

"We had the house," she argued, feeling that his words somehow implied criticism of her beloved parents.

"A big, run-down house that sucked up money and energy."

"A house that we were able to turn into a money-making enterprise," she corrected.

"That's what I was saying...you survived because of initiative and hard work. The two of you are worth all of last season's Nob Hill debs put together."

Kate didn't return his smile, but she was pleased nonetheless. "Well, I'm glad you're not ashamed to have me working here," she concluded.

Sean boosted himself off the table and spoke seriously. "Katie, I'm more proud of you than I've ever been able to express. It's myself that I've been ashamed of."

She met his eyes, not sure what to say. His expression was as humble as the dirty mining clothes he wore. It was hard to see any traces of the cocky, spoiled charmer he'd been when he first came to Vermillion. "You'd better get back to work," she said finally. "Or the foreman will cause trouble for us both."

He nodded and turned to leave the kitchen, but just before he left, he turned back to her and asked, "Will Jennie and Carter be back tonight?"

"I don't think so. They'll likely be staying a couple more days." Carter had asked Kate if she would mind if he kept Jennie in Virginia City for a short vacation.

"She needs the rest, and, besides, the International Hotel there has special memories for us," Carter had explained. Then he'd added with a grin, "I figure I'd better take advantage now before I have to share her attention with my son."

"I think it would be a great idea if you two stayed a couple of days for her to get some *sleep,*" Kate had agreed, smiling. "I'll expect to see you both well rested when you return."

At her answer, Sean's expression appeared to brighten, but all he said was, "Ah. Well, I hope she finds out that everything's all right with the baby."

"So do I."

"See you at lunch, Katie." She noticed that as he turned down the path toward the nearest mine tunnel, he was whistling.

As usual, Sean was exhausted by the end of his day of hauling carload after carload of ore up the long tracks from the back of the mine. It was "mule" duty, one of the worst, but he liked it better than working the pickaxes. At least this way he got to emerge regularly into the bright sunlight. The pickers, though they earned a dollar more a day, descended into the bowels of the mine in the morning and came out at dusk, covered in soot and blinking their eyes at the fading light like some kind of night creatures.

But tired as he was, Sean detoured into town on his way home to make a stop at the general store. The young clerk looked at him in his grimy miner's outfit as if he were out of his mind, but when Sean produced a twenty-dollar bill from the depths of his blackened coveralls, the boy snapped to attention and took care of Sean's purchases with total courtesy.

By the time he reached the Sheridan house, it was almost supper time. Omitting his usual after-work visit with Caroline, he raced upstairs to wash off the dust, change clothes and get his purchases ready.

He came into the dining room just as Barnaby was entering from the kitchen with a basket of freshly baked rolls. Sean could smell them all the way across the room.

He took an approving whiff. "Mmm. Fresh bread."

"And pot roast," Barnaby added. "With gravy."

Sean's eyes danced. "Pot roast and gravy. Just the thing for a birthday party."

Barnaby put the basket on the table and looked up with a frown of confusion. "It's not anyone's birthday," he said.

Sean merely smiled and handed Barnaby the bottle of wine he was carrying. "Give this to Kate to open in the kitchen," he said. Then he walked over to kiss Caroline, who was already in place in her high chair, gnawing on a biscuit.

In a moment Kate's head poked through the door. "Did you bring that wine, Sean?" she asked.

He nodded.

She looked puzzled. "There's just the two of us to drink it, unless Barnaby wants to try a sip."

"That's all right," he replied. "We're celebrating."

"Celebrating what?"

"I'll tell you in a minute. Shall I get the wineglasses out of the hutch?"

She shrugged, then disappeared again into the kitchen.

Barnaby brought out the pot roast on a big platter adorned with carrots and onions, and Kate followed with a steaming bowl of mashed potatoes.

She looked at Sean, who was still standing next to Caroline. He'd taken one of the rolls and was shaping it into little figures. There was a miniature bread person and a four-legged something, perhaps a dog, already on her tray. Caroline explored them gently with the tip of her finger.

Kate smiled and asked, "Will you carve the roast?"

Sean looked up in surprise. "Me?"

"You appear to be the man of the household tonight. Unless you want Barnaby to do it."

Barnaby eyed the platter doubtfully. "Sean better do it," he said.

Sean moved around to the head of the table and picked up the carving knife, then hesitated.

"It's already dead," Kate said, amused. "It won't get up and charge at you."

Sean grinned. "I've never done this before. It's odd—makes me feel kind of like a real father."

"You're Caroline's father," Barnaby observed, as if Sean might not be entirely sure.

Kate and Barnaby sat down and left Sean standing at his place at the head of the table to serve their plates and pass them down. He filled a tiny plate with shreds of meat, two carrots and a glob of potatoes for Caroline, who immediately mashed a fist into the potatoes, then stuffed it into her mouth.

"Where's the wine?" Sean asked.

"Oh, I left it…" Kate started to stand up, but Sean waved her down and went to the kitchen himself to fetch it. He poured a glass for her and himself.

"So now do you want to explain the special occasion?" she asked.

Finally taking his seat, Sean raised his glass and said, "I was in the mood to celebrate, so I thought it would be a good time to catch up on the celebrating I missed—Caroline's first birthday."

Kate had begun to eat, but she set down her fork and uncertainly lifted her glass to clink it to his. "Here's a toast to my family and my new life," Sean said softly.

Their eyes held for a long moment until Barnaby asked, "Do you mean it's like a party?"

Sean broke his gaze away from Kate and answered the boy. "Yes, like a party."

"With presents?"

Sean smiled. "Maybe."

"She's weeks past her birthday," Kate reminded him.

"Well, she doesn't know that. This pot roast is incredible, sweetheart."

Unlike earlier in the day, she made no objection to the endearment.

By the end of the dinner, Kate had accepted a third glass of wine and Barnaby had decided to go along thoroughly with Sean's game. "Did you know you're going to get a birthday present, Caroline?" he asked her eagerly.

"I suppose it's time," Sean said, getting up from his chair. He disappeared into the hall and came back with three wrapped packages. He put one on Caroline's high chair tray, gave one to Barnaby and set one down in front of Kate.

"Is this one for me?" Barnaby asked, wide-eyed. "Are we pretending it's my birthday, too?"

"Well, I wasn't around for Caroline's birthday, but then, I wasn't around for yours, either. So I figured we'd just kind of have a general birthday for everyone."

That was all the invitation the boy needed to tear into the brown wrapping and uncover a shiny harmonica. "Wow!" he exclaimed. "Freddie Colter can teach me how to play it."

Sean smiled. "I'm glad you like it, sprout. Now maybe you can help Caroline open hers."

Barnaby jumped up and ran around to Caroline's chair. "Let's see your present, Caroline," he said, and put his own hands on the baby's so that together they could tear off the paper, revealing a small fur muff in the shape of a bunny.

"Oh, my goodness! It's adorable," Kate exclaimed.

"It's for her hands the next time we go on a drive in the mountains," Sean said, obviously pleased at her reaction.

Barnaby didn't seem too impressed, but Caroline was delighted with the soft fur and began pounding away at it.

"Careful, Barnaby, she'll get food on it," Kate admonished.

But Sean said, "Don't worry about it. I'll clean it afterward. You haven't opened your present."

She looked down at the square package, then up at Sean. "It's definitely not my birthday. I shouldn't—"

"Just open it," Sean said.

Inside the wrapping was a polished wooden box, inlaid with other kinds of wood in the shape of flowers. She slid her fingers over the smooth top.

"Now open that," Sean urged.

She pried back the lid to reveal a tiny singing bluebird. "It's a music box," she marveled.

Even Barnaby was impressed. He walked around the table to Kate's side and reached out. "Could I try?" At her nod he opened and closed the lid several times, starting and stopping the tinny music.

"It's a happiness bluebird, like the one that brought

me happiness long ago on Pritchard's Hill," Sean said to her in a low voice.

She blushed and looked away. "It's lovely," she said. "Thank you."

Sean leaned back with a satisfied smile and watched the reaction to his gifts. The choices had been more than satisfactory, he decided. Kate looked pleased and, more important, *softened,* which was what he had been hoping for.

When Barnaby started clearing the table, he rose and helped. The three did the washing up together while Caroline toddled around the kitchen, underfoot.

When they were finished, Sean said, "If you'd like to relax in the parlor, Kate, I'll put her to bed. Does she need a bath?"

Kate shook her head, relaxed and sleepy from the wine and the long supper. "It's late," she said. "She just needs a change of diaper and gown. If you'd like to take her up, that would be very nice."

Sean nodded and scooped her up. "C'mon, pumpkin, Papa's going to put you down to sleep tonight. Would you like me to sing you a lullaby?"

Barnaby giggled, then said, "I can play her a lullaby on my harmonica, when I learn how."

"You sure can, sprout. She'll like that. I'll be back down shortly," he said to Kate.

"I'll wait for you in the parlor," she replied, which Sean decided was more encouragement than she'd given him all week.

He didn't hurry, enjoying the moments alone with his daughter, but he was conscious of the fact that Kate was waiting for him. As soon as Caroline was settled and he saw her eyelids drooping, he wasted no time in finding Kate in the parlor. He was pleased to see that she was alone.

"Barnaby?" he asked casually.

"He's gone to bed."

"Ah." He walked across and put another couple of logs on the fire.

When he turned back to her, he asked, "So, you liked the presents?"

Her expression was unreadable. "The muff was darling. And practical. Her little hands get so cold."

He glanced at his accustomed chair, but instead took a seat next to her on the settee. She slid away six inches.

"I hope she can use it. But what about the music box?" he persisted.

"It's lovely, too, of course."

Sean was puzzled. He could tell she'd been pleased with the box, but she was bothered by something. He'd wanted to make her happy, to show her how much he cared for her and Caroline, but instead she seemed almost more distant than she had earlier up at the mine. "So what's wrong with you?" he asked with a frown.

"Nothing."

"Kate," he admonished gently. "Tell me."

She leaned back against the cushions and let out a deep sigh. "Oh, Sean, it's just that…you've still got it *wrong*. Caroline and I don't need presents from you for us to accept you. That's thinking the way your mother would think."

Sean's face tightened. "I just wanted to please you."

Kate looked tired. ''I know. You did please me. The gifts are very nice. Barnaby's thrilled.''

''But you're not.''

''Of course I am. I've never had anything quite like that. But what would make me happier would be for you to understand that gifts and luxuries are not what I want from you.''

Sean leaned forward, his voice low. ''Then help me to understand, Kate. What exactly *do* you want from me?''

His face was only a few inches from hers. He could feel her gentle breath on his lips.

Kate took a deep, shaky breath. ''I don't want *things,* Sean. I want *love.*''

Chapter Sixteen

Kate knew from the minute the word left her lips that she'd once again lost her carefully fought battle. Because she *did* love him. The truth was she'd never stopped, not all through the months she thought never to see him again, not through all those nights of waiting while he caroused at the gaming houses in San Francisco. She'd tried to stop loving him. She'd *wanted* to stop. But she never had.

"Kate," he said, reaching for her across the settee. "My love you already have...you've always had it." His voice was raspy.

When she shook her head in denial, he pulled her into his arms. "I know, I haven't always shown it," he said. She could hear the tears filling his throat. "But, I love you, Kate. I love you for the way you stood up against the town in order to have my baby. I love you for raising her to be as bright and sweet and loving as her mother."

She tried to pull back, out of his arms. He loosened his hold, but continued the onslaught of his words. "I don't deserve your love in return, sweetheart. At every turn, you've been strong and I've been weak. But I want the chance to prove to you that I'm worthy of you, of you and my daughter.''

It seemed almost ridiculous to her that Sean Flaherty, handsome, rich son of one of the West's most influential families was saying that he wasn't worthy of her love, but Kate could hear the sincerity in his tone, could feel his intensity in the shaking of his hands. She chose the most pressing issue. ''Caroline needs a father, Sean,'' she said. ''Not someone who will be there while he's enjoying himself and then head off for other amusements or in some other direction when he gets discouraged or bored.''

At that he released her entirely and put his hands up. ''I know,'' he said, his voice more under control. ''That's exactly what I've been trying to become ever since I left San Francisco. A father. And I'd like to be a husband to you, too, Kate.''

She averted her gaze. It was too debilitating to see his crystal blue eyes looking at her so intently. ''You weren't here Saturday night when I looked for you,'' she said.

He muttered an oath, low and under his breath, then he seized her shoulders and turned her, forcing her to look at him. ''I was *jealous,* Katie. I was drinking myself sick because every time I stopped drinking, all I could see was the picture of you here with Lyle, his hands on you, perhaps his lips on you, just as I wanted *mine* to be.''

Kate was breathing heavily. ''The only thing that happened with Lyle Saturday night was my telling him that there could never be anything between us.''

The lamps were dim, leaving Sean's face illuminated mainly by the firelight. In its reddish glow, his eyes gleamed with sudden brightness. "Truly, Katie?" He seemed to hold his breath as he waited for her answer.

"Truly, Sean. I told him he had my blessing to go find some of the many women in town he claims are wanting to throw themselves at his feet." She smiled as she made the comment, and Sean smiled back broadly.

"He accused me of sending him packing because of you," she added.

"And what did you say?"

She cocked her head a little and said in a teasing tone, "I told him I'd be plumb out of my mind to give my heart yet another time to a no-account, blarney-spouting Irishman who never seems to be around when I need him."

Sean hesitated a moment, as if trying to be sure that she was in jest. Then he flashed a grin and said, "Out of your mind, eh? You know, I've heard that mountain air can turn people that way."

"Well, I guess it's turned me," she said ruefully.

"So going back to last Saturday night. You sent Lyle off and then you say you *looked* for me?"

Kate nodded, her smile fading. "You weren't there."

"I wasn't *where?*"

She licked her lips. "In your, ah, bedroom."

Sean slid backward on the settee and folded his arms. "Now tell me, Katie Marie, what would a decent girl like you be doing coming to a man's bedroom late on a Saturday night?''

Kate felt the heat of the fire in the flush on her cheeks. "Maybe she would be looking to have a conversation," she said in a soft voice.

"A conversation? I don't think so." He continued to sit leaning against the arm of the settee without moving.

"Perhaps she would be wanting to say good-night."

He nodded. "That would have been polite of her. But, no, I don't think so. I think she wanted something more. What did she want, Katie? Tell me."

His voice was low and smooth as velvet. Kate felt it curl all the way into her toes. Her answer was scarcely audible. "She wanted *him*."

Sean moved then, all at once, powerfully, like a tiger unleashed from a cage. He leaned over, lifted her off the couch and stood. "I'm so glad," he whispered before he tucked his head down and began to kiss her neck.

Kate hardly felt the movement as he carried her upstairs, still kissing her, sending flickers of heat up and down her body. All at once they were in his room, on his bed, and he was continuing the kisses, marking a trail from her chin and across ivory skin to her breasts which he had bared to his gaze.

"There's not a single day since you left San Francisco that I haven't thought about doing this again," he said, kissing first one nipple, then the other. "Sometimes I burned so hot, I thought whiskey was the only thing that could quench the flames."

"I was afraid you were getting as bad as Charles Raleigh," she whispered.

"Hell, I started outdrinking Charlie ten to one after you left. It's a wonder I didn't kill myself. At that point, I wouldn't have cared."

It was the first account Kate had heard of Sean's activities after she had run away, and the description made her feel sick. "Perhaps I was wrong to leave so abruptly," she admitted.

"No. You did exactly right. You did what you thought was in the best interests of your child and yourself. I was the weak one for not taking off after you that first day."

He had continued making gentle circles on her breasts with his fingertips. She gasped as he touched a particularly sensitive spot. "I thought you didn't want me," she stammered.

"Most of the time, Katie Marie, you're an intelligent woman, but every now and then you say something quite foolish." He kissed her mouth, gently at first, then with deepening strokes of his tongue. "Not want you?" he asked, pulling back. "Saints preserve us, the woman is daft."

She giggled at his teasing, light tone. The conversation had been too intense, and all at once she didn't want to talk anymore. She wanted him to continue his exploration of her body with his fingers and lips and tongue. She reached to unfasten the rest of the buttons on her dress. "Is it warm in here?" she whispered.

Sean grinned looking down at her. "No. We just have too many clothes on."

They undressed, heedless of how they looked rolling

awkwardly around to shed the last bit of clothing. Suddenly both felt the need to hurry. "Ah, my love," she moaned with a sigh as he eased himself over her.

He smiled against her cheek. "I'm thinkin' that perhaps *this* is what that lass was looking for in the gentleman's room last Saturday," he teased.

She moved underneath him, feeling his aroused manhood swell against her soft stomach. "You could be right," she agreed.

"And a gentleman would always oblige a lady in this regard," he said, putting his hand between them to adjust his position.

"Yes, he would. Ah, Sean," she ended with an urgent little gasp.

He put his lips to her ear and murmured, "I'm thinking you might be ready for me now, Katie Marie. What are you thinking?"

The only answer she could manage was a nod. Then they started to move together, the moonlight dancing across their glistening bodies. After a few moments, Sean rolled over to let her move above him. Still connected, she straddled him and let the natural movements of their bodies fuel the rising passion. His hands on her hips guided her motion. Opening her eyes, she could see his were open, too, watching her. And the look of pure desire was enough to send her hurtling over the edge. He stiffened and joined her climax.

The spasms left her entire body weak. She collapsed on top of him and his arms came around her gently. "I love you," he said, kissing her hair.

For a long moment, she couldn't speak. When she twisted her face so that she could look at him, there were tears on both her cheeks and his. "You never said that to me before," she whispered.

He kissed a teardrop that was about to run off her chin. "I've never said that to anyone before. I don't think I knew how to say it."

She put her head down on his chest, pondering his words. "Not even to your family?"

"No."

Her tears started in afresh. "My love, that's so sad."

He rocked her back and forth on top of him. "Perhaps. But it's past. You're my family now—you and Caroline. And I intend to say it to each one of you every day for the rest of my life."

"Mmm." She slipped off to one side of him and let him enfold her in his arms. "Will you stay here beside me tonight?" he whispered.

She hesitated. "Caroline…"

"She sleeps through the night these days, and I'll go open the door to your room. If she cries, we'll hear her."

"Barnaby…"

Sean chuckled and squeezed her against his chest. "Sweetheart, it's not scandalous for us to spend the night together. We're *married,* in case you've forgotten."

She gave a happy sigh and let her head drop on his shoulder. "I haven't forgotten."

"You would have had every right to forget it," he said, more seriously. "I've not been the ideal husband."

"There's no such thing as an ideal life, Sean. I've

certainly learned that well enough in the past couple years.''

''Well, things are about to change. From this day on you're going to see a husband so ideal you'll think he was invented by a storyteller.''

Kate laughed and pulled away to look down at him. ''I'd just as soon have a real man in my bed, if you don't mind.''

''Katie Marie,'' he said softly, pulling her back into his arms. ''From now on that's exactly what you're going to have.''

By the time Carter and Jennie arrived home two days later, Kate had almost become convinced that this time Sean's promises were for real. She knew that her sister could tell the difference in her attitude immediately.

''You look happy, sis,'' Jennie said as Kate sat on Jennie's bed watching her unpack her valise.

''Of course, I'm happy. The hospital says you're normal and healthy and should have every expectation of a healthy, normal baby. It's wonderful news.''

Jennie raised her eyebrows. ''Oh. So this blush on your cheeks has nothing to do with Sean?''

Kate looked down and rearranged her skirts. ''We made love, Jennie,'' she admitted.

''I thought there was a glow,'' Jennie teased.

Kate flopped back on the bed. ''Oh, Jen, I don't know. I'm probably the world's biggest fool. He says he means it this time—he loves me. He wants to make a life together.''

''Well, perhaps he *does* mean it this time.'' Jennie

moved her valise to the floor and sat on the bed next to her sister.

"Perhaps. But in the back of my mind I have to wonder how long he'll be content to go up to the mines every day like a common laborer. He's never had to work like this in his life."

"I haven't heard him complaining."

"No, but it's still something of a novelty. When he and Charles Raleigh were here prospecting that spring, he stayed for three months before he got bored and went back to his easy life at home."

Jennie appeared to be considering her sister's words. She knew that deep down she wanted things to work out between Kate and Sean, but she would be careful with her advice. Finally she said, "I'm not sure that Sean's life at home has ever been such an easy one, Kate. But in any event, that was a different situation. He went home that spring because his prospecting was a bust—he and Charles didn't find any silver. Now he's got you and Caroline to consider."

"He had me to consider back then, too."

Jennie sighed. "Yes, he did. I don't know, sis. I don't blame you for being cautious, but I certainly don't think you're a fool for wanting to give it another try."

Kate sat up and grinned mischievously at her sister. "My mind says I am, but the rest of me is voting to take him back."

Jennie laughed and gave her sister a friendly shove. "My sister is shameless."

Kate shoved her back. "Oh, am I now? Maybe you'd like to explain, darling sister, why you and Carter stayed three nights in Virginia City for a one-day doctor visit?''

"We were seeing the sights."

"Certainly you were. Did you even go out of the hotel?"

"Of course we did. Once," she added with a giggle.

They sat on the edge of the bed looking at each other in the easy silence of years of affection. "Seriously, Jennie. I'm so happy the doctors said that everything's going well."

Jennie nodded and reached to squeeze her sister's hands. "And, seriously, Kate, I'm happy you've decided to try to make things work with Sean."

"After Mama and Papa died, I wondered if life would ever be joyous again," Kate said. "But I must say, it looks as though things might be finally heading in the right direction for the Sheridan sisters."

Jennie smiled at her sister. "I'd say it's about time."

They were saying it was the coldest February anyone could remember. The foreman up at the Wesley mine had ordered kerosene heaters placed inside the tunnels so the men could periodically warm their hands without having to come all the way out to the bonfire that they kept burning all day near the cook shack for the men on the mule shift.

In town, school was canceled as the first cases of flu began to strike. Memories were still vivid of the epidemic two years ago that had proved fatal to so many, including Francis and John Sheridan.

Barnaby and his friends took the school closing news with high spirits. Ignoring warnings to stay inside at home, they spent the sunny, chill days exploring the hills, marveling at the rare beauty of hoarfrost on the fir trees.

Kate had started taking over Jennie's cooking duties at the mine three days a week. Jennie had mostly stopped being sick in the morning, but she still tired easily, and neither Carter nor Kate liked the way her face had grown paler with dark circles under her eyes.

"I should probably insist on taking over every day," she told Sean one night as they lay nestled in his bed. Kate's bedroom was used solely by Caroline these days, prompting Kate to tease Sean that he was determined that his daughter would have a nursery one way or another.

"Yup," he'd teased back. "I was forced to entice her mother into my bed so that my poor child could have a room."

After two weeks, the arrangement seemed to be taken for granted by everyone, though Kate still felt a niggling worry that all this happiness could be snatched away from her at any moment. It had happened before. There was a quick moment of relief each night when Sean came home to her, whistling and obviously content.

"But you told me that Jennie wanted to keep working," he answered.

"She does, but maybe it's not good for her. Though the way Caroline's running around, I don't know which is more work—cooking for forty miners or keeping track of one little girl."

Sean chuckled and juggled her in his arms. "She

can tucker me out quicker than ten loads of ore,'' he agreed.

"I thought you were going to talk to the foreman about a different job than hauling.''

"Hauling's not so bad. At least I get out into the open now and then to ogle the pretty cook.'' He gave her bottom an affectionate swat.

She kissed his chin in return, but returned to her subject. "I just worry that you're going to get tired of that job. It looks so exhausting.''

"Sweetheart, one of these days you're going to stop being so worried that something's going to make me change my mind about being here with you. I've told you that this is where I'm going to stay—with you and Caroline.''

"Even if you have to push ore cars the rest of your life?''

At one point Sean would have gotten touchy at the question, but he only laughed easily and said, "I'll be finding something else to do one of these days. For now I'm happy concentrating on spending the evenings with my daughter.'' His voice grew low and sensual as he added, "And the nights with my wife.''

She wanted to believe him. She wanted it more than anything she'd ever wanted in her life. But once bitten, twice shy, as her mother used to say. She sat up and reached for the covers, though she didn't feel the least bit cold. "Your wife appreciates the nights, too,'' she told him.

She settled down in his arms, but thoughts kept whirring through her head as she tried to sleep. Jennie…her baby coming…Sean's lean aristocratic hands now welted with blisters…Barnaby and his friends….

She sat up. Sean blinked up at her, half-asleep. "Barnaby could take care of Caroline, while I cook at the mine. That would keep him home during the day."

"Sweetheart, why don't you let Jennie work another month if she wants to? By then she'll be showing, and she'll have to stop anyway."

"I don't like Barnaby roaming about with the other children when the sickness is back," she explained.

"I don't either, Katie. But it's hard to keep a boy of his age at home."

"Hmm. If Jennie—"

Sean reached up and pulled her back down beside him. "It'll keep until morning, my love. Tomorrow we'll take a look at all your plans and see how we're going to make life right for everyone."

Within minutes she could hear his breathing turn deep and even. Poor Sean, she thought. He *did* work hard every day. He did appear to be trying. She wasn't totally convinced that he would keep up such a difficult life, but at the moment, she had to admit that, as she and Jennie had observed, for once life at Sheridan House seemed pretty close to perfect.

"So I decided that I'm taking over the mine job for good, at least until after the baby's born. Barnaby can help you take care of things down here," Kate said. "It'll work until they start up school again, anyway."

She and Jennie were packing up the food Kate would take up to the mine that day. She'd lain awake for a long time the previous night thinking about it, and she'd decided that her decision to take over for Jennie was a good idea.

"I'm perfectly capable of walking up to the mine," Jennie argued.

"It's not just the walk up. It's walking up, then standing on your feet for four hours cooking and serving and washing up. You've got to begin to consider your limitations, Jennie."

"You and Carter are in a conspiracy," Jennie said, and smiled.

"Well, good. If you won't listen to me, maybe you'll listen to him."

"I don't intend to listen to either of you until I'm good and ready."

Kate jammed a loaf of bread into the bag. "Well, maybe you'll think about Barnaby, then. He's out running wild every day with his friends. It would do him good to have to shoulder a little more responsibility around here."

"He's still a boy, Kate," Jennie admonished.

"Yes, and there's flu abroad."

This statement sobered them both. Even the word itself was enough to evoke memories of those horrible two weeks when they had had to stand by and watch their parents die, one after the other.

"I'll tell him to stay home," Jennie agreed, her eyes worried.

"We should all stay in as much as possible. We don't want to bring anything back to the house that might put you at risk...and the baby."

"Or Caroline," Jennie added.

Kate felt a wave of panic in her stomach. Her parents had been healthy and strong, yet the scourge had taken them both. Caroline was still so tiny. "Lordy," she said.

Jennie gave her shoulders a shake. "Well, now we're asking for trouble to jump into our basket, as mother used to say. This time around's not anywhere near like it was two years ago, according to Dr. Millard."

"The school closing was just a precaution," Kate agreed as they gave each other reassuring smiles.

The back door banged and Barnaby came in, carrying a dead rabbit. "See what I shot?" he asked. His face looked flushed with triumph.

"Good job, Barnaby," Jennie said. "We'll have it for dinner. You can help me skin it when I get back from the mine."

He let the rabbit fall right in the middle of the kitchen floor. "I don't know, Jennie. You might have to skin it yourself." His voice sounded odd. The flush in his face suddenly looked more ominous than a boy's hunting triumph.

"What's the matter?" Kate asked in alarm.

Barnaby's eyes rolled around. "I don't feel so good," he said, then he slowly slid to the floor.

Chapter Seventeen

They'd put Barnaby immediately to bed. Then Kate had taken the food up to the mine, prepared a hasty lunch and had hurried back home, after telling the foreman not to expect her services for a while.

Sean and Carter each arrived home early from work and joined their wives for a somber dinner, all utterly conscious of Barnaby's empty chair. Kate and Jennie took turns sitting with him all evening. Dr. Millard came by about nine o'clock. He'd been seeing flu patients since sunup.

"Try a cool cloth on his head for the fever," he'd said. "But don't let him take a chill. Keep him well covered up. And get some soup down him."

The instructions were dismal echoes of what they'd been told when their parents had been taken sick. Jennie and Kate had exchanged scared glances across Barnaby's bed.

To everyone's relief, by morning, it appeared that Barnaby's fever had broken. He asked for some water and even managed a smile when Sean came to see him and teased him about trying to get out of rabbit-skinning duty by feigning sickness.

They'd been lucky, Kate told Sean, who was taking the day off from the mine. But by afternoon, her words proved to be ominously premature.

"Kate, this doesn't feel like the morning sickness," Jennie had told her sister after running out the back door of the kitchen to lose her lunch on the cold ground.

Kate looked at her sister with a sinking heart. "Dr. Millard says the strain's not as bad as two years ago," she said, trying to keep her voice calm. The strain may not be as bad, but Jennie was already fatigued from her pregnancy. She looked ghastly, her face flushed red except for a deadly whiteness around her mouth.

Sean went to the law office for Carter, who came home immediately to put his wife to bed and insisted on sitting right beside her the rest of the day. Kate went back and forth from Jennie to a recovering Barnaby. Sean fixed dishes of nun's toast for the patients. Barnaby ate the cut-up bread and hot milk readily. Jennie could not even look at the dish without becoming once again sick to her stomach.

Dr. Millard arrived and took her pulse. "Try chicken broth," he told Kate, his voice grave. "If she gets too weak, she won't be able to fight it."

"Will you come to bed, sweetheart?" Sean asked, meeting Kate on the stairs as she continued her trips back and forth between Barnaby's little bed behind the kitchen and Jennie's bedroom. "It's nearly midnight, and you're exhausted yourself."

Kate shook her head. "No. I'll stay up."

"You were up all night last night with Barnaby."

Kate's eyes filled with tears. "I was up every night for two weeks nursing my parents." She leaned forward and let her head rest against his chest for a moment. Then she straightened up, rubbed a hand at her back and said, "I'll be all right. You go on to bed."

Sean shook his head. "If you're not going to sleep, I won't either."

"But you have to work tomorrow."

"No. I'm not going back until everyone's healthy again. I've sent word."

She smiled at him gratefully. "Well, you could check on Caroline, then. Just be sure she's sleeping peacefully."

But, to Sean's horror, Caroline wasn't sleeping peacefully at all. Her eyes were open and glazed. Her tiny body was drenched in sweat. "Good Lord," Sean whispered. He picked her up and cradled her in his arms for a long moment, then placed her back in her crib and went running to fetch Kate.

He found her in Carter's arms. His brother- in-law looked up as Sean entered the room. "She walked over to the bed and collapsed," he said.

"Is she…?" Sean began.

"Burning up," Carter confirmed. "God Almighty, Sean, they've both got it." His normally calm gray eyes were frightened.

Sean sagged against the door frame. "Caroline, too."

Carter swore under his breath. "What are we going to do?"

Sean pushed himself upright and took a deep breath. "We're going to get them well," he said.

Sean had never worked so hard in his life. With two men who had never had the running of a household to themselves trying to take care of four patients, there was not even a minute for rest. Sean did not leave the house. Carter brought in food, since he had to make periodic trips to his office to deal with urgent legal matters.

Barnaby was recovering, but stayed weak. When he was told that Caroline was sick, he insisted on going to her room to see her, but just the effort of walking down the hall and back had him wringing wet, and Sean told him he'd have to stay in bed another day.

Sean put Kate to bed in her own bedroom so that he could care for both her and Caroline together. The first night and day of the illness, Kate wasn't coherent enough to understand that Caroline was sick. When the baby would occasionally begin a feeble cry, Sean would drop everything else and hold her until she was comforted again. Every spare minute that he wasn't preparing food, hauling water, washing out drenched linens, emptying waste basins, putting cold cloths on the patients' foreheads or spooning soup into their mouths, he'd take Caroline in his arms and rock her. Feeling delirious himself from lack of sleep, he'd croon to her, talk to her, kiss her soft cheek, and then he'd put her back into her crib, look down at her fragile listless form and do what he hadn't done since he was a child—pray.

By the third day things seemed to be reaching a

climax. Sean's eyes stung from weariness and his head was muddled, but he was encouraged that Kate was sleeping peacefully and seemed to be breathing easily. Her color was returning to normal.

Barnaby was definitely on the mend. The boy had gone down to the kitchen earlier and helped Sean prepare a chicken for soup.

But Caroline still lay weak and quiet, far too quiet, in her bed. And Jennie was once again thrashing with fever as the sun began to set. Sean closed his eyes in relief when the front door slammed and he heard Carter's voice calling to him that he was back. The two men had become as close as real brothers during their ordeal.

"I'm in Kate's room," Sean called down to him.

In a minute, Carter appeared in the doorway with Dr. Millard.

The old town doctor had been concerned at first about leaving the two men as nurses. "I could ask around in town for someone to come give you men a hand," he'd said, "though there's hardly a family left that's not dealing with the sickness themselves."

But Carter and Sean had assured the doctor that they would take care of their own families, and after watching the two men these past three days, Dr. Millard had admitted, with admiration, that he couldn't have found more attentive nurses in a big city hospital.

"How are the patients tonight?" the doctor asked, entering the bedroom.

Kate opened her eyes. "Caroline?" she asked weakly.

Sean was at her side immediately. "The doctor's

here to see the two of you, sweetheart. You're doing much better. You slept nicely most of the afternoon. Caroline's sleeping, too," he answered evasively.

"What about Jennie?" she asked.

"Dr. Millard will see Jennie next. You just worry about getting well yourself."

"I want to hold her," she said, nodding toward the crib. Her voice was hoarse.

Sean looked at Dr. Millard, who nodded, then he picked Caroline up from her crib and laid her in Kate's arms.

"She's lost weight," Kate said.

It was true. In three short days, she'd changed. The baby chubbiness was gone from her cheeks. "She'll gain it back when she starts feeling better," Sean said, straining to keep his voice from reflecting his worry.

Kate's eyes drifted closed again, and Sean picked up Caroline, hugged her to his chest, then placed her back in her crib. "There must be something else we can do, Doctor," he said, keeping his voice low. "Caroline's not getting better, and she's wasting away."

Dr. Millard shook his head. "These things hit harder with babies and old folks. We don't know why."

Sean shook his head to clear his suddenly blurred vision. "We're not going to lose her. Or Jennie, either."

Carter had already disappeared into his and Jennie's bedroom. The doctor looked at Sean, from his uncombed hair to his rumpled clothes. "You're doing all you can, Sean. And if you don't get a little sleep yourself, you'll be the next patient."

"I'm fine."

Dr. Millard shook his head, picked up his black bag from the bed and started out of the room. "Kate's doing much better. By tomorrow you'll see her starting to get back to herself. Why don't you lie down there next to her and rest?"

"I think I'll just rock Caroline for a few minutes, then I'll see if that soup's ready."

Dr. Millard fixed him with a hard look. "I don't mind telling you, son, that I was mighty angry with you when Kate first came to me a couple years back about the baby. With her own pa dead, I considered oiling up my old shotgun myself and going out in search of you. But I'm starting to think that I might have been wrong about you. When you see a man battle for his family the way you've been doing the past few days, it says something about his character."

Sean was too tired for the doctor's words to have much impact. At the moment, he didn't give a damn what anyone thought of his character. He just wanted his family to be well again.

The main wave of infection seemed to have passed, the toll far lighter than the previous epidemic. They'd been lucky, most of the townfolk agreed. Three dead, all older folk who wouldn't have had too many years left on this side of the vale by any account. The only still questionable case was the Sheridan baby, as she was still called, though she was a Flaherty now. She was hanging on by a thread, according to Henrietta Billingsley, who made it her business to know.

The Sheridan sisters had recovered, as had their adopted orphan boy. The two husbands had not been infected. Carter Jones was keeping regular office hours again, but Kate Sheridan's husband had not returned to his mine job. He was sharing his wife's vigil at their child's bedside.

Dr. Millard had been effusive in his description of Sean Flaherty's heroics during his family's illness. The man hadn't slept for a week, according to the doctor. He'd bathed and clothed and ministered to not only his wife and daughter but his sister-in-law and Barnaby, as well. He'd carried bedpans and administered tonics, and one account had him sitting out on the back stoop all by himself plucking a chicken.

There was reluctant admiration among some of the families, even some of those who had been eager to condemn the San Francisco blue blood for leaving poor Kate Sheridan to face the consequences of his seduction. Some even expressed a willingness to finally welcome him as a bona fide citizen of the town.

But others said that the issue was probably moot in any case. Now that the patrician young man's father and grandmother had come all the way from San Francisco to fetch him, there were few who believed that he would be content to stay in a backwater place like Vermillion. Whether little Caroline lived or not, the betting in town was that Sean Flaherty would soon once again be on his way out of town.

They had just finished a delicious supper that, amazingly, Sean and Barnaby had prepared entirely themselves.

"I offered to help," Nonny said, "but I was run out of the kitchen."

"Barnaby and I make a good team, don't we, sprout?" Sean asked.

Barnaby grinned. "We sure do. But Sean has to do the gooey part."

"Taking out the innards of the chicken," Sean explained.

Patrick Flaherty shook his head in wonder. "I've heard it said that mountain air changes people, but I never would have credited this if I hadn't seen it with my own eyes."

Sean smiled tiredly. "I hope you didn't have a problem with my cooking, Father," he said dryly.

Patrick harrumphed and said, "On the contrary. I just find it quite...extraordinary."

Nonny looked at her grandson fondly. "I'm proud of you, Sean. And you, lad," she added, including Barnaby in her praise.

"And you can give my husband part of the credit," Jennie put in. "I never thought I'd see the day that Carter Jones would be emptying out slop jars."

"A good lawyer's ready for any contingency," Carter said, reaching across the table for his wife's hand.

At the gesture Sean looked across the hall toward the stairs. "I think I'll let the washing up be contingent on the lawyer this evening," he said. "I'm going back to Caroline."

The faces around the table became serious. "Do you want me to come, Sean?" Nonny asked.

"Later, if you like. We'll be there all evening."

"I'll help Carter, and then I'll be up," Jennie said.

"Oh no, you won't help Carter," Carter disagreed. "You're not strong enough. You'll rest right here at the table while Barnaby and I do the dishes.'' He motioned to Barnaby, who jumped up and headed toward the kitchen. ''Keep her occupied, will you, Mrs. Flaherty?'' he said to Nonny. ''Tell her what one's supposed to do with babies.''

Both Nonny and Jennie laughed at his rather vague suggestion, but Jennie stayed seated and let Barnaby and Carter clear the table by themselves.

''The answer to your husband's question about babies, my dear,'' Nonny said after a moment, ''is that you love them. And it appears you have a perfect example to follow watching your sister and my grandson.''

''They haven't left Caroline alone for an instant,'' Jennie said. ''Sean will hardly let her out of his arms.''

Patrick was shaking his head again. ''It's hard to believe.''

Nonny shook her head. ''I'm sorry, Patrick, but it's not hard to believe at all. You've always underestimated Sean—all his life. He's a warm, intelligent person, and I've always known that he was capable of giving so much. He was just waiting for the right opportunity...and for someone to give *to*.''

''He's certainly found that in Kate,'' Jennie observed. ''And as much or even more so in his daughter. Now if only...'' She paused and her lip trembled.

''If only he doesn't lose her, just when he's discovered exactly how precious she is,'' Nonny finished gently.

Patrick pulled off his spectacles and cleaned them with his napkin. ''Don't talk nonsense. No one's going to lose anyone. That little colleen is Flaherty stock. We breed 'em strong.''

Jennie and Nonny turned in unison to cast worried glances up the stairs. ''Dear Lord,'' Jennie said. ''I hope you're right.''

Kate was lying in her bed, but she was not asleep. As he had every night since she'd recovered, Sean insisted she lie down and try to rest. ''You're not strong enough yet to sit up all night,'' he'd said. ''Caroline's right here with you, and I'll be here. I promise to wake you if there's any change at all.''

But she found sleep difficult, though she dozed off and on, as did Sean, sitting up in the rocker, unable to stay totally awake after so many days of exhaustive nursing.

Sean was right, she did still feel the effects of the illness. She was as weak as she had been at the hospital after she'd had Caroline. The weakness made tears spring easily to her eyes, and made it more difficult to keep up her normally strong spirits when she looked at the slowly wasting body of her only child.

It was Sean who'd had to be the strong one. In spite of days without sleep, he seemed to have indefatigable energy, and refused to hear one word of pessimism about Caroline's condition.

''She's breathing more easily than this afternoon,'' he'd say. Or, ''Look at how her color's improved.''

Kate's gratitude for his optimism was boundless, and though she hadn't taken time from her vigil to tell him so in words, she felt he understood. It was apparent in the silent clasp of their hands, in the looks they exchanged over her crib, in the myriad things he did all day long to keep both Kate and Caroline comfortable.

The man who tenderly tucked her into her covers each night, then went to sit by his daughter's bedside, was quite simply a world removed from the cocksure charmer to whom she had lost her heart all those months ago. And her love for him was tenfold what it had been then.

Her eyes drifted shut. What seemed like minutes later, Sean was gently shaking her shoulder. "I think she's doing better, suddenly. Truly better," he said excitedly, his voice swollen with tears.

Kate sat up in her bed and blinked. Out the window she could see the first streaks of dawn in the dark blue sky. As his words began to register in her brain, she jumped out of bed and ran to the crib. Caroline was awake, her eyes clear, looking up at her mother with interest. Her complexion was pale, without the flush it had had for days.

"How's my sweetie?" Kate asked softly.

Caroline reached her arms toward her. With a little cry, Kate picked her up and clasped her to her chest. "Oh, Sean!" she said, meeting his moist eyes with tears in her own.

"The sheet's dry for the first time in days, Kate," he said. "I think the fever's gone entirely." He put his hand out to touch the baby's back. "She feels normal."

"*Normal.* What a wonderful word," Kate said with a laugh.

"Kee," Caroline said, pointing out the window.

"Oh, baby," Kate said, crying now in earnest. "Yes, sky. Pretty, pretty sky."

"Pity kee," Caroline mimicked.

Sean put his arm around them both at once, his head against Kate's. With tears streaming down both their faces, they stood together at the window, rocking their child and watching nature's spectacular announcement of a new day.

"Well, son. You know why I've come," Patrick Flaherty said brusquely.

He and Sean were having the conversation both had avoided since the two older people had arrived in Vermillion to find a house still recovering from the epidemic. It had been two days since Caroline's fever had broken. She was now eating almost normally, though she still slept much of the day and did not have the strength to walk more than back and forth across the room.

In spite of Kate's and Sean's objections and fear that she would be infected, Nonny had insisted on taking her turn at Caroline's bedside while they finally got some real sleep. Patrick had waited patiently throughout the ordeal, had not even broached the subject, but Sean had known since he'd seen his father's hired carriage pull up in front of the house that this moment would come.

"I've received your wires, Father," he said. "But this time, for once, I meant what I said. I'm no longer a part of Flaherty Enterprises, and I don't intend to change my mind."

The two men looked at each other from the straight

chairs they'd pulled out to sit on opposite sides of the parlor fireplace. Both had seemed to feel that the cushiony settee or the deep rocker were too soft for this particular meeting of wills.

"It's the issue of a house, isn't it?" Patrick asked. "I've done some thinking about that, and have decided that perhaps you were right. I can see how Kate would be more comfortable raising your child without being quite so close to Harriet's hovering."

Sean gave a slight smile. "I'm sorry to say that we've discovered that a four-day stagecoach ride is just about the right distance away from Mother's hovering. Though we'll be happy to have both of you visit us anytime."

Patrick frowned and leaned forward, his elbows on his knees. "Sean, you've got to think of your future...and your child's." He looked around at the simple parlor furnishings. "Think of all the things you can give Caroline back in San Francisco."

Sean leaned back. "Things like what?"

"Why...fine clothes, a beautiful home, servants, the best schools—"

"Now you're sounding like Mother yourself. And perhaps I would have sounded the same way a couple years ago, but not anymore. I've changed. Something happened to me."

Sean's voice held a new degree of confidence, and for once in his life, Patrick appeared to be genuinely listening to his son.

"What happened was I met two sisters," Sean continued. "I didn't fully understand it at the beginning, I'll admit, because I was too besotted by the younger sister's beauty to give the rest of it any thought. But now, almost two years wiser, I realize that the Sheridans had something that the Flahertys never had for all our fine furniture and clothes. They had strength of family. They had love.''

Patrick's blue eyes, so like Sean's, narrowed with hurt. ''You're my only child, Sean. I've always loved you.''

''I know. Or at least, I'm beginning to know that. Loving Caroline has helped me understand that special love between parent and child—that special and *complicated* love. I'm beginning to understand that much of what you did with your life was *because* of me, even if I resented it.''

''But, of course. Why else have I devoted my life to Flaherty Enterprises if not for you, Sean?''

Sean could have told him the story of John Sheridan. He hadn't built a fortune for his family, but he'd given them a much more important legacy of family loyalty and mutual support, qualities lacking in the Flahertys. But Sean had lost any desire he might once have had to hurt his father.

They were products of two generations and totally different life circumstances. His father had had to claw and fight for what he had, whereas Sean had never really worked in his life up until the past few weeks. But some part of him, the child still inside, wanted to gain his father's understanding, if not his approval.

''I'm grateful for all the things you were able to give me growing up, Father, but now I need the chance to be able to provide a home for my own family.''

''I'll help you,'' Patrick interrupted, straightening

up. "They're building down on Van Nuys—fabulous houses that'll dwarf the Nob Hill set. Your mother will be green with envy."

Sean listened calmly, shaking his head. "Our place is here," he said finally. "It's where Kate's home is and her family, and it's where we'd like to raise our child."

Patrick stood up from his chair and paced across the small room in agitation. "You can't seriously think you're going to dig in the dirt the rest of your life."

"You dug in the dirt a number of years, as I recall," Sean pointed out with a smile. "It didn't appear to hurt you any."

"That was different. Back then there were still riches for the picking, a man could turn millionaire overnight."

"I've already got my riches, Father. They're both upstairs sleeping right now."

Patrick went back to his chair and sat down again, heavily. He drummed his fingers on his knees with the air of a man who was not used to being contradicted. "What do you do up at that mine anyway?"

"I push ore carts. Back and forth all day long."

His father gave a kind of shudder.

They were both silent a long moment. "You should see my arms," Sean joked. "I could take on a whole slew of sailors down at the wharf."

"How much is that mine worth?" Patrick asked finally, his expression changing from despair to calculation.

Sean laughed. "Are you planning to buy it and give

it to me for Christmas?'' he asked. ''You'd probably get it for a bargain price—the ore's playing out.''

''Well, there you have it. What's wrong with the idea? You could manage the thing instead of scrabbling in the dust every day.''

''Father, I don't intend to scrabble in the dust the rest of my life. You didn't. I have several avenues I'm beginning to explore. In spite of what Mother might think, this isn't the end of the world. New industries are starting—not just mining, but lumber, ranching. Carter has talked about investing in a shipping line. The freight service here leaves a lot to be desired. I've money set aside, as well. A business like that would need a manager.''

Patrick sat up and rubbed his hands together with enthusiasm. ''Why, that's a brilliant thought. A freight line to link up with Flaherty shipping. It's perfect. Just tell me how much you need to get it started.''

Sean was shaking his head again. ''Father,'' he said gently. ''I'm done letting you provide me with everything. You've given me more than I can properly thank you for. I was raised with many luxuries and a fine education. But now I need to show myself that I can do something on my own.''

''There's nothing wrong with taking a little help,'' Patrick argued.

''Maybe I will someday. But for now I'm happy with things the way they are. I intend to stay at the mine another year or so. The money's better than I could earn anywhere else. Then I'll make some decisions. In the meantime, I'm busy learning.''

''About shipping?'' Patrick asked.

Sean shook his head. "About life," he said with a smile.

Kate was waiting for him in his bedroom. That afternoon Nonny had bustled into Kate's room with her carpetbag, informing Kate that she would be sleeping at Caroline's side for the next couple of nights until she and Patrick left to return home.

"Your place is next to your husband, dear," she told her, then added with a sly wink, "now that you're well enough again to be of some entertainment to each other."

Kate had blushed but had accepted her grandmother-in-law's offer. She was feeling healthy again, and the thought of an uninterrupted night in Sean's arms was making her feel pleasantly jumpy inside.

The feeling had lasted all through supper, but her anticipatory mood vanished after the meal when Patrick had taken Sean aside and asked to speak to him in private. Though Sean had sent her a reassuring glance as he followed his father into the parlor, Kate had worried. She'd helped Jennie with the cleaning up, then she'd climbed the stairs with a familiar feeling of foreboding.

It had lasted all the while she bathed and changed Caroline and bid good-night to Nonny, thanking her again for her help. "Run along, child," Nonny had said with a careless wave. "Your husband's waiting."

But he hadn't been waiting. He was still closeted in the parlor with his father, the father who once before had ordered him home, leaving Kate to face her pregnancy alone. In the past few weeks, Sean had been a changed man—humble, attentive, affectionate, hard-working. He'd finally been ready to express his love for her and his daughter in words as well as deeds. But now his father had come to fetch him back to his old life, and Kate was not sure what Sean's answer would be.

It was nearly ten o'clock by the time she heard his footsteps coming up the stairs. She was still wide-awake, in spite of her lingering exhaustion from recent days. The delicate thread of her life was being twisted in that parlor downstairs, and she wasn't about to fall asleep before she found out if it was once again going to end up in a tangled mess.

His face was unreadable when he came in the door, but it brightened when he caught sight of her, already lying in his bed. "I went to look for you in your room," he said. "Nonny and Caroline are both sleeping."

She nodded. "Nonny moved me out. I had to seek refuge elsewhere."

He walked over to the bed and leaned down to give her a kiss. "You chose the right place," he said, his voice vibrating close to her ear.

She smiled at him as he began unbuttoning his shirt. "Did I now?" she asked archly, mimicking the slight brogue he sometimes adopted.

"Yes, ma'am," he confirmed. He quickly shed his clothes, leaving them scattered carelessly behind him on the floor. Then he lifted the covers to slide in next to her. His eyebrows went up in pleased surprise. "Didn't Nonny let you take any nightclothes when she moved you out?"

"I didn't ask to take any," she answered, sliding her naked body a little farther down in the bed. "I thought you might prefer me like this."

"You thought right," he said, his voice thick.

He spent a moment admiring her before he moved over to gather her in his arms.

"But first you have to tell me what happened," she said.

He buried his face in her neck and groaned. Kate's spirits sank. She pulled away from him and sat up. "What is it?" she asked tensely. "Are you going back with him?"

Sean looked at her in surprise, then pushed himself to a sitting position beside her. "I'm sorry, sweetheart. My groan was because you were making me wait, not because of my conversation with my father."

Her heart slowed its accelerated beating. "Then your conversation was…satisfactory?"

"He offered to buy us a house after all," he replied. "Fancier than the Nob Hill house, just to make my mother envious." But his mischievous grin told Kate that he had not looked at his father's offer seriously.

"You turned him down."

Sean picked her up and set her on his legs, her bare bottom rubbing against his thighs. "I turned him down, Katie Marie. I told him I'd much rather stay in the mountains pushing mine carts all day and making wild love to my wife all night."

"Sean, you didn't!"

He leaned forward and nipped her ear. "No, but it's the truth."

She pounded on his chest in frustration and asked, "So what happened?"

He grew serious. "My darling wife, I'll be happy to give you a blow-by-blow account of every minute of our conversation, but could it please wait until afterward?" He slid her toward him so that she could feel the extent of his arousal, pressed between her leg and his stomach. "Have pity," he pleaded.

"Just tell me quickly—are you going back to San Francisco?" she demanded. She, too, was beginning to feel the urgency in the lower portions of her body.

"We'll go back for a visit to show them our son," he murmured, moving sinuously underneath her.

Kate smiled. "We don't have a son."

He lifted an eyebrow in mock astonishment. "We don't? Well now, darling, I'd suggest we remedy that situation right away."

She squirmed, adjusting the juxtaposition of their bodies below. "The sooner the better, my love," she agreed.

Epilogue

Vermillion, November 1883

It was satisfying to see John Sheridan's big oak dining table full again. Dennis, Smitty and Brad, the three silverheels, had come all the way from Virginia City to help celebrate Caroline's second birthday and, not incidentally, to give an official welcome to little John Sheridan Kelly Smith Connors Jones.

"The poor lad will spend twenty years in grammar school just learning to spell his name," Sean had protested.

But Jennie had wanted to honor both her father and the three caring miners who had been such an important help to the sisters after their parents' deaths. Carter, who had never had a legitimate last name of his own to claim, was delighted that his young son would have a whole passel of them.

And since he'd been the one to file the newly required birth records, the name had been duly registered.

"Now I have two sons," Carter had observed, taking Barnaby in an affectionate headlock that turned into a hug. Shortly after Caroline's birth, Carter had filed adoption papers to make the young orphan officially Barnaby Sheridan Jones.

"The lad is as bonny as his namesake," Dennis observed with a twinkle when the supper was finished. Jennie had just brought the tiny bundle to the table for all to admire.

"Depends on what namesake you're meaning," Brad objected. "He's a sight prettier than you, you big Irish lug."

"I think he looks like Jennie," Smitty observed, giving his former landlady a big smile.

"If he's as kindhearted as his three namesakes, I'll be happy," she said, beaming at the trio.

Sean, sitting at the end of the table with Caroline on his lap, cleared his throat. "We're all happy about little Johnny, Jennie, but there's just one problem."

Jennie looked up. "Problem?"

Sean looked at Kate, who blushed and nodded her head. "He's only one little tyke, but you've used up all the names."

Carter went to stand behind his wife, putting his hands on her shoulders and smiling down at his son in her arms. He appeared to find some significance in his brother-in-law's remark, but Jennie still looked puzzled.

"Shall we tell them, Caroline?" Sean asked his daughter, who seemed too interested in her new birthday doll to notice. It was an expensive fashion doll with ruffles all down the dress and a real bustle in back, much too fine a toy for a two-year-old. But Sean had said to Kate, "It's from her grandparents. Let her play with it."

Sean bounced her on his knee a little to get her attention. "Pumpkin, let's tell Aunt Jennie and Uncle Carter our secret." The doll fell to the floor with a thud as Caroline turned her attention to her father. He asked her again, "What do we have cooking in Mama's tummy?"

Caroline looked around the table and announced, "Baby."

Sean leaned toward her ear and whispered in mock correction, "Baby boy."

"Baby boy," Caroline obliged.

"Or girl," Kate added with an indulgent shake of her head.

"Oh, Kate…how long have you known?" Jennie exclaimed. She turned around and deposited little John in Carter's arms, then ran over to her sister's chair to embrace her.

Carter juggled the baby a little uncertainly. "A fine couple of partners we'll make, Sean," he said. "How do we expect to get a freight company up and running if we're both walking the floors every night with babies?"

Kate and Jennie both began to object at the same time, so Jennie fell silent and let her sister defend her.

"Jennie's the one I see up every morning before dawn feeding your son, Carter. I haven't seen any dark shadows under your eyes."

"I wake up when she does," he protested. "It's just that I don't have the particular equipment that

Johnny's interested in at this stage of the game. So I go back to sleep,'' he ended lamely.

"I think we'll manage, brother-in-law," Sean observed. "In fact, you and I might find it a lot more restful down at the shipping office than here at home with so many little ones underfoot."

"Can I come to the shipping office, too?" Barnaby asked wistfully.

Everyone laughed, but Sean said, "You can come anytime you want to, Barnaby. And if you want, in a few more years we'll give you a job. But I promise you, it would be a real job, one of substance." He exchanged a meaningful glance with Kate. "And only if you like it there."

"Once you two get started maybe we'll come back and work for you," Dennis suggested. "Mining's not what it used to be in the boom days. What do you say, boys?" He turned to Brad and Smitty. "Are you two ready to become mule skinners?"

"Sounds good to me. At least we'd see the sunlight," Smitty replied with an emphatic nod.

And Brad added, "Count me in."

Barnaby wrinkled his nose. "Hey, then you all would have something other than silver on your boots. Instead of *silverheels,* you'd be…"

"That's enough, Barnaby," Jennie admonished gently, but laughed along with everyone else.

The merriment could have lasted well into the night, but both babies started getting crabby and the miners got to their feet and said that since they still *were* silverheels, they'd better start out on the road back to Virginia City.

Jennie said a hurried good-night and rushed upstairs to feed Johnny, while Carter walked with the three miners out to the horses they had borrowed for the trip.

Caroline was falling asleep in Sean's arm. He put his other arm around Kate as they mounted the stairs together. "We won't give her a bath tonight," Kate said. "She can just go right down to sleep."

Together they placed her in the crib in what was now exclusively her bedroom, then walked down the hall to their own.

"How are you feeling, sweetheart?" Sean asked. "You're not too tired?"

Kate gave him an arch smile. "Too tired for what?"

Sean grinned. "I didn't mean that. I'm thinking about my son. Unlike the first time around, this time I'm here to take care of you, and I intend to do it."

Kate leaned her head on his shoulder. "Sometimes it's hard for me to believe how much richer my life is than it was two years ago as I lay all by myself in that hospital in Virginia City."

"Mine, too." He stopped at their doorway and suddenly scooped her up in his arms.

"What are you doing?" she exclaimed.

"I'm carrying you across the threshold."

Kate giggled. "That's for honeymoons."

"That's all right. You and I have done a number of things backward, but eventually, we'll get them all worked in. Tonight I'm in the mood for a honeymoon." He stopped and looked down at her with a little frown. "That is, if you're sure you're all right."

Kate clasped her arms more tightly around his neck

and thought about her daughter sleeping peacefully in her bed down the hall, about the new little one already growing within her and about her thoroughly-at-peace husband. "My darling Sean," she told him, "I've never been more all right in my whole life."

Looking For More Romance?

Visit Romance.net

Check in daily for these and other exciting features:

Hot off the press

View all current titles, and purchase them on-line.

What do the stars have in store for you?

Horoscope

Hot deals

Exclusive offers available only at Romance.net

Plus, don't miss our interactive quizzes, contests and bonus gifts.

PWEB

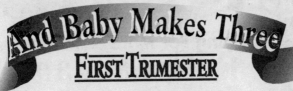

And Baby Makes Three

FIRST TRIMESTER

by

SHERRYL WOODS

Three ornery Adams men are about to be roped
into fatherhood...and they don't suspect a thing!

And Baby Makes Three

APRIL 1999

The phenomenal series
from Sherryl Woods has readers
clamoring for more! And in this special collection,
we discover the stories that started it all....

Luke, Jordan and Cody are tough ranchers set in
their bachelor ways until three beautiful women
beguile them into forsaking their single lives for
instant families. Will each be a match made in
heaven...or the delivery room?

Available at your favorite retail outlet.

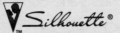

Look us up on-line at: http://www.romance.net
PSBR499

COMING NEXT MONTH FROM

HARLEQUIN HISTORICALS